one small thing

Books by Erin Watt

One Small Thing
When It's Real

**The Royals series
(in reading order)**

Paper Princess
Broken Prince
Twisted Palace
Fallen Heir

erin watt

one small
thing

HARLEQUIN®TEEN

Recycling programs
for this product may
not exist in your area.

ISBN-13: 978-1-335-01727-7

One Small Thing

Printed in U.S.A.

This book is dedicated to the assistants and publicists who help manage our lives:

Nicole, Nina, Natasha and Lily

1

"Hey there, pupster." I laugh as Morgan, the Rennicks' dog, races across the lawn and jumps up on my khaki pants.

"Morgan, come here," yells an exasperated Mrs. Rennick. "Sorry, Lizzie," she says, rushing over to pull the big black mutt off me without much success. She's small and he's so big that they're about the same size.

"It's no big deal, Mrs. R. I love Morgan." I crouch down and scratch the big boy behind his ears. He yaps happily and slobbers all over my cheek. "Oh, and it's Beth now," I remind my neighbor. I'm seventeen and Lizzie is a name I wish would go far, far away. Unfortunately, no one seems to remember.

"That's right. Beth, then. Don't encourage him," she scolds, tugging on his collar.

I give him a few more rubs behind his ears before releasing him.

"Your mom's going to have a fit." Mrs. R frets.

I look down at the dog hairs that are now dotting my white button-down shirt, which was already spattered with food stains from work. "I need to wash up anyway."

"Still. Tell her I'm sorry." She drags Morgan away by the collar. "I promise to watch him better."

"Don't," I say. "I love all the time I get with Morgan. It's worth the punishment. Besides, it's not like there's any reason for us to not have a pet now." I stick out my chin. The reason for our pet-free house has been gone for three years, even if my parents don't like acknowledging that fact.

Mrs. R falls silent for a moment. I don't know if she's holding back curt words toward me for being callous, or toward my mom for being too strict. And since I don't know, I'm too cowardly to press.

"I'm sure she has her reasons," Mrs. R says finally and gives me a small wave goodbye. She doesn't want to get involved. Good choice. I wish I wasn't involved, either.

Morgan and Mrs. R disappear inside their garage. I turn and squint at my house, wishing I was anywhere but home.

I check my phone. There aren't any messages from my best friend, Scarlett. We talked this morning about going out tonight after my shift at the Ice Cream Shoppe. School starts on Tuesday. For Scarlett, the summer of fun is over. For me, it means I'm one day closer to true freedom.

I roll my head around my shoulders, trying to loosen the tension that always appears the minute I see my house. I exhale heavily and order my feet to move forward.

Inside, Taylor Swift's "Bad Blood" trickles into the mudroom. Mom's playlist is set in an eternal 2015 loop of Sam Smith, Pharrell and One Direction, back when One D was still a group with five members. I toe off my ugly black work shoes and drop my purse onto the bench.

"Is that you, Lizzie?"

Would it kill her to call me Beth? Just once?

I grit my teeth. "Yes, Mom."

"Please tidy up your locker space. It's getting messy."

I glance down at my section of the mudroom bench. It isn't *that* messy. I've got a couple of jackets on the hooks, a stack of Sarah J. Maas books that I'm rereading for the eightieth time, a box of mints, a bottle of body spray that Scarlett bought me at the last Victoria's Secret sale and some random school supplies.

Stifling a sigh, I pile everything on the Maas books and walk into the kitchen.

"Did you pick up in there?" Mom asks, not bothering to look up from the carrots she's chopping.

"Yeah." The food looks unappetizing, but then all food does after I'm done with work.

"Are you sure?"

I pour myself a glass of water. "Yes, Mom. I cleaned up."

I guess I'm not believable, because she sets down her knife and goes into the mudroom. Two seconds later, I hear "Lizzie, I thought you said you tidied up."

Ugh. I slam down the glass of water and join her. "I did," I exclaim, pointing to the neat pile of supplies and books.

"What about this?"

I follow the line of her finger to the messenger bag hanging on the hook in the section next to mine. "What about it?"

"Your bag is in Rachel's section," she says. "You know how she didn't like that."

"So?"

"So? Take it off of there."

"Why?"

"Why?" Her face grows tight and her eyes bulge. "Why? You know why. Take it off now!"

"I— You know what, fine." I reach past her in a huff and drop the bag in my section. "There. Are you happy?"

Mom's lips press together. She's holding back some scathing comment, but I can read the anger in her eyes clear enough.

"You should know better" is what she says before spinning on her heel. "And clean off that dog hair. We don't allow pets in this house."

The furious retorts build in my mouth, clog up my throat, fill up my head. I have to clench my teeth so hard that I can feel it in my entire jaw. If I don't, the words will come out. The bad ones. The ones that make me look uncaring, selfish and jealous.

And maybe I am all those things. Maybe I am. But I'm the one still alive and shouldn't that matter for something?

God, I can't wait until I graduate. I can't wait until I leave this house. I can't wait until I'm free of this stupid, awful *fucking* prison.

I tear at my shirt. A button pops off and pings onto the tile floor. I curse silently. I'll have to beg Mom to sew this on tonight because I have only one work shirt. But screw it. Who cares? Who cares if I have a clean shirt? The customers at the Ice Cream Shoppe will just have to avert their eyes if a few strands of dog hair and chocolate sauce are sooooo offensive.

I shove the dirty shirt into the mudroom sink and strip off my pants for good measure. I saunter into the kitchen in my undies.

Mom makes a disgusted sound at the back of her throat.

As I'm about to climb the stairs, a stack of white envelopes on the counter catches my eye. The writing is familiar.

"What are those?" I ask uneasily.

"Your college applications," she replies, her voice devoid of emotion.

Horror spirals through me. My stomach turns to knots as I stare at the envelopes, at the handwriting, the sender addresses. What are they doing there? I rush over and start ri-fling through them. *USC, University of Miami, San Diego State, Bethune-Cookman University.*

The dam of emotions I was barely holding in check before bursts.

I slap a hand over the pile of envelopes. "Why do you have these?" I demand. "I put them in the mailbox."

"And I took them out," Mom says, her eyes still focused on the carrots in front of her.

"Why? Why would you do that?" I can feel myself tearing up, which always happens when I'm angry or upset.

"Why would you apply? You're not going to any of them." She reaches for an onion.

I place my hand on her wrist. "What do you mean I'm not going to any of these colleges?"

She plucks my hand off and meets my glare with a haughty, cold stare of her own. "We're paying for you to go to school, which means you'll go where we tell you—Darling College. And you don't need to keep asking for applications. We've already filled yours out for Darling. You should be accepted in October or so."

Darling is one of those internet colleges where you pay for your degree. It's not a real school. No one takes a degree from Darling seriously. When they told me over the summer that they wanted me to go there, I thought it was a joke.

My mouth drops. "Darling? That's not even a real college. That's—"

She waves the knife in the air. "End of discussion, Eliza-beth."

"But—"

"End of discussion, Elizabeth," she repeats. "We're doing this for your own good."

I gape at her. "Keeping me here for college is for my own good? Darling's degrees aren't worth the paper they're printed on!"

"You don't need a degree," Mom says. "You'll work at your father's hardware store, and when he retires you'll take that over."

Chills run down my spine. Oh my God. They're going to keep me here forever. They're never, ever going to let me go.

My dream of freedom has been snuffed like a hand over a candle flame.

The words tumble out. I don't mean for them to come out, but the seal breaks.

"She's dead, Mom. She's been dead for three years. My bag hanging from her hook isn't stopping her from coming home. Me getting a dog won't stop her from rising from her grave. She's dead. She's *dead!*" I scream.

Whack.

I don't see her hand coming. It strikes me across the cheek. The band of her wedding ring catches on my lip. I'm so surprised that I shut up, which is what she wanted, of course.

Her eyes widen. We stare at each other, chests heaving.

I break first, tearing out of the kitchen. Rachel might be dead, but her spirit is more alive in this house than I am.

2

"I don't want to go." Scarlett's firm tone doesn't waver. We've been standing in front of the gas station for twenty minutes arguing about our plans, and my best friend isn't budging.

Neither am I. My cheek still throbs from Mom's earlier strike.

The girls who invited us to the party lean against the side of a black Jeep with its top down, their heavily made-up faces wrinkled with annoyance. The dark-haired guy in the driver's seat looks impatient. I'm surprised they're waiting around. I mean, it's not like they know us. Their invitation was the result of a five-second conversation in the potato chip aisle after I told the blonde that I liked her shirt.

"Fine. Then don't go," I say to Scarlett.

Her brown eyes flood with relief. "Oh, okay, good. So we're not going?"

"No, *you're* not going." I lift my chin. "I am."

"Lizzie—"

"Beth," I cut in sharply.

I don't miss the irritated flicker in her eyes. "Beth," she

corrects, dragging out the one syllable as if it's *so* inconvenient for her to utter.

Like my parents, my best friend is having a tough time adjusting to my new name. Scarlett doesn't think the name Lizzie is juvenile at all—*It's more juvenile suddenly calling yourself something else after going your whole life as Lizzie!* was her response when I announced at the start of the summer that I was now going by Beth. But of course, she'd say that. Scarlett is a badass name. Who would ever dream of changing it?

"You don't even know these girls," Scarlett points out.

Another shrug. "I'll get to know them."

"Beth," she says miserably. "Come on."

"Please, Scar," I say, equally miserable. "I need this. After what happened today, I just need a fun, crazy night where I don't have to think about anything."

Her features soften. She knows all about the slap and the college application betrayal—it's all I've been talking about since I got to her house tonight. I think that's one of the reasons she suggested going out and driving around. She was tired of hearing about it.

"I really don't want to go, though," she admits. "But I don't want you to go alone."

"I'll be fine," I promise. "I'll go for a couple hours, scope out the scene and then come back to your place, and we can stay up all night eating ice cream."

She rolls her eyes. "The ice cream's all yours. I'm on a crash diet 'til Monday. I need to look hot for my first day of senior year."

A loud honk comes from the direction of the waiting Jeep. "Yo! Come on!" the driver shouts.

"I'll see you later, Scar," I say quickly. "Leave the back door unlocked for me, 'kay?" Then, before she can object, I hurry over to the Jeep. "I'm coming," I tell the girls, because if I don't do something outside my parents' perfectly prescribed routine, I will implode. There won't be anything left of me but scraps. That's how I feel right now, actually, like I'm nothing but scraps pasted together by my parents.

"'Bout time," one of them mutters, while the other blows a bright pink bubble with her gum.

"Beth!" Scarlett calls.

I glance over my shoulder. "Did you change your mind?"

She shakes her head. "Just be safe."

"I will." I climb into the back seat next to the blonde. Her friend hops into the passenger seat and whispers something to the driver. I lean over the side to address Scarlett again. "If my parents call, tell them I'm asleep. I'll be back in a few hours. Promise."

I blow her a kiss, and, after a beat of hesitation, she pretends to catch it in her hand and smacks it on her cheek. Then she heads for her car, and the boy behind the wheel of the Jeep revs the engine and we tear out of the gas station parking lot.

As the wind snakes under my hair and lifts it up, I count all the sins I've just committed.

Accepting a party invite from kids I don't know.

Going to a party in the next town over, an area that's not exactly white picket fences and apple trees like my pretty, safe hometown.

Getting into a car with strangers. That's probably the biggest sin. My parents will ship me off to a convent if they find out about this.

But guess what?

I. Don't. Fucking. Care.

They've already announced that I'm expected to spend my college years with them. We're at war now.

I feel trapped in my own life, weighed down by their rules and their paranoia and their fears. I'm seventeen years old. I'm supposed to be excited about my senior year. I'm supposed to be surrounded by friends and dating cute guys and having the time of my life right now. People say it's all downhill from here, and that's just depressing because if these are supposed to be the best years of my life, exactly how much crappier is life going to *get*?

"What's your name anyway?" the blonde girl asks.

"Beth. You?"

"Ashleigh, but you can call me Ash." She points to the front seat. "That's Kylie and Max. We all go to Lexington High. Gonna be juniors this year."

"I'll be a senior at Darling," I tell her.

A slight sneer mars her red-lipsticked mouth. "Ah, okay. You're a Darling girl."

I bristle at the implication. "Not everyone in Darling is rich, you know." I'm not lying; my family definitely isn't as rich as some of the other families in town. Our middle-class suburb is safe and quiet, though.

The party we're going to is in Lexington Heights—or Lex, as its residents call it—a working-class neighborhood where the houses are smaller, the people are poorer and the kids are rowdier. In Darling, coke and molly are passed around along with hash. In Lex, you're more likely to be offered meth.

My parents would freak out if they knew I was here. Scarlett nearly had a panic attack when we had to stop for gas in Lexington tonight.

"So whatcha doing over in Lex on a Saturday night?" Kylie twists around from the front seat to voice the question to me. "You looking to score some party favors?"

I offer a shrug. "I just want to have a good time before school starts."

Max whoops loudly. "Girl after my own heart! What's your name again, good-time girl?"

"Beth," I repeat.

"Beth." Driving one-handed, he reaches his other hand toward me. "Gimme some sugar, Bethie. Time to get our party on."

I awkwardly slap his hand and manage a smile. I suddenly feel really bad about ditching Scarlett, but I tamp down the guilt until it's buried deep and forgotten. Besides, she was okay with me going in the end, even though I don't think she totally gets why I had to go. Scar's parents are cool. They're laid-back and hilarious and they give her so much freedom she doesn't even know what to do with it.

I get it. I really, totally get it. I *do.* Mom and Dad lost a daughter. I lost a sister. We all loved Rachel and we all miss her, no one more than me. But my sister's accident was just that—an accident. And the person responsible was punished for it. Isn't that all we can ask for? Rachel's never coming back—that's not how life works. But justice was served, as much as it could've been.

And I'm still alive. I'm alive and I want to *live.*

Is that such a bad thing to want?

"We're here!" Ashleigh announces.

Max parks across the street from a narrow house with a white clapboard exterior and an overgrown lawn that's littered with teens. Beer bottles and joints are being passed around right there in the open, like nobody even cares if a police cruiser drives by.

"Who owns this place?" I ask.

"This guy Jack," Ash answers in an absent tone. She's too busy waving to some girls on the lawn.

"Are his parents home?"

Kylie snorts. "Um. No."

Okay then.

We climb out of the Jeep and weave our way through the crowd toward the front door. Kylie and Max disappear the moment we enter the house. Ashleigh sticks close to me. "Let's grab a drink!" she says.

I can barely hear her over the deafening hip-hop song that's shaking the walls. The house is crammed with bodies, and the air smells like a combination of perfume, body spray, sweat and stale beer. Not exactly my scene, but the bass line is sick and the kids look friendly enough. I half expected to see bare-knuckle brawls and people screwing against the walls, but it's mostly just dancing and drinking and very loud conversation.

Ash tugs me into a small kitchen with linoleum counters and outdated wallpaper. Half a dozen boys crowd around the open screen door, smoking a joint.

"Harley!" she shrieks happily, and then she lunges forward and throws her arms around one of the guys, who separates himself from the group. "Omigod! When did you get back?"

The tall boy lifts her off her feet and gives her a very sloppy-looking kiss right on the mouth. I think he's high, because his eyes are almost completely glazed over. I awkwardly lean against the counter and pretend like I belong here. This is what I want, I tell myself. A hard party that would drive my parents insane.

"Really late last night," he says. "We stopped for dinner in Chicago and then powered through for the rest of the drive. Marcus said he'd rather drive through the night than pay for a motel."

"You shoulda called me first thing this morning," Ash whines.

He slings an arm around her shoulders. Is he her boyfriend? She hasn't introduced us yet, so I have no idea.

"I didn't even wake up 'til like an hour ago," Harley says with a laugh. "Otherwise I would've called." His eyes narrow. "You seen Lamar yet?"

"Nope. Don't plan on it, either."

"Tonya says she saw him with Kelly at the arcade last night."

"Goody for Kelly. Can't wait for Lamar to dump her skanky ass just like Alex did."

Harley. Marcus. Tonya. Kelly. Lamar. Alex.

Who the heck are all these people? I stand there by the counter, growing more and more uncomfortable as Ashleigh and her maybe boyfriend toss random names back and forth to each other.

I look around the kitchen. Ash and Harley are still talking, arguing almost, about their friends. It doesn't matter. I didn't come here to listen to gossip. I'm tired of being passive, of allowing myself to be controlled. For the past three years, I've done what I've been told, taken the electives recommended, gotten the job that my parents set up for me.

And what's my reward?

Another four more years added to my sentence. The cell door got slammed shut before I even got a chance to step outside. I glance at the case of beer. I could get drunk, but that's too easy. I could get high, but that's too dangerous. I need to do something between drunk and high that would make me feel good and piss my parents off.

A flash of movement catches my attention, and I turn to find a very good-looking guy stopping and leaning in the kitchen doorway. He has the darkest blue eyes I've ever seen.

They're incredible. Over the left one, his eyebrow has a gap. It looks like a scar from this distance. Or a bad plucking accident, but he doesn't look like the type to manscape.

His jaw is covered with dark blond stubble, making him look older than all the other guys here. The boys in the kitchen, Harley included, don't have any facial hair. And they aren't nearly as tall as Blue Eyes or as built or as attractive.

Him. That's what I need. A very bad boy to take me down a very bad path.

A sense of power sweeps through me. This would make my parents angrier than anything. All kids drink, but hooking up with some random stranger? It would drive my proper mother nuts.

Internally, I rub my hands together with glee and start plotting. He's not making eye contact with me, but he's not staring at someone else, either—guy or girl. He's not exactly aloof, but there's space between him and the others. As if they're afraid to approach him. He's got an aura of someone cool and together.

The very things that I'm not.

I glance down at my ripped skinny jeans and skimpy yellow halter top and confirm that my zipper's zipped and my boobs are sufficiently covered. I'm not the hottest girl here, but he's alone and so am I.

Besides, if he says no, who cares? I won't see him again. And the whole point of coming out tonight was to do things that I wouldn't ever do. To get a taste of real life.

"Who's your friend?"

I jolt at the sound of Harley's voice. He's finally noticed me. "Hey," I say, tearing my gaze off Blue Eyes to smile at Harley. "I'm Beth."

"Harley." He releases Ashleigh and wanders over to hug

me. Harley's a hugger, it seems. "Nice to meet you. Wanna get high?"

"Um, maybe later?" I say coolly, hoping he doesn't notice the flush on my cheeks and realize I've never smoked weed before.

"Yeah, let's save that for later," Ash agrees, much to my relief. "Let's dance." She moves to my other side and links her arm through mine.

Dance? I sneak a peek at the doorway, only to find that Blue Eyes is gone. Disappointment washes over me. I wonder where he went. Maybe he's also heading to the dance floor—um, no. He didn't look like the kind of guy who would "shake his ass" to a techno beat. Way too intense for that. Most guys won't dance anyway. They think they're too cool for it.

"Come on," Ash says, tugging on my arm.

I place Blue Eyes on the shelf. I'll dance with Ashleigh and then pursue him. I let my new friend drag me into the living room, where the music is louder and the air is hotter. I start sweating, but it's okay because everyone else is, too. Ash bops her butt against my hip and the two of us laugh and whip our hair around and dance until we're breathless.

This is what I wanted tonight. To have fun and feel young and not think about the fact that my life is a joke. I don't *have* a life. I'm not allowed to go to parties, only to my friends' houses, and only if their parents are home. Driving around with Scarlett tonight was a huge no-no. Scar's folks knew it, too—my parents have been embarrassingly vocal to all my friends' families about the rules. I think Scar's mom feels sorry for me. When Scar and I were leaving, Mrs. Holmes pretended not to notice and I love her for it.

And I love this. The music and the noise and this room full

of strangers who don't know who I am. Nobody knows about
Rachel. Nobody feels sorry for me. Nobody cares.

I toss my hair back and bump hips with Ash again. Then I
stumble midstep when I catch another glimpse of Blue Eyes.

It's fate. We're supposed to meet tonight.

He walks over to the L-shaped couch and leans down to
say something to a stocky boy in a red T-shirt. His hair is
longer than I realized, curling under his ears and falling onto
his forehead. The dirty-blond color is almost the same shade
as my own.

I grab Ash's arm. "Who is that?"

"What?" she shouts over the beat.

I bring my lips close to her ear. "Who is that?" I repeat,
louder. "The guy by the couch."

She frowns. "Which one?"

I look back and tamp down a groan. He's gone again! What
the hell. This guy appears and disappears like a ninja. This
time, I'm not letting him get away.

"I have to pee," I tell Ashleigh.

She nods and turns to dance with someone else. I make
my way out of the crowd. Blue Eyes is back, leaning against
the kitchen doorway.

I take a deep breath and force myself forward. I've never,
ever hit on a guy before. This is going to be disastrous.

I spy a row of shot glasses on a table. I grab one and throw
it back. The foul liquid burns on the way down. I slap a hand
up to my mouth to cover a cough. Over my fingers, I meet
Blue Eyes's gaze.

With courage I didn't know I had, I pick up two more shot
glasses and carry them over.

"You look like you need a drink," I say, offering him one.

He takes it. "You look like that was the first shot you ever drank."

I'm so glad it's dark in here so no one can see me blushing. "Nah, I've drunk a few in my time," I lie.

"Mmm-hmm," he says before lifting the shot glass to his lips. He downs it cleanly and then tucks the empty in his front jeans pocket. My eyes wander downward and then flip back up to see him staring at me in bemusement.

"Do you know who I am?" he asks.

I run my tongue across my lower lip, wondering what I should say. Is he famous? I don't want to seem uncool. "Of course." I shrug as carelessly as possible. "Doesn't everyone here?"

Something dark passes over his face. "Yeah, probably. But you're still here talking to me. Bringing me drinks." He taps my shot glass.

"Like I said, you looked like you needed one."

He scrubs a hand down his face. The dark shadow is gone, only to be replaced by a weary expression. "I guess that's true. So why are you here? Want to take a walk on the wild side?"

His last sentence is said with great scorn. Intuitively, I know that the truth is not my friend, because if I admit I came here to piss off my parents, Blue Eyes is going to disappear, and I desperately do not want that to happen.

Not because I think this is the perfect way to get back at my parents, but because there's something interesting about him. Because I want to get to know him. Because I want him to want to get to know me.

I can't tell him the real reason, but I can be honest, as embarrassing as it is. "Can't a girl bring a hot guy a drink? I tried to get your attention before, but you disappeared. You were standing here by yourself and I took a chance. If that's wild behavior in your book, then you must not get out much."

He cocks his head. "Is that a joke?"

"Yes. But not a good one because you're not laughing." I stare at the shot in my hand. This has gone more terribly than I imagined.

He exhales heavily. "Because my people skills suck. Joke or not, we both know I *haven't* gotten out much in the past three years."

I have no idea what that means, but since I already pretended to know all about him, I can't ask for an explanation. "Does that mean I should go?"

"No. You should stay." The corner of his mouth curves up. "Not gonna lie. This is all very good for my ego."

"It hasn't been good for mine," I admit, a bit testy.

The half smile turns into a full one and my breath catches at how gorgeous he is.

"I've never had a girl as pretty as you say so much as hello to me."

My heart flips over and I'm so dumbstruck I can't summon a witty reply.

He ducks his head in embarrassment. "Too corny?"

I find my voice. "Too amazing. My head is so big right now I don't think this house can contain me."

"Then let's get out of here."

"Really?" My eyes grow wide. "Where?"

"Just outside. I like it outside."

"Me, too."

He holds out his hand. Mine slips easily into his. His long fingers curl around the back of my hand. Against my palm, there are hard calluses. We leave the shot glasses on the kitchen counter we pass. I don't need the alcohol now. I'm holding hands with the hottest guy on the planet, and I feel like I'm floating on air.

We maneuver through the crowd. Some people stare. I lift my head. *Yeah, I'm with this hottie.*

Outside, the noise thins out and so do the people. He leads me down the deck and toward a small shed.

"Do you keep the bodies in there?" I joke.

He halts suddenly. "You have a dark humor, don't you?"

The remark makes me think of the hysterical laughter that burbled in my throat during Rachel's funeral. How I covered my face to keep it from spilling out and everyone thought I was sobbing. It wasn't so much dark humor as a defense mechanism.

"I'd rather laugh than cry," I admit. "I cry too easily. It's one thing I hate about myself."

He lowers himself onto the grass. "That's not a bad philosophy—the laughing over crying thing."

"I wish I had more control over my tears. It's frustrating when I'm mad but everyone thinks I'm sad." I drop to the ground beside him, wondering why I'm spilling these things to him. I shut up then, and listen to the crickets sing as the faint music in the house plays in the background.

"You have a name?" he teases.

"I'm Beth."

He rakes a hand through his messy hair. My gaze doesn't miss the way his biceps flex from that action. He's got incredible arms. Sculpted.

"I'm Chase." He tilts his head toward me. "And I still feel like you're too good to be sitting out here with me."

"You aren't holding me down," I point out. "Are you telling me to leave?"

"No. I don't want that." He exhales again and his perfect body is momentarily framed by the thin cotton of his T-shirt.

Gosh, he's gorgeous.

"It's beautiful out here, isn't it?"

I glance up at the night sky and then at Chase's upturned face. It's so cloudy you can barely make out the moon, let alone the stars. "I guess?" He's beautiful. The sky? Not so much.

He chuckles to himself. "It could be raining buckets and I'd be happy."

"Me, too." *Because I'm with you*, I think. I haven't felt this at peace with myself for weeks, maybe months. The fight with my mom seems like a long-ago bad memory.

His hand is pressed against the ground between us. I edge mine closer to his until our pinkies touch.

"Your fingers are long."

He turns his head away from the sky to peer at our fingers. "Maybe yours are really short."

"I have normal-sized hands."

"Let's see." He slides his hand over mine and my fingers disappear under his.

My heart begins to beat wildly and my mouth goes dry. Body parts start tingling in places I didn't know could tingle.

"Are you going to kiss me?" I blurt out.

His lips curve into that gorgeous smile of his. "Yeah. I think so. You okay with that?"

I nod.

"It's been a long time for me," he admits.

His honesty catches me off guard. "Me, too."

"Good." He tucks my hair behind my ear. He moves closer. "Then we can mess up together. Tell me if I do something wrong."

He palms my cheek, strokes it gently. Ever so slowly, his lips meet mine.

3

Chase rolls onto his side. He reaches for something on the nightstand of the bedroom we wound up in. I hear the hiss of a lighter. The scent of smoke soon fills my nostrils as I lie there, staring at the ceiling. Taking a deep drag, he shifts onto his back and does the same. The crisp cotton sheet covers his lower body. His chest is bare.

Me, I threw my clothes on the moment it was over. Second thoughts are chased by third thoughts chased by so many thoughts that I'm paralyzed. What do I do now?

What have I done, period? My entire body is hot with embarrassment and my heart is pounding harder than the bass line that's still shaking the house.

Chase takes another drag on his cigarette. He's acting like what we just did was no big deal. But maybe it's not to him. It probably isn't. He probably has sex with hundreds of girls at parties.

I didn't tell him I was a virgin.

I—

"I have to go," I blurt out, shooting to my feet.

He doesn't say a word. Doesn't meet my gaze. I'm glad, because I don't particularly want him to see the shame swimming in my eyes.

It's not until I'm about to turn the doorknob that he speaks.

"Where's your phone?"

My head swivels toward him, and, finally, our gazes collide. His expression reveals nothing. His chest still has a slight sheen of sweat on it from… I tear my eyes away.

"It's in my purse," I mumble. "Why?"

"Take it out."

I'm helpless to say no when it comes to this guy. Face burning, I fish my phone out of my bag and wait.

He rattles off a number.

I stare at him, still feeling dazed. And my body, despite being sore, is responding to the sight of his abs.

"Put that number in your phone." His voice is rough. "Text me when you get back to your friend's place so I know you made it back okay."

I keep staring.

"Beth," he prompts, and I finally manage to find my voice.

"Give me the number again," I whisper.

He repeats the digits and I dutifully type them into my phone.

"And, yeah, call me if you ever need me," he says gruffly.

I nod, but I think we both know that aside from the one text I'll send from Scarlett's, I will never, ever, ever use his number again.

4

Tuesday is the first day of school. The first day of my last year, and I should be rejoicing. One year is all I have left under this roof. One year until I'm in college, the college *I* want to attend, free from my parents' constant, watchful control.

Their eyes are pinned on me right now. They have questions. I can feel a heaviness in the air. Mom's disappointment mixed with Dad's frustration and resentment have formed a black thundercloud that clings to the ceiling and walls like smoke after a pan fire.

I try to act normally, as if I didn't do things last night I sorely regret. Things I've lied about to Scarlett, to my parents, to myself. Since I opened my eyes this morning, I've been forcing myself not to think about Chase. But it's so hard not to. And when the thoughts of him do surface, I feel like sobbing.

I had sex for the first time yesterday. I wanted to, and I enjoyed it. I really did—at the time. But it didn't take very long for the glow to fade. For the thrill of doing something new and exciting and rebellious to be replaced with bone-deep shame.

My first time was with a stranger. It was a one-night stand.

What the hell do I do with that? I can't even begin to process it, and I wish my parents would stop staring at me. I'm afraid if they stare long enough, they'll be able to read my thoughts.

"Did you have a nice time at Scarlett's?" Mom asks, breaking the silence.

The sound of her voice brings a phantom pain to my cheek. She *hit* me yesterday. She's acting like she doesn't remember. Or maybe she's just trying to forget. Or hoping *I'll* forget. Fat chance.

"Lizzie?" she prompts. "Did you have a nice time?"

"Uh-huh." I push the sautéed zucchini to the edge of my plate. Scarlett had been sleeping when I crawled into her bed. When morning came, I barely spoke a word to her. She kept pumping me for details about the party, but I could only manage vague answers. I don't want Scarlett to know that I gave it up to some hot stranger at some random party. It's way too embarrassing.

"What did you do?"

My fork halts its trek to the side, a pale green half-moon stuck on one of the tines. This type of question is asked only when your parents are suspicious and want to catch you in a lie. The less said in times like these, the better. "Stuff."

I force my hand to move, to pretend like my heart rate hasn't picked up and my body isn't tense with fear.

"Like what?" Mom's tone is light, but probing.

"Same stuff we always do."

There are several beats of silence during which I realize that they know something and are waiting for a confession. I keep my eyes pinned to my plate.

Next up for separation are the mushrooms. I hate those. I always have and yet Mom continues to cook with them.

Mushrooms were Rachel's favorite.

There's a shuffling of papers. White appears at the corner of my eye. I don't want to look but I can't help it.

"Do you know what this is?" It's Dad's turn to question me now.

This is a good cop/bad cop routine that they do. Mom pretends concern and when I don't show any remorse, Dad steps in with his stern voice and even sterner commands.

"No." That's honest, at least.

"It's a printout of your text messages."

"What?" Jaw dropping, I grab the sheaf of papers. My eyes skim down the page in total disbelief. Either I'm hallucinating, or I'm actually reading a transcript of the texts I exchanged with Scar when I was leaving the party last night.

217-555-2956: How's the party? U OK?
217-555-5298: I'm fine. Party's lit. omw back now. cabbing it.
217-555-5298: Prnts call?
217-555-2956: No
217-555-5298: kk cover 4 me if they do
217-555-5298: Made it back, safe and sound.

My stomach sinks. That last one was the message I sent Chase. I almost cry with gratitude that I didn't say anything more damning.

I flip backward and see more messages.

217-555-2956: party 2nite?
217-555-5298: yessss
217-555-2956: what abt prnts?
217-555-5298: Ill tell them have 2 wrk

Fear, anger and frustration spin around in my head. I don't even know what to say. And in the back of my mind, all I can think is *Thank God*. Thank God I didn't text Scarlett about Chase and confess to having sex for the first time. Thank God I didn't message Chase about what happened between us. The mere thought of my parents finding out about it, reading it firsthand on some text message, makes me nauseous.

"I can't believe you're spying on me!" I shout, slamming the papers onto the table. Unwelcome tears prick the corners of my eyes. "You don't have any right to read my text messages!"

"I pay for that phone of yours," Dad thunders.

"Then I'll pay for it myself!" I jump out of my chair and push away from the table.

Dad grabs my wrist. "Sit down. We aren't done."

The look in his eye says that I better sit or he'll make me. He never used to be this hard, this strict. Before Rachel died, he was the fun dad. He told the cheesiest jokes because he liked hearing us groan and cringe at them. Now I don't think he even remembers how to smile.

I gulp, try to find my bravado, but come up empty. I sit.

"It's not your actions that disappoint us," Mom says, "but your lying. We simply can't trust you."

"Which is why your car is being taken away," Dad adds.

"My car?" I gape at them. My car is one of the single instances of freedom I have. They gave me Mom's old hatchback the second I got my learner's permit. I would've been fine taking the bus or walking, but my parents felt I'd be safer behind the wheel of a car than on foot at crosswalks or bus stops.

Rachel was on foot when she was killed after all. Apparently that means I can't walk within five steps of a motor vehicle ever again.

God, I sound bitter. I hate feeling this way, especially when deep down I know my parents aren't bad people. They just haven't recovered from Rachel's death. I doubt they ever will, not without years and years of therapy—which they refuse to go to. The one time I suggested it, Mom stiffly informed me that everyone grieves differently, and then she got up and walked out of the room.

But they're hurting me as a result of their unending grief, and I *am* bitter. And now they're taking away my car?

In my car, I can blast my music, scream profanities and give voice to all my inner frustrations. Losing it would be awful.

I grapple for reasons that'll convince them that this is wrong. "How am I supposed to get to work? Or the animal shelter?" For the past year, I've volunteered at a local animal shelter twice a month. Rachel's allergy made it impossible for us to have pets at home and even now that she's gone, the no-pets rule is still strictly enforced. So volunteering is the only way I get to be around dogs, who are way better than people, in my opinion.

Mom doesn't meet my eyes. Dad clears his throat. "You won't be doing, either. We've informed your boss at the Ice Cream Shoppe and Sandy at the clinic that you'll be too busy with school to be able to work or volunteer."

"You…" I take a breath. "You *quit* my jobs for me?"

"Yes."

I'm so stunned I don't have a response. All I can see are the doors slamming closed in my already-constrained life. No car. Slam. No part-time job. Slam. No volunteer work. Slam. Slam. Slam.

"You're saying I go to school and come home. That's it?" The knot in my chest threatens to choke me. It's my senior year. I should be looking forward to my world getting bigger, not smaller.

"Until you can prove to us that you're worthy of our trust, yes."

I turn toward Mom. "You can't agree with this. I know you know that this is wrong."

She refuses to meet my eyes. "If we were stricter before..." She trails off but I know what *before* means. Our lives are strictly bisected into BR and AR.

"Marnie, let's not talk about that." Dad likes to pretend that BR never happened.

"Right, of course, but it's because we love you that we're doing this. We don't want a repeat of the past. Your father and I discussed—"

"This is bullshit!" I erupt. I spring to my feet and out of my dad's reach.

"Don't use that tone with us." Dad shakes his finger at me.

This time I don't cower. I'm too angry to be afraid. "This is bullshit," I repeat recklessly. Tears are dropping—which I hate—but I can't stop. I can't stop my words, my anger or my tears. "This is punishment because I'm the one alive and Rachel is the one who's dead. I can't fucking wait until I leave here. I'm not coming back. I'm not!"

Mom bursts into tears. Dad yells. I spin on my heel and race to my bedroom. Behind me, I hear my parents shouting. I climb the stairs two at a time and slam my bedroom door shut. I don't have a lock but I do have a desk. I break three nails and knock the wood against my shin twice, but I finally drag it in front of the door.

Just in time, too, because Dad's at the door, trying to shove it open.

"You open this door right now," he demands.

"Or what?" I cry. I've never felt more helpless. "Or what? You'll ground me? You've taken away my job, my car, my

privacy. I can't make a call or write a text without you knowing. I can't even breathe without having to report to you. You
don't have anything left to punish me with."

"We're doing this for your sake." That's Mom, pleading
for me to be reasonable. "We're not punishing you because
of your sister—" she can't even say Rachel's name "—we're
trying to help you. We love you so much, Lizzie. We…" Her
voice cracks. "We don't want to lose you."

I lie down on the bed and pull the pillow over my head. I
don't care what they have to say. There's no justification for
what they're doing. I wouldn't be sneaking out if they let me
have some freedom. Scarlett's parents don't hold her down and
she never sneaks out. If she goes to a party, she tells them. If
she gets drunk, she can call them and they'll come pick her
up. And the truth is she rarely gets drunk, because they'll let
her have the occasional beer or glass of wine. It's my parents'
fault I'm this way. They've made me into this girl—the one
who doesn't listen, the one who sneaks and lies and breaks
promises, loses her virginity to some stranger.

I dig my face into the mattress as hot shame roils through
me. I hate them. I hate Rachel. I hate myself most of all.

Because of my actions, the sweet animals at the shelter are
going to suffer. Who's going to take the doggies for a walk?
Who's going to feed Opie his medicine? I'm the only one that
can handle the rottie. He hates everyone else at the clinic. And
George, the snake? The techs there are scared of the python.

The sound of metal clanking against metal and the whir-
ring of a drill grab my attention. I sit up and search for the
source of the construction sounds.

My eyes clash with my dad's, visible above the door he's
holding. He glares grimly at me before walking away. I gape

at the open doorway. He removed my door. He fucking removed my fucking door.

I leap to my feet and rush over to the desk that's still in the
doorway. "What are you doing?" I say helplessly.

Mom appears in the hallway. "Sweetheart, please."

"Are you serious?" I reach out, still in disbelief that my dad
removed the door from the wall, but the empty hinges hang
there in mocking proof.

"This is only temporary," she says.

"It'll be permanent if she can't clean up her act," Dad yells
from below.

"Mom. I'm seventeen. I need a door to my bedroom." I
can't believe my voice is so stable when my insides are riot-
ing. "Even prisoners have a door!"

Her gaze falls to the floor. "It's only temporary," she repeats.
"Until we can trust you again."

I stumble back. "I can't believe this. I can't fucking believe
this."

"Don't curse," she snaps. "You know how much I hate
that."

"Right, because Rachel never cursed."

"It's not about Rachel."

"Of course it is. Everything in my life is about Rachel.
You let Rachel do whatever she wanted. She didn't have to
follow a single rule and it backfired on you, so now you're
doing the exact opposite with me," I spit out. "You've kept
me on a leash since she died, and now the collar's so tight it's
going to choke me to death."

"Don't say that." Mom's eyes glitter dangerously. She ad-
vances, stopped only by the desk. "Don't you say that. Don't
you say that word."

"Or what?" I challenge. "You're going to hit me again?"

Her face collapses. "I'm sorry I did that," she whispers. "I—"

"What's going on?" Dad has returned. He looks at me and then at Mom.

"Nothing," we say at the same time.

And then we all fall silent because there's nothing left on our tongues but caustic, hurtful words and we've done enough to inflict pain on each other. I return to my bed, shut my eyes and ignore the grunts from my father as he lifts the desk away from the doorway, the mewling noises of my mother as she frets over how our household is a war zone.

This is my life now. I'm imprisoned in my own home, with no privacy and no escape. Graduation can't come soon enough.

5

The bus stinks of nerves and cold sweat. The freshmen are huddled toward the front, but the smell of their fear drifts all the way to the back. Next to me, Sarah Bunting chatters on about her new manicure and the "lit as fuck" Converse sneakers she scored at the Premium Outlets in Rosemont.

I turn my music up even louder and slouch down in the seat. Seventeen, licensed, has her own car, but still rides the bus. How lowering.

I keep my head down as I walk to my locker in the seniors' wing. I don't greet anyone and whether it's the surly look on my face or something else, everyone leaves me alone.

I spin the locker combination, jerk my door open and stuff my backpack inside. My first class is AP Calc. Woo-hoo. At least there won't be some long lecture—only a bunch of practice problems. I grab my supplies for the next three classes and slam the door shut. Scarlett's face appears and I try not to jump in surprise.

"Hey," I mutter.

"I'm so sorry." She looks genuinely regretful.

First thing I did this morning was IM her with the heads-up that I'd been busted. With my parents having evidence that Scar and I have sneaked out to parties before, I had to warn her in case my parents snitched to hers.

"Forget it." It's not her fault, really.

"Everything is just going to shit, huh?" She sighs. "You're having the worst luck—first your parents and TextGate, and now this."

I guess she means the grounding. "They took my phone away, too," I say glumly.

"Oh, okay, so *that's* why you haven't responded to the million messages I've sent you."

"Yup."

She clucks her tongue sympathetically. "I don't know, maybe it's a good thing you don't have a phone right now. I can't imagine what people are texting you. Kids can be so dumb."

My cheeks feel hot. Why would anyone be texting me? Did someone see me at the party? Did they know what happened with me and Chase? Do they know what's going on in my house? Did my parents actually tell other parents that they took the door off my room? God, this year is going to be nothing but one set of humiliations after another, all courtesy of my parents.

"Whatever." I force one shoulder up in a careless gesture. "It doesn't matter what anyone thinks. After this year, we probably won't see half these kids ever again."

"Gosh, I hope not." Scarlett tugs on my books. "Let me carry those."

"Why? I can carry my books."

"I know you can. I just… Forget it." She slips her arm through mine. "Let's go to Calc."

"Why did we ever decide taking AP Calc was a good move?"

"Something about it looking good on our college apps. Have you decided what visits you're going to do this fall?"

My mood dives even lower thinking of the applications Mom has stolen. Guess what. I'm going to get new ones and reapply. The problem is I can't do it online because I need a credit card to pay the fees. I was able to mail a money order. I'm not sure how I'm going to pull off future applications, but I'm going to make it happen. Somehow.

"USC, Florida, Miami, San Diego State." I rattle off my dream destinations. Granted, I have no clue what I want to major in, but at least I've got the location category confidently checked off.

Scarlett grins. "Hmm. I'm sensing a beach theme."

"You're so smart, Scar."

"I know, but you don't really want to go so far away, do you? I'll miss you so much."

Any response I would've had dries up at the sight of a tall, broad frame at the end of the hall. I wouldn't have noticed him, if not for the fact that the entire senior hall has fallen silent.

My heart rate speeds up as my eyes meet familiar blue ones. Oh my God. Oh my *God*. What is he doing here?

"What is he *doing* here?" I say out loud before I can stop myself.

Crap. Now she's going to ask how I know him and I'll have to admit to meeting him at the party, and she'll read between the lines and know exactly what I did. Or maybe someone from Darling saw Chase and me together and told everyone, and Scarlett already knows. Either way, embarrassment is burning holes in my cheeks.

Scarlett follows my gaze and halts in her tracks. "Right? The nerve of that guy! To show up here." She steps forward and then turns to try to block my view of Chase. "I can't believe they didn't make him go to a different school, but I'm sure it has to do with his mom being the mayor's wife now." She tsks again. "Favoritism is so gross."

"He's the mayor's stepson?" I say blankly.

"I didn't know that either until this morning. Wendy Bluth said that his mother was secretly dating the mayor for years and they just tied the knot this spring. I don't think anyone would've voted for him if they'd known the truth."

"The truth?" I'm so confused.

Scarlett's mouth turns into a sympathetic frown. "I get it. You don't want to talk about it." She glances over her shoulder to check if Chase is still there. "It's weird. I didn't even recognize him at first because he looks totally different, but you can't mistake the scar."

My bewilderment deepens. There's no reason for Scarlett to recognize him at all. She wasn't even at the party.

I turn back and stare. He doesn't look any different from Saturday night. He looks exactly the same. Breathtakingly attractive. His chin is completely clean today. His dark blond hair sweeps down in the front, almost, but not quite, covering the scar that bisects his eyebrow.

I kissed that scar a few times that night.

The heat of embarrassment creeps through me again. I can't believe he's standing ten feet away from me right now. I thought I'd never see him again, and I was okay with it because that was the less humiliating option. Coming face-to-face with him again after what we did is a million times more humiliating.

Our eyes lock. My breath catches. Scarlett's saying something, but I can't hear her over the roaring mortification in my ears. Or is that something else I'm feeling? I swallow and it feels like there are razor blades in my throat.

"Come on," she says. "Just ignore him. He isn't worth your time."

How does she know? "Does he have a rep?" I ask hoarsely, because it suddenly occurs to me what might've happened. If Chase has the reputation of being a player, maybe he bragged about Saturday night to anyone who'd listen. Darling and Lexington Heights are neighboring towns—word travels fast if the right people are talking about it.

"Meaning does everyone know about him?" she asks.

I nod without looking at her.

"Of course everyone knows about him." She huffs in disgust. "Oh, there's Jeff."

A flicker of green catches my eye. Directly over Chase's shoulder, Jeff Corsen's dark head appears.

I'm not too surprised to see him. I heard he was coming back to Darling. After Rachel died, Jeff totally broke down. Barely managed to finish his sophomore year and then disappeared for more than two years. Grief, his parents said. They sent him to England to live with his grandparents, but apparently he didn't finish senior year over there because he's back at Darling High. It's weird that my sister's boyfriend, who used to be two years ahead of me, is now in the same grade.

In his forest green hoodie and faded jeans, Jeff strides forward, his shoulder deliberately bumping Chase's. It breaks our eye contact. Chase's mouth thins and I tense up, anticipating a confrontation. But then Chase merely turns aside, ignoring the insult.

He's not fazed by a thing. Not by seeing his hookup standing at the end of the hall on the first day at a new school. Not by being physically brushed aside by another guy. Not by the stares and silence of his new classmates.

I envy that. God, I envy his composure a lot. It reminds me of why I was attracted to him in the first place. There's a surety about him. Like, a hurricane could sweep through and he'd still be standing in the hall, feet firmly planted, shoulders back.

I bet his parents wouldn't have the nerve to take the door off his bedroom.

Noise penetrates my brain. Jeff's appearance has broken the spell cast by Chase. A few classmates laugh. Others rush up to greet Jeff. He was popular before he left. He and Rachel were the golden couple. If she'd lived to her senior year, the two of them would've been king and queen of homecoming and the prom.

If she'd lived… My heart seizes up and a familiar discomfort churns in my stomach. I'm not going to think about that.

Instead, I wonder what it was like for Rachel, to be so loved by a guy that he had to move to another country to recover from her death. Did he love her more than I did? I know my parents think I didn't love Rachel enough, that I don't mourn her like I should. If I did, I'd behave.

I did love her, though. We were two years apart, but she never treated me like I was a bratty little sister, not even when she started high school and I was still in middle school. We helped each other with homework. We played volleyball. We had slumber parties in her room. She was my big sister. *Of course* I loved her.

I swallow the pain again. Banish it. Unlike my parents, I won't let myself obsess over Rachel. I can't.

"Hey, Lizzie," Jeff says when he reaches me. His hand, the one with the long, elegant fingers that floated across the piano keys, reaches out and curves around my ear. "Long time, no see."

"It's Beth." When he makes a quizzical face, I repeat, "Beth. I don't go by Lizzie anymore."

"All right. Beth it is. How are you?"

"Hi, Jeff!" Scarlett chirps at my side before I can respond.

"Scarlett," he says. His voice is different, accented.

Scarlett notices. "Oh my God. You came back with an accent. That's so cool."

"Is it?" Jeff cocks his head. Behind him, I spot Chase again. His face is half-hidden by the locker door, but I know it's him.

My body tingles. I guess I'd know it was him if I was blindfolded. A connection was made the other night—one that neither of us can really deny by the looks of the way we stared at each other before Jeff appeared.

Why am I the one ashamed of what happened? It was my choice. I wanted it. The thing I should be embarrassed about is running off like a scared girl. But I can't help it.

I've never been one of those girls who pictured candles and rose petals for her first time, but I at least thought I'd be going out with the guy I gave my V-card to. He'd be my boyfriend, and we'd take it slow and make out a bunch and fool around until we eventually did the deed. But that didn't happen, and I don't know how I feel about that.

What I do know is that I can't let him, or anyone else, see how shaken up I am. I straighten my shoulders. Confidence is what Chase has. I want that.

"Nice to see you, Jeff," I say, and then I take a few steps forward, in Chase's direction.

"Wait—" Scar catches my arm. "Do you really think this is a good idea?"

"Why not?" I shrug. "He obviously goes to school here. I might as well face up to him now instead of trying to hide from him for the next nine months."

"There's no reason for you to talk to him," Jeff says. "We'll keep him away." He throws a dark look over his shoulder toward Chase, who's gathered his books and is walking away.

Yeah, Chase definitely has a rep. Even Jeff, who's been gone for so long, has apparently heard that something went down between me and Chase. That means word's gotten around.

A spark of anger lights my belly as I picture Chase bragging to all those Lex kids that he bagged a Darling girl.

I speed up, walking fast down the hall with my eyes pinned on Chase's back.

He's an island. Like, there's literally a bubble of space around him, which is shocking given the size of my class. Three hundred seniors attend Darling. The halls are packed this morning, yet no one seems to be able to penetrate his personal space. Fuck. I kinda love that.

I walk faster, waving hello to classmates but not stopping until I reach Chase. He's halted in front of the AP Calc room. How convenient.

I hug my books close to my chest and clear my throat. "Chase."

He spins slowly until we're facing each other. "Beth."

Despite my anger that he might've told people about us, I appreciate that he calls me Beth. He knows me only as that. I don't have to remind him that it's my name now.

"Who'd you tell?" I say bluntly.

He wrinkles his forehead. "Tell?"

"Yeah, who did you tell?" I repeat, sounding way more confident and confrontational than I feel right now. Just being in his presence is fogging my mind. "About Saturday night."

Rather than flush or look sheepish, he meets my gaze head-on. "Nobody."

"Nobody," I echo, still suspicious.

"Yeah. Why would I tell anyone?" he says simply.

For some inexplicable reason, I believe him. I believe he's kept quiet about what we did at the party. Someone else must've seen us. Maybe someone saw me coming out of that bedroom. Ashleigh, or the guy who owned the house. Whoever it was, I know it wasn't Chase.

"All right, then," I say with a nod.

The corners of his eyes crinkle in humor. "All right, then," he echoes.

Anger dissipating, I brush by him, open the classroom door and then reach back and grab the sleeve of his untucked and unbuttoned denim shirt to pull him inside. "So I don't know if you've heard the scoop, but the AP Calc teacher is a monster. Rumor has it she stays up nights and spends her weekends thinking of new ways to torture us. Expect constant pop quizzes and no-mercy midterms."

He sounds amused. "Okay."

There are a few other students inside. Macy Stedman waves to me until she notices Chase. Then her hand falls and her face grows anxious.

"Lizzie, come here." She motions me over.

"Lizzie?" asks Chase, an odd note in his voice.

"It's Beth," I tell him. "Elizabeth Jones."

There's a long, strained beat.

"Elizabeth Jones?" he chokes out.

"Yes. But everyone calls me Beth."

He jerks his arm out of my grip. My hand drops to my side. I flush lightly, embarrassed by his sudden need to get away from me.

"Did you tell me your last name the other night?" His voice is low and harsh. I have to lean in to hear him.

"Maybe. No. Probably not." I don't know his, either, I realize. "Why? What's yours?"

"Lizzie! I need to talk to you!" Macy calls shrilly.

"It's Beth," I tell her between gritted teeth. "And I'll be

there in a sec." I turn back to Chase, whose face is chalk white. "What's yours?" I repeat.

He licks his lips and takes another step back. And then another. Until two desks are between us. "I'm Charles Donnelly. And I'm sorry."

With that, he turns on his heel and walks out of the classroom. Charles Donnelly.

My stomach lurches. "I thought your name was Chase!" I yell after him.

Macy appears at my shoulder. "Are you all right? Did he hurt you?"

I turn bewildered eyes to her, hoping for some help in processing what I just learned. "That was Charles Donnelly?"

"Uh-huh." She nods and rubs a hand up my arm.

"I didn't recognize him." My head's clogged up. I can't stop blinking.

"He's changed a lot. Prison will do that for you," she sneers toward the empty doorway. "Come on. I bet you're in shock. I can't believe you have classes with him. Admin sucks. They are so incompetent." She leads me over to the desk next to hers. "Should I get you a water? Or, um, a Coke maybe? I'll get a Coke. Be right back."

I barely register her leaving because my mind is still whirling over the fact that I slept with Charles Donnelly.

The guy who killed my sister.

I barely make it to the trash can before my breakfast surges violently up my throat.

6

"Are you sure you're okay?" Macy asks for what feels like the thousandth time.

"Yep," I answer as brightly as possible. The lunchroom's familiar buzz isn't settling my nerves like I'd hoped. Instead, I keep wondering how many of those conversations are about me. I'm not blind to the fact that there was a shit ton of head turning when I entered.

"You didn't stay in the nurse's office very long," Scarlett says quietly. "I would've lain in there all day."

"He shouldn't even be here," Macy insists. "Like why isn't he at Lexington Public or Lincoln?"

"The mayor lives in Grove Heights and that's Darling school district," Yvonne, one of my other friends, points out.

A voice of reason. I throw her a small relieved smile. She frowns in return, as if smiling is not permitted at a time like this, so I let my gaze fall back onto my unappealing salad.

"The mayor should open enroll him into Lex. Isn't that where all the delinquents hang out?" Macy asks.

with my toe. I want to get over Rachel's death, but here, in this house, in this town, it's impossible.

Rachel is everywhere. Her room is in the same exact condition it was the night she died, except Mom has made the bed. Rachel never made her bed. She'd wake up late, throw the covers on the floor and rush to the bathroom we shared. Downstairs in the mudroom, Mom still has her name in white chalk over her section of the storage bench. The piano that only Rachel ever played still sits in our living room, meticulously dusted each and every day by my mother. The wood-and-rope swing Dad constructed for Rachel is still hanging in this yard, even though no one has used it since she died. If I go into Rachel's room, I'll see her volleyball uniform hanging on the back of her door. Even her toothbrush is still in her side of the Jack-and-Jill bath.

I once asked Mom why. She broke down and shut herself in her bedroom for an hour. Dad glared at me the whole time. I never asked again, but Mom told me later that it was so we would never forget.

Forget Rachel? How could you? Even if you razed this house and all its possessions to the ground, you wouldn't forget her. I don't say any of this to Mom, though. The grief counselor they sent me to after Rachel's death says everyone grieves in their own way and that no way is wrong. But I can't help but measure my sadness, or lack thereof, against my mom's or dad's or, hell, even the kids at school.

All of them expect me to react a certain way, but I just want to be me. If I knew who *me* was. I'm trying to figure that out. It's why I keep trying different things. I don't fit in here. None of the Darling crowds feel right to me. That's why I went with Ashleigh the other night. It's one of the reasons that

I slept with Chase—no, sorry, Charlie. I thought, wrongly, that I'd find out something about myself.

I guess I did. I found out I make shit choices when it comes to guys.

Shame tickles my throat. I gulp it down, because really, I have to cut myself some slack about this. Having sex isn't a crime. I'm seventeen—most of my friends, Scarlett included, have already lost their virginity. Macy had sex for the first time in freshman year, Yvonne when she was a soph. Technically, I waited way longer than most of my peers.

But if I had to do it over again, I'd turn around and walk away.

Wouldn't I?

I scrub my hands over my face, but a soft whining noise has me lifting my head. For the first time in what feels like years, a genuine smile tugs on my mouth.

I hop off the swing and wander over to the wooden fence that separates our yard from the Rennicks'. The sweetest sight greets me—big brown eyes and a wet black nose and the sloppy, drooly tongue of the big black mutt whose head is popping out from between two slats. The gaps in the fence are just big enough for Morgan to stick his head through, but not enough that he can wiggle his whole body free.

I wish he could, though. I'd love nothing more than to run around in the yard with him and be the receiver of his doggy kisses. Actually, I want *all* the neighborhood dogs to join us—Morgan, Mr. Edwards's yappy terrier and the Palmers' labradoodle. That would be a thousand times better than sitting here thinking about what a failure I am.

"Hey, buddy," I greet the dog, kneeling down to pet his face.

His tongue instantly comes out to lick my hand. He looks so happy to see me that I want to cry. Animals break my heart sometimes. They love you so unconditionally, so deeply. Even when you've mistreated them—and I've come across many abused animals at the shelter—they still want nothing more than to please. Fucking heartbreaking.

"How was your day, cutie?" I ask him. "Did you chase any squirrels? Find any sticks? Tell me everything."

A male chuckle sounds from behind me, and I shoot to my feet in surprise. When I turn around, I'm expecting to see *him*.

Only it's not him.

It's Jeff.

7

"Hey there, Lizzie." Jeff smiles at me, then at the furry head sticking out of the fence. "Cute pup."

"He is. And it's Beth," I correct by rote.

A crooked smile appears. "Right. Beth. I forgot. You're all grown-up now." He reaches out and pulls on a lock of my hair, something he did back when I was fourteen and had a giant crush on my sister's boyfriend.

I try not to blush and fail. "You've been gone awhile," I say to cover my embarrassment. I head back to the rope swing and plop down on the wooden seat.

His crooked smile grows into a full-blown grin. He doesn't look any different than when he left Darling two years ago. He still has that solid square jaw and dark eyes that crinkle at the sides when he smiles. My sister thought he was the most beautiful boy in the world. I didn't disagree.

"Two years," he confirms. "But Darling hasn't changed at all, has it? The same stores, streets, people."

"Yup."

"I like it." He brushes some nonexistent dust off his jeans.

"Everything overseas was foreign and different, but Darling is the same. That's why we always want to come home, yeah."

"Yeah? You picked up an accent," I tease.

He grabs the rope and gently pulls me forward. "Hard not to after two years there, but I'll lose it in time."

"Do you miss England? I'd like to go sometime."

"Would you?" He chuckles. "I don't think you'd like it. You're made for small-town America, Lizzie. It fits you. There's no point in going away from here. It's got everything you need. People you love and who love you back. Out there, no one really knows or gets you."

"Dinner!" Mom calls from the back door.

"Great. I'm starved." Jeff waves a hand toward my mom to let her know we've heard her. "Come on."

"Are you staying?" I drag my toes into the ground to bring the swing to a stop.

"Yeah. I miss your mom's roast beef. Can't get that over there in the UK. The meat's not the same, you know?"

"Aren't they famous for their cows? I read that on the internet somewhere."

He throws an arm around my shoulders. "Didn't they teach you in fifth grade that seventy-five percent of what's on the internet is trash? You going to trust me, your old friend Jeffrey, or some online rag?"

"You."

"That's right." He squeezes me.

His arm feels strange around my shoulders. It doesn't belong there. This is Rachel's boyfriend. It's her shoulders his arm should be around.

Dinner is less of a mess than I'd imagined it would be. My parents love Jeff and are thrilled he's back at the table.

"It's like old times." Mom sighs.

"Only better because we're older and Lizzie is prettier and I've been lifting." He flexes and Mom laughs at his playful antics.

Dad grunts some form of approval.

"How are sales at the store?" Jeff asks my dad. "I heard they might be opening up a Home Depot in Lincoln, so some competition might be cropping up, huh?" Lincoln is a town twenty minutes east of us.

"They've been saying that for years and it still hasn't happened. And even if does, I'm not worried. Those big-box people don't know the difference between an Allen wrench and a Phillips screwdriver, son. As long as they keep employing ignorant boys, the folks here will always come back to me."

Jeff and my dad talk about the store some more, and then Jeff tells us about his grandparents' apartment in England, except he calls it a flat and his accent bothers me a little but I can't explain why. Of course you're going to pick up certain phrases and mannerisms when you live somewhere else for two years.

It's not Jeff, I guess. I'm just on edge from everything that happened today. Seeing Chase at school. Finding out that Chase isn't Chase. He's Charles. Charlie. The boy who, in my house, is looked upon as a villain. A murderer.

I'm Charles Donnelly. And I'm sorry.

As I pick at my dinner, moving my mashed potatoes around on my plate, my mind drifts. I try to recall what I know about Charlie. He was a summer kid, as far as I remember. His parents were divorced, and he visited his mom in Darling during the summer and lived with his dad the rest of the year. His dad lives in Springfield or Bloomington or something. Definitely a city, but I can't remember which one. And I only know this because my parents told me. I'd never met Charlie before Saturday night.

I shove some mashed potatoes in my mouth and chew quickly.

I don't think Rachel ever met him, either. He was a stranger. A teenage boy who came to stay with his mom one summer, stole a car, took it for a joyride and ran over my sister.

Again, I know those details only because of my parents. I wasn't allowed to read the newspapers after it happened. There was no trial. No media storm. My parents shielded me from the whole thing. Charlie took a plea deal and was whisked off to juvenile detention. It was all very nice and tidy.

Except it left my family a mess. In pieces.

And, ironically, Chase wasn't the only one who wound up in prison.

I snort at that thought, and everyone turns toward me.

"Ah. Sorry," I mutter, staring down at my plate. "I was just thinking about…something funny."

My father's tone is tinged with disapproval. "There is nothing funny about what we're discussing, Elizabeth."

What *are* they discussing? I'd completely tuned them out. When I lift my gaze, I find three grim faces staring back at me.

"Anyway," Jeff says, picking up wherever he'd left off, "I also disagree with the administration's decision to let him attend Darling High."

My pulse kicks up a notch. They're talking about Chase.

Dad nods tersely. "We're planning on voicing that sentiment when we meet with the school board."

My gaze swings toward my father. "What? Why are you meeting with them?"

"Because it's necessary. They need to know that we don't

take kindly to that *boy* being allowed back into the community. I don't give a shi—a damn," he says hastily, "who his mother is married to these days. He should not be allowed to attend the same school as my daughter, as my—" Dad's voice gets louder "—my surviving child!"

I cringe. Is that how they think of me? As their "surviving child"?

I scrape my chair back. "May I be excused?" I mumble under my breath.

"No," Dad says. "We have a guest, Lizzie."

"It's Beth now." This time it's Jeff who does the correcting. I glance at him with grateful eyes.

"And I should probably take off anyway," Jeff continues, even though his food is only half-eaten. "I've still got a ton of unpacking to do at home."

"Tell your mother I'll give her a call tomorrow," my mom says. "I'd love to catch up with her and your father."

"They'd love that, too. Maybe we can have a barbecue this weekend, while the weather's still nice. Like old times," Jeff says, winking at my mom.

"That sounds lovely. Lizzie, why don't you walk Jeff to the door? And then you may be excused to your room."

I don't thank her for that, but I do thank Jeff when we stand in the front hall. "Thank you for backing me on the name thing. They refuse to call me anything but Lizzie." I swallow. "And I'm sorry if you felt like I was trying to run you off. I just… I'm not in the mood for family togetherness."

He nods. "I get it. My mood sank pretty fucking fast when I saw that killer at school today."

Guilt arrows into me, and suddenly I find myself praying that nobody at the party on Saturday saw me going into the bedroom with Chase. That nobody saw either one of us walking out of that room hours later with our clothes disheveled.

It never happened. Maybe if I just keep saying that, over and over again, I'll actually be able to forget it.

"Don't worry, though." Jeff's voice lowers ominously. "He won't get away with what he did to us."

I eye him warily. "What do you mean?"

"I mean he won't get away with it." Brown eyes glinting with fortitude, Jeff pulls me in for a tight hug. "He took away the most important person in my life, in *our* lives. Trust me, he'll pay for that."

"He did pay for it," I point out, but my voice comes out weak and shaky, hardly a firm objection.

"Three years in juvie?" Jeff spits out. He's still holding me, and his breath fans hot against my cheek with each angry word. "You think three years makes up for the loss of a life? He killed someone."

"It was an accident," I whisper. "He didn't hit her on purpose."

"That doesn't make her any less dead, now does it?"

The venom in his tone makes me flinch. Gulping nervously, I ease out of his embrace. "I'll see you at school tomorrow. I'm glad you're back, Jeff."

The anger in his eyes dims, replaced with a flicker of joy. "I'm glad I'm back, too."

I close and lock the door after him and then hurry upstairs to my bedroom. Once again, the lack of a door throws me for a loop. Frustration has me stomping forward with more force than necessary. My room happens to be directly above the dining room, and I smile with grim satisfaction at the thought of my parents hearing my angry footsteps thudding on the ceiling.

They might have taken away my phone, but I'm still in

possession of my laptop and an internet connection. For all I know, they hacked into the computer and set up a bunch of spy programs or parental controls, but I don't care if they did. I know they'd never take away the laptop. I need it for schoolwork, and school is very important to my parents.

I flop onto the bed and open up a search engine. It doesn't take long to find out everything I can about Chase, and it's not much more than I already knew. He pleaded guilty to reckless homicide. As a minor, he was sentenced to three years at a juvenile correctional center in Kewanee. I heard it was a harsh sentence, because most of those cases get only probation. Chase—I mean Charlie—started serving his time when he was sixteen. That'd make him nineteen now.

The only valuable piece of information I discover is the picture. All the papers ran one photo of Charles Donnelly, and the kid on those front pages looks nothing like the guy I met at the party.

No wonder I didn't recognize him. Back then, his hair was cropped short, almost completely buzzed off. His features were smoother, giving him almost a baby face. He had no facial hair. His mouth was more sullen, whereas now it's...tighter, resigned.

I run my finger over the computer screen, tracing Charlie's grainy lips. Does he regret what he did? Does he wish he never stole that car? Never drove over the speed limit? Never hit my older sister and sent her flying onto the pavement?

The gruesome image brings bile to my throat, but it doesn't make me want to circle the wagons and raise the pitchforks and march to Chase's house in a violent mob.

If anything, I want to talk to him. If I had my phone, I'd use the number he gave me and... And what? Text him? Call? What the hell do I say to the boy who ran my sister down with his car?

Ding.

An IM screen pops up with a chime. It's Scarlett. I glance toward my gaping doorway. Luckily, my parents aren't lurking there. I mute the volume of the chat window and read Scar's message.

You there, bb?

Yes, I quickly type back. The parentals didn't take my laptop away.

Oh, perfect! This is just as good as texting.

Yup.

Can't believe your parents didn't tell you about CD coming back.

They were too busy taking my door off the hinges.

WHAT? jk, right?

Not jk at all. 1 sec.

I pick up the computer and turn it around so that the webcam has a view of the door. I snap a picture, load it into the IM screen and send it. Scarlett's reply is swift and appropriately shocked.

OMG! THEY DIDN'T!

Oh they did.

I hear soft footsteps coming up the stairs and curse under my breath. Wonderful.

Gotta go, I type to Scarlett. Bbiab.

I minimize the chat screen just as Mom appears in the doorway. "Can we talk?" she asks quietly.

"I'm doing homework," I answer in a curt voice.

"Lizzie."

"Beth."

She sighs. "Beth."

I pretend to be focused on the screen. Mom can't see it so she has no idea I'm just staring at a screensaver picture of me, Scarlett and Macy at the lake last summer. But Mom's not going away, either. I can make out her slender frame from the corner of my eye.

She stands there, silently, patiently, until finally I release a loud groan and say, "Fine. Talk."

Mom steps into the room and sits on my desk chair. I close the computer and wait for her to speak.

She begins with "Your father and I are concerned—"

I can't stop a snort. "What else is new?"

"Beth," she chides.

"Sorry."

"We're concerned that the *boy* might harass or upset you at school."

My gaze flies to hers. "Why would he harass me?"

"Because you're a reminder of what he's done to our family, to this town. People don't like to be reminded of their mistakes. Sometimes they lash out as a result." Her lips thin out. "I don't want that boy anywhere near you, Lizz—Beth."

Despite my anger, I soften slightly, because I appreciate the effort she's making to call me Beth. She's trying. More than Dad is willing to try.

"Your father and I will try to have him removed from your school, but I can't promise that we'll be successful."

I arch a brow. She's acting as if I'm the one who requested they do that. Which I didn't. "I'm not asking you to do anything. I don't care if he goes to school with me."

"Just the sight of him made you sick to your stomach today!" Mom is visibly stricken. "He's a threat to your mental health and your well-being, and I promise you we'll do what we can. But on the off chance that we fail, we need you to promise that you'll stay away from that boy."

Hysterical laughter burns my throat. *Too fucking late, Mom.*

"We won't let him hurt you or our family ever again," she says, and the ferocity of her tone startles me. "*I* won't let him. He already took one daughter from me, and…" Her voice catches, and she takes a long, deep breath.

The pain in her eyes chips away at more of my resolve. We used to be so close. When I was growing up, she'd take me on an outing once a month, just me and her. I think it was her way of showing me she loved me as much as Rachel, even though deep down I knew Rachel was her favorite. Rachel was Dad's favorite, too. I guess the firstborn daughter always is. But I didn't care about being their favorite. At least when Rachel was alive, I had parents who loved me.

I miss that.

"He won't hurt me, Mom."

She doesn't seem to hear me. "What you said yesterday. About…about this being a prison." She lifts her gaze to mine. There's so much anguish there. "This house isn't a prison, Beth. It's a safe haven. It's the only place where you're truly safe. Where nothing can hurt you."

I stare at her. Really? I *am* hurt in this house. They're suffocating me with their fears. They took away my door, my privacy.

She's delusional if she believes I feel safe here.

About as delusional as me thinking I can pretend I didn't sleep with the boy who killed my sister.

8

The next morning, I find Scarlett and Jeff waiting by my locker. Scarlett immediately throws her arms around me and whines, "It *sucks* that you don't have a phone."

"I know," I say glumly.

"Your dad said he took it away because you snuck out to a party?" Jeff prompts.

I narrow my eyes at him. I don't remember that coming up at all during dinner last night. "When did he tell you that?"

"This morning. I stopped by the hardware store to say hello before school."

The revelation bugs me a little, but I can't explain why. Jeff was over at our house all the time when he was with Rachel. He practically lived there. But it's been ages since anyone has seen him, and Rachel is gone, so this insta-closeness with my family is weird to me.

"Where was this party?" Jeff keeps pushing for details. "Was it just you and Scar?"

"I didn't go," Scarlett, the traitor, tells him. "Beth went on her own. With a bunch of kids from Lexington Heights."

I scowl at her and she shrugs as if to say *I didn't know it was a big secret.*

"Lexington kids?" Jeff says with visible disapproval. "All those Lex kids are total trash, Lizzie. Everyone knows that."

"Not all of them," I say in the defense of Ashleigh and Harley and the rest of the kids who were nothing but nice to me on Saturday. "I had a good time."

"Yeah? Doing what?" he says suspiciously. "I've heard about the kinds of drugs that float around at those Lex parties."

"I don't do drugs," I say stiffly.

"I should hope not."

The judgment in Jeff's eyes grates on me. Who is he to judge? He doesn't even know me anymore. The last time he saw me, I had a mouth full of braces and a face covered with zits. I don't think I'd even kissed a guy at that point.

"Anyway, it was fun," I tell Jeff and Scarlett. I slam my locker shut and shift my backpack onto my shoulder. "I have to go. I want to talk to my Calc teacher before the bell rings. I'm already a day behind because I missed class yesterday."

I leave before they can respond, waving a hurried goodbye over my shoulder. Truth is, I do want to get to AP Calc early. But not to talk to the teacher.

My heart is racing as I lurk outside the classroom door. Kids stream past me up and down the hallway. Some duck into the classroom I'm waiting by, others dart through the other open doorways in the corridor.

Where is he?

Impatience has me tapping my foot and playing with the straps of my backpack. I search the hall for him, scanning every boy that comes near. I dismiss the ones with dark hair, the gangly ginger-haired one, the one with the dreadlocks and his buddy with the shaved head. I wait in the hall, even after the bell rings, even after the classroom door closes.

And finally, my patience pays off.

Charlie Donnelly appears at the end of the hall. He's wearing black cargo pants and a black T-shirt, and a harried look on his face. He rakes a hand through his dirty-blond hair as he rushes down the tiled floor. He's clearly pissed at himself for being late.

When he sees me, he stumbles to a dead stop.

"Fuck," he murmurs.

"Chase," I say awkwardly.

I take a step forward, and he takes a very fast one to the side.

His hand shoots out for the doorknob. "We're late for class," he says, and his tone is so cold, so aloof, that I frown deeply. He won't even look at me.

"I don't care if we're late. I need to talk to you."

"Got nothing to say," he mutters.

"Please," I beg.

I grab his hand before he can turn the knob. He flinches as if I've burned him with a hot iron. Hurt trembles in my belly. A few days ago, he was begging me to touch him. Now it's like he can't stand the sight of me, the feel of me, the—

And why the *hell* do I care? A wave of anger and self-reproach washes over me. This guy hit my sister with his car and went to jail for it. I shouldn't give a flying fuck if *he* isn't into *me*.

"Well, I have something to say," I grind out. "And it doesn't matter if we're one minute late or five minutes late—late is late. So you might as well give me a few seconds of your precious time."

His hands drop to his sides. He's still making a very obvious effort to not look at me. Those blue eyes focus on a spot a few feet above my head. I feel stupid talking to his chin, but I do it anyway.

"You're going to school here now," I start.

"Are you asking me or telling me?" His gaze swings briefly to mine before sliding away.

"I'm stating a fact. You go here now. I go here. We have classes together." I awkwardly jerk my hand at the door behind me. "So…yeah. Given that this is the situation we're in, I think we should…clear the air, I guess."

His dumbfounded gaze collides with mine. "Clear the air." He makes a choked noise. "I…" He wrenches his gaze away again. "You're Rachel Jones's sister."

My heart clenches. "Yes."

"So there's no air to clear, Elizabeth."

"It's Beth."

He ignores me. "Move away from the door."

"No." I stubbornly plant my feet on the ground and cross my arms. "You can't pretend I don't exist. You can't pretend that we didn't have se—"

"Shut up," he growls.

My eyes widen.

Almost instantly, his features twist with distress. "I'm sorry for snapping," he says roughly. "And I'm sorry for the other night…" He trails off, and I realize that the dark emotion swimming in his eyes isn't quite remorse.

It's shame. He's ashamed of what we did, too.

"You regret it," I mumble.

This time, he looks right at me, and his stare doesn't waver. "Yes."

I can't explain the wave of hurt that crashes into me. "Because I'm her sister?" I have to ask. My voice shakes wildly with every word.

"Yes," Chase says again.

That gives me pause. "But if I wasn't her sister..." I draw a quavery breath. "Would you regret it?"

He eyes me for a long moment, those blue eyes sweeping over my face, then shifting lower. "No," he finally admits.

It's my turn to feel ashamed. That one tiny syllable—*no*—brings a flash of relief, a flicker of happiness. Nausea burns my throat and I want to throw up at my response to this guy.

While I stand there immobile, Chase gently moves me aside and opens the classroom door. He disappears inside without another word.

I turn and watch his broad back as he makes his way to his desk. He folds his tall frame into a chair and stares straight ahead.

At the front of the room, Mrs. Russell is talking about Mathematical Practices for AP Calculus, or MPACS, that will dictate our course of study this semester. She notices me in the doorway and a slight frown creases her lips. She glances at Chase, then at me, then says, "Beth, why don't you take a seat? There's an empty one in the back." AKA as far away from Chase as possible.

I trudge into the classroom, making a pointed effort not to look at him. Our conversation was too short. I have more to say to him. I'm not entirely sure what, but I do know one thing. Chase and I have unfinished business.

I check my watch. Our next class together is Music History. That gives me two hours to plot. Even a stone can be worn away by a constant drip of water. Well, watch out, Chase. Here comes a flood.

9

I haven't passed a note since the fourth grade and that was to Scarlett asking her if she wanted to learn how to skateboard. I'd watched a YouTube video of some girls in Afghanistan burning it up and wanted to be as cool as them. Scarlett had said no.

We need to talk. Meet me at my house. Midnight, I scribble while Ms. Dvořák talks about the dead white guys we'll be studying in Music History. *I'll be sneaking out.*

Eh. I erase the last part. He doesn't need to know that. Besides, it'll be kind of obvious. I fold the notebook paper and glance over my shoulder. He's two rows over and one row back, staring intently at his textbook. How do I get his attention while not creating a spectacle of myself?

I cough lightly.

"You okay?" Scarlett hands me a water bottle, but Chase doesn't move.

I wave her off. I tap my pencil on my desk. Ms. Dvořák pauses in midsentence. I lay my pencil down. Still nothing from the boy in black. Isn't it kind of clichéd of him to wear all black? Is he trying to announce that he's a bad guy? He has a *record* and everyone knows it. He could wear white every day, and half the school would still mark him down to star as all the villains in the school play.

I wiggle in my seat, trying to make it squeak.

"Ms. Jones, do you need to use the restroom?" Ms. Dvořák asks. "Then, please, enough with the background noises, all right?"

I could die of embarrassment. "Yes, ma'am."

My gaze drifts over to Chase again, only this time I'm not terribly covert about it because Ms. Dvořák notices.

"Ah," she says. She clucks her tongue sympathetically. Rapping her knuckles on the table, she calls out, "Mr. Donnelly."

His head pops up. "Yes, ma'am?"

"Please go sit in the hall. You are disturbing the class." Her plump, friendly face has grown cold.

What? I straighten up and lift a hand to motion that I'm all right. A few boys in the back snort and chuckle.

"Mr. Donnelly. Did you hear me?"

Everyone is staring at him now. Someone throws a crumpled piece of paper at him. He doesn't flinch, but there's a red flush creeping up his neck. Silently, he gathers his books and rises.

The whispers grow, like a wave, pushing at his back. One of the football players loudly proclaims that this day is going to be killer. The whole classroom erupts into laughter. Even Ms. Dvořák's lips twitch.

I track Chase's path with stunned horror. The muscles of one defined arm flex as he twists the doorknob.

The door closes softly behind him and the sound crescendos.

"God, I cannot believe he's allowed in this school," Scarlett says.

"I don't know why he would want to come here," I reply. I wanted to crawl under my desk earlier, but whatever I'm feeling can't begin to compare with Chase's humiliation.

But why am I sympathizing with him, dammit? I'm supposed to hate him, just like everyone else hates him. I'm supposed to feel *sick* that I allowed him to touch me.

Maybe I shouldn't hate him, then. Maybe I should hate *myself.*

I groan in distress, causing Scar to glance over. "You okay?" she asks.

No, I'm not okay. At all. But I manage a nod.

"Did you see how he walked out of here? All swagger and shit. Like he's proud of what he's done. It's disgusting." My friend's face screws up like she's smelled one of Allyn Todd's infamous farts.

"Yeah," I echo vaguely. He didn't seem intimidated at all— not by the other students, not by the teacher, not even by me. There's something intriguing about that. It's what drew me to him before, when I only knew him as Chase, a random hot guy at a party who gave me attention when I needed it.

Ms. Dvořák calls the class to order and continues her lecture, but my attention is broken. Shouldn't I be having the same feelings as Scarlett? Shouldn't I be mad at this guy? Shouldn't I be horrified that I have to breathe the same air, sit in the same class? What's wrong with me that I'm not?

Why do I feel like it's my classmates and Ms. Dvořák who are the problem here and not Chase? I half expected the class to rise up and yell "Shame" like some scene out of *Game of Thrones.* And that doesn't sit right with me.

It's been three years since Rachel died, but no one wants me to let go.

After the bell rings, I linger at my desk until Ms. Dvořák notices me.

"Is there something I can do for you, Elizabeth?"

I pick up my supplies and make my way to the front. "About Charlie—"

"I can't kick him out of the class every day," she interrupts. "You'll have to talk to the principal about that."

"I know. I…I'm actually not bothered by him."

"You don't need to say that. I'm not thrilled to have to teach him, either."

I grapple for an argument that she'll buy. "My family believes in forgiveness," I lie. "That an eye for an eye makes the whole world blind. That sort of thing."

Ms. Dvořák's face softens. "That's very generous of you." She leans forward and pats me on the shoulder. "I'll do what I can to minimize his disruption. I suppose I can ask Principal Geary myself to have him transferred to another class. If he needs a fine arts credit, he can take something else."

My mouth falls open slightly. She totally mistook my attempts to smooth things over as a complaint in disguise.

"He's not a disruption," I repeat.

"You don't always have to put on a brave front, Elizabeth. I'll see what I can do, all right? Now, you'd better go so you're not late for your next class." She gives me another distracted, condescending pat.

Frustrated, I stomp out of Dvořák's classroom and go hunting for Chase, the note I wrote him firmly in hand. Of course, he's not readily found. I walk down to the lockers, but there are so many people around that I can't slide the note into his locker without being seen.

Or can I? Who says I shouldn't talk to him?

"Lizzie! Are you okay?" Macy throws her arms around me.

"I heard that—that *criminal* was bothering you in Dvořák's Music History class. How horrible. This school is the worst."

"It's Beth," I mutter, but nobody's listening to me.

"You let me know if he's bothering you and we'll teach him a lesson." This is from Troy Kendall, a football player whom I've never said more than two words to.

"We should do it anyway," another thick-necked jock says.

"Tell your parents," Yvonne murmurs at my side. "They'll get this straightened out. You could put something in the paper, rally public support behind you."

Stomach churning, I crumple the note in my hand. Who says I shouldn't talk to him?

Only everyone.

I arrive home after a forty-five-minute bus ride. I hate the bus. I hate it with the heat of a thousand fiery suns. It smells like a rancid mix of sweat, bad gas and garbage. The seats look like a thousand middle schoolers spit on them and then rubbed their dirty butts all over the covering. And it's bumpy as hell. I feel sick to my stomach by the time the ride's over.

No one's home when I walk in. Mom's at work and Dad's at the store. Normally I'd be at the Ice Cream Shoppe, but I've been banished from working. Losing the spending money from my part-time job sucks. Plus, I need to save up for the college application fees.

Not being able to volunteer at the animal clinic? Not bearable at all. I'm supposed to be there this weekend, and I'm already planning on broaching the subject again on Friday. Maybe Mom and Dad would be willing to let me keep at least one shift.

I drop my stuff onto the bench, not caring that one of my notebooks falls into Rachel's space. She's not here after all. If she was, she'd yell at me.

Stop being so sloppy! she'd say. *This is my stall and that one is yours.* And then she'd shove my stuff on the floor.

Once, when we were driving to Grandma's house, she didn't want to share the seat with me and forced me to sit on the floor. God, Rachel could be mean sometimes. Doesn't anyone remember that? If you ask my parents, Rachel spoke the language of unicorns and pooped out rainbows. She was a perfect, wonderful angel.

That isn't true, though. Rachel was amazing sometimes and bratty at other times. She had her flaws, just like everyone else.

I wander through the house, stopping at the piano. The washi tape that Rachel plastered on the expensive piano is peeling at the corners. I pull one strip off and then stare guiltily at the naked black key. Mom will notice if it's not there. One time the cleaners moved a small tray from the bedside table in Rachel's room and left it on her desk. Mom yelled at them on the phone for over an hour. They don't clean Rachel's room anymore. Only Mom does.

I replace the tape.

I wonder how my parents know that I'm even home. Mom usually doesn't get off work until five—she's an accountant for a real estate agency. Dad could come home at any time if Kirk, his part-time worker, is on the schedule. But it's Wednesday. Kirk doesn't work Wednesdays, which means Dad will be at the store until closing.

It's four o'clock. Mom won't be back until sixish. Dad, even later. That gives me about two hours to try to track down Chase. His mom's married to the mayor, so it'll be easy to find out where they live. If I had my phone, I'd just call him, but—

An idea pops into my head. I make a beeline for Dad's office and stare at his desk.

My phone is in this desk. It's the only one in the house that has drawers that lock. If I was going to confiscate a phone, this is where I'd stash it.

I sit in Dad's chair and jiggle the drawer handle. Locked, of course. I sigh and wake his computer.

The fourth YouTube video gives me fairly explicit instructions on how to pop the drawer open.

Amazing what you can do with office supplies. I stare with satisfaction at the open drawer. Plucking my phone out, I cradle it in my hands like a precious baby.

Chase's number is there in my notes app. My heart pounds as I open up a new message box and shoot off a quick text.

Meet me at midnight. My house. There's a swing in the backyard— I'll wait there for you.

I send him the address and then drum my fingers against the desk as I wait. And wait. And wait. Thirty minutes pass. He hasn't even read the damn thing.

Antsy, I clean out the browser history on Dad's computer and slam the drawer shut. The phone, I take with me. I'll put it back before Mom and Dad get home, but there's no rush right now.

I go into the hall bathroom, the one room upstairs that I can sit in that does have a door. I put the toilet seat down and wait for Chase to respond. After a few more intolerable minutes, I text him again.

I'm calling you in five minutes if you don't respond.

The response bubble immediately appears.

At work. Sorry, no meeting.

Oh no. He's not blowing me off.

I stare at the screen in frustration. I have to talk to him. I don't care that he doesn't want to—I need this. What we did at the party… He's the only other person who knows about it, the only person I can talk to about it. I don't care what I have to do to get him to talk to me. I'll do anything.

So even though it makes me sick to my stomach, I force myself to type two words.

I'm late.

???

My period. I should've gotten it yesterday.

There's a prolonged moment of silence.

C u at midnite.

I feel a bit guilty about lying to him, but not as guilty as I feel about losing my virginity to Charles Donnelly.

I delete our text exchange, run down to Dad's office, and stick the phone back in its hiding place. I can't figure out how to relock the drawer, so I leave it, hoping my dad thinks that he left it open.

Mom comes home at five-thirty, bringing with her burritos for dinner. Dad arrives shortly after, like they planned it. We sit down to eat. Mom asks questions. I refuse to answer. Dad makes unhappy grunting sounds. As soon as dinner is over, I escape outside to the swing until night falls and Mom calls for me to come inside.

I get undressed in the bathroom because my bedroom has zero privacy. Once I'm in bed, I pull on leggings under the covers, along with a Darling sweatshirt. Then I curl over on my side with a copy of *The Great Gatsby*, which we're reading for AP Lit.

The hours drag on. Time moves more slowly than a snail crossing a river rock. Gatsby keeps staring at the end of the dock at the green light, waiting for *his* green light. I'd like my own go sign. I keep reading until, finally, it's five to midnight.

I slide out of bed and creep down the hall toward the stairs. The lights are all off. Dad's snoring can be heard from the kitchen. The lock on the back door makes an overly loud sound as I flip it to the open position. I freeze for a moment. Hearing nothing, I pull open the door and sprint outside.

When I reach the swing, my heart's pounding a thousand miles a minute, but there's no one there. The swing hangs empty. The night's so still. I don't even hear crickets or cicadas. I twirl in a circle and see nothing.

Disappointment crushes me. He didn't come. I had so much to say to him and he didn't come!

"Argghhhhh!" I quietly scream, hands fisted at my sides. Angrily, I kick at the grass. Fuck him. Fuck him. Fuck my parents. Fuck the school. Fuck everything.

"You come off a little spoiled sometimes, you know?" a voice near the tree says.

I spin toward the sound and see a dark form peel away from the shadows.

"Chase?"

"Yeah. It's me."

He steps forward into a pool of moonlight. My breath catches. He looks like a fallen angel, glowing from the night's light.

"You're late," I manage to say.

"That's my line," he replies grimly. "Have you gone to the doctor? Is there one you can go to?"

Shame tightens my throat. "Oh. I..." I swallow hard. "I lied about that. I'm sorry. I really am, but it was the only way to get you here."

"Right." He looks away, showing off his perfect jawline. The stubble sparkles where the moonlight touches it. Then he says, "I take that back. You're a lot spoiled."

He starts to leave.

I panic and grab his arm. "Please, wait. We need to talk."

"About what?" He shrugs me off. "What happened at the party? We both know that was a mistake. If I knew..." He trails off. He clears his throat and continues, "If I knew you were Elizabeth Jones, I would've never touched you."

My heart squeezes tight. "Why? Why does that matter?"

He cocks his head. "Did you hate your sister or something?"

His words strike me in the gut. I stumble back, blinking back hot tears. "I didn't hate her. Why would you even say that?"

"Because if the guy who killed my sister was standing in front of me, I wouldn't be looking at him like I wanted to rip his clothes off."

I gasp in shock. "I...don't want to do that."

"Yeah, you do." He rakes me from head to toe in one cool, dismissive gaze. "You think you're the first chick who's thrown herself at me since I got out? I spent three weeks in Springfield after my release, stayed with my uncle because my dad wants nothing to do with me, and trust me, all the girls I grew up with were suddenly all over me. Now I'm the bad boy everybody wants to tame."

His dad wants nothing to do with him? Is that why he had to move to Darling and live with his mom? I want to ask him so many questions, but he's not done.

"Grow up, *Beth*. In the real world, bad boys are actually bad. They aren't heroes. It's not dope to hook up with them. Your home life problems aren't solved with my dick. Bad boys do bad shit and eventually drag everyone around them into the same hell pit. Go home to your bed and forget about me. I'll be doing the same about you."

With that, he turns and disappears into the night, his black-hoodie-clad form swallowed up by the dark.

10

On Thursday morning, a mere five minutes into AP Calc, Chase gets a new nickname. Troy Kendall, the football player from Dvořák's Music History, calls it out as he's passing back a worksheet Mrs. Russell produced.

"Don't cut yourself, Williams," Troy says as he passes the papers behind him. "Manson over here might get turned on by the scent of blood." Troy smirks at his own joke and exchanges a hearty high-five with another jock.

Half the room gasps. The other half laughs. Manson, as in Charles, the serial killer, Manson. What an awful joke. I can't help but look at Chase to see how he's taking it. Then I realize everyone's staring at him, waiting for him to react. I wince in sympathy. I know just how uncomfortable it is to be the center of everyone's attention, except I was the focus of pity while he's the subject of scorn.

It's a lot worse for him.

Our eyes meet and I swear I see a hurt betrayal in them. A whole lotta *et tu, Brute* is swimming in those blue eyes of his. But what does he want me to do? Stand up and defend him in front of the entire class? Last night he told me to grow up. He told me to mind my own business, so that's what I'm going to do.

I break the eye contact and spin toward the front and fixate on Mrs. Russell instead. Her back is turned to the classroom. Either she's intentionally tuning us out or she didn't hear Troy's comment.

"Manson's the perfect name for him," Scarlett says next to me.

"Manson was a serial killer," I mumble.

"Yeah, and I bet Charlie's had more than one road rage incident."

"It wasn't road rage," I say, feeling suddenly tired. Why am I even bothering to explain Chase's actions away? He made it perfectly clear that he wanted nothing to do with me.

"I can't wait to tell Jeff," Scar continues as if I hadn't even spoken. Maybe I hadn't. Maybe it was all in my head.

With Mrs. Russell not paying attention to us, everyone else is talking, too.

"You got a basement over in Grove Heights," Troy says loudly. "Maybe stashing a few bodies down there?"

"He used to live in Lincoln before his mom married Mayor Stanton," volunteers a girl in the back. "I read it in the paper."

"Someone should go dig up his old backyard."

"Oh my God. He should go to jail while that's being done instead of sitting here with us."

"What if there *are* bodies back there? Can he be tried again? What about that double-double thing?"

I can't take it any longer.

"Shut up!" I roar at my classmates.

Silence crashes over the room. At the front, Mrs. Russell turns around in alarm.

"Elizabeth," she says in a soft tone reserved for hysterical children. "Please sit down."

Sit down? I didn't even realize I was standing. I guess I jumped out of my chair. Everyone is staring at me. Except for Chase. He's staring straight ahead at Mrs. Russell. I swear I see a tic in his jaw, though, as if he's trying very hard to keep his composure.

Scar's hand reaches for mine. "Shut up, you guys. You're making this harder on Lizzie than it already is." She tugs. "Sit down, Lizzie."

She thinks I just yelled at the entire class because their whispered gossip and accusations were upsetting me.

I yelled because the whispers were upsetting *him*.

Helplessness lodges in my throat. I let Scar pull me down to my chair and then clasp my shaky hands together on my desk. "I'm sorry," I tell Mrs. Russell. "I'm fine now."

She eyes me for a moment before nodding. "Let's focus on our assignment, everyone. Since you have so much energy, Mr. Kendall, you can come up and do the first problem."

Looking sheepish, Troy gets to his feet and walks over to the blackboard. The class quiets down. For the rest of the period, I don't pay much attention. I just sit there and try not to cry.

The moment AP Calc is over, I go to my locker even though I don't need anything from it. But my next class is Physics, and Scarlett's in that class, too, and I don't want to walk with her. She gave me so many sympathetic looks and arm squeezes this past hour that I need a break.

I rest my forehead against the locker and wonder how and when my life got so out of control. Well, when Rachel died, obviously. Three years of dealing with my helicopter parents have completely worn me down. But I feel like in these past days, I've been more powerless and upset than in those three years combined.

This is what I get for trying to rebel. I wanted *one* night. One fun, amazing night before summer ended and school started. One night where I didn't have to think about my dead sister or my overprotective parents. One night where I could be whoever I wanted to be without the dark cloud of my sister's accident hanging over my head.

Well, I got what I wanted. I went to a party where nobody knew me, nobody knew Rachel. I got away from my parents and could finally breathe, even if it was only for a few hours. I had fun. I met a boy. I *liked* that boy. I really, really did.

And now everything is a big fat mess and all I want to do is bawl.

I draw a deep breath. I won't cry. I'm stronger than that. I'm just going to go to class and—

A large hand grabs my arm and twists me around.

"Hey!" I object. "What—" The words die when I realize it's Chase. "What do you want?" I ask weakly. So much for being strong. One second in his presence and my hands are shaking and my pulse is thudding in my ears.

He gives an incredulous laugh. "What do *I* want? I came over here to ask what the hell *you* want."

I blink in confusion. "What do you mean?"

"I mean, you invite me over to your house. You stand up for me in class—"

"I didn't stand up for you," I cut in, but I think he knows I'm lying. I wanted everyone to stop saying mean things about him back there. That's why I told them to shut up.

"Stop sticking your nose in my business, Beth. I can handle whatever they throw at me."

Can he? "Can you?"

"Yes, I can. Trust me, I've dealt with a lot worse. You think a bunch of high school bullies scare me?" He laughs humorlessly. "I spent three years in juvie with actual criminals. You think Troy's the first one to think of Manson as a nickname? These are kids' games here."

I shouldn't feel sorry for him, but I do. "Can we...please talk about all this?"

His dark blond eyebrows crash together. "Talk about what?" Frustration rings in his tone. "Fuck, Beth, what's your problem? There's no reason for us to talk, okay? We're not friends and we're never going to be friends. We can't. Your sister's dead because of me."

My eyelids start to sting.

He lowers his voice. "We had sex, all right. Big deal. It's not like either of us were virgins or anything—"

A strangled sound flies out of my mouth.

I hope, no, I *pray*, that he doesn't notice, but one thing I've learned about Chase—he doesn't miss a thing. Maybe he learned to be this vigilant in juvie because he constantly had to keep his guard up, or maybe it's a skill he's always had. Either way, his blue eyes narrow on my face.

"Beth..." His voice is slightly hoarse. He clears his throat. Swallows, and his Adam's apple bobs a little. "Don't tell me you were a virgin."

"Okay," I whisper.

"Okay what?"

"Okay, I won't tell you."

It's his turn to make a choked noise. Then he slams one hand on the locker behind me. I jolt at the unexpected sound, but I'm not afraid of him getting violent toward me.

God, why aren't I afraid of him? He mowed someone down with his car! I should be afraid, dammit.

"Beth," he says again. "Look at me."

Miserably, I lift my head. "This is embarrassing enough, Chas—Charlie," I correct.

"Chase," he says, and it reminds me of how adamant I am about people calling me Beth. We're more alike than he realizes, I think. "I go by Chase now."

"Why?"

"It's a nickname I got when—" He stops abruptly, shaking his head. "No, we're getting off track. I need to know if..." He raises a hand and lets it hover near my cheek, as if he wants to stroke me. Then his hand drops to his side.

I quickly look around to make sure no one saw him almost touch me, but the hallway is still empty. Class started a while ago.

"Were you a virgin?" he finally asks, unhappiness swimming in his blue eyes.

I draw a slow breath and then exhale in an even slower rush. "Does it really matter?" I answer sadly.

I don't look back as I walk away, but I can feel his gaze on me the entire time.

11

At lunch, I sit with Scarlett and the girls. Jeff joins us half-way through, which I find weird, but everyone, especially Scar, looks happy to see him. I want to ask him why he's not sitting with his friends, but then I realize… He doesn't have any. Everyone from his grade graduated already. Like Chase, he's a nineteen-year-old senior.

I don't contribute much to the conversation. As usual, my thoughts are muddled. I can't erase Chase's expression from my mind, the one he got when it occurred to him that I was a virgin. It hadn't been horror, per se, but concern, maybe? Shock, definitely. And yeah, I think horror did play a small part.

Trust me, Chase, nobody's as horrified as I am.

I almost wish I hadn't walked away from him earlier. We could've talked more about it. The sex, that is. I *need* to talk to someone. The secret is eating me up inside, but who can I confide in?

Scarlett? She'd be horrified, too. And even if she believed that I didn't know who Chase was beforehand, she'd probably still be a bit disgusted with me for sleeping with a stranger. Scar lost her V-card to Matty Wesser, a boy she dated seriously for two years. The only reason they're not still together is because his dad was transferred to Denver for work and Matty's family had to move away halfway through junior year.

Macy and Yvonne? They'd absolutely judge me for what I did.

My parents? They'd lock me in the basement for the next thirty years if they knew what happened between me and Chase.

Everyone else at school, I'm not close with, and it's not like I can confide in Sandy at the animal shelter. She's in her midtwenties and would probably offer some really good advice, but she was also my sort of boss, even if I wasn't paid for the work I did.

That leaves Chase. But he doesn't want to talk to me, and I walked away from him when the opportunity arose. I regret that now.

"...Kav's place. His parents are out of town."

I swear, Troy Kendall has the loudest voice in the world. No matter where I am, I always seem to overhear some BS he's rumbling about.

"And they just got a new hot tub," Landon Rhodes, another football player, says gleefully. "A ten-person one."

"Sweet."

"I know, right."

"Yo, Yvonne!" Troy calls over to our table. "You coming to Kav's tonight?"

Yvonne rolls her big gray eyes at our resident loudmouth. "Who the fuck is Kav?" she calls back.

"Greg Kavill? Kav? Kavi? Kav-ster?"

"Saying it in a hundred different ways isn't going to make

me know who he is," Yvonne says haughtily, and everyone laughs, even me.

"Quarterback over at Lincoln Public," Landon says helpfully. "He's having a thing at his place tonight. Open invite."

Troy glances in my direction, then Scar's and Macy's. "You girls are welcome, too, obvs."

Yvonne shrugs. "Text me the deets. We'll decide later."

"Word," Troy says before he and Landon turn back to their friends.

The moment the football players are occupied again, Jeff speaks in a low, displeased voice. "You shouldn't go to that," he warns us.

That gets my attention. I'd actually been considering going to this thing. If I can't spend the evening with the dogs at the clinic, a party in Lincoln could be fun—

I almost burst out laughing. Fun? *Elizabeth*, I chastise myself, *do we not remember what happened the last time you went to a party in a different town?*

"Why not?" Macy asks Jeff.

"First of all, it's a school night—"

The girls burst out laughing. "We're seniors," Yvonne tells him, still giggling. "We're all allowed to go out on school nights."

"Fine. Well, that's not a good crowd. I've heard bad rumors about Kav and his buddies."

"They can't be all bad if Troy and Lan are friends with them," Yvonne points out. "Besides, football parties are usually lit."

"I'm in, then," Macy chirps.

"There isn't going to be anyone there but the Lincoln crowd and *maybe* a few Darling kids," Scarlett says scornfully. "And the Lincoln crowd is so trashy."

"Then I don't want to go," Macy says.

Beside her, Yvonne rolls her eyes. Macy's flakier than dandruff. She jumps on and off bandwagons at the drop of a hat. If the Charlie Manson fan club did become a thing, she'd be the first one to sign up.

As for this Lincoln party, it's sounding more and more appealing, at least if I can convince one of my friends to come. This time, I can't take the risk of going alone, but the fact that it's a different crowd is exactly why I want to go. None of Darling's students looking at me with pity? Sounds like heaven.

"I want to go," I say slowly.

"Me, too," Macy pipes.

Yvonne snickers softly.

I glance at Scarlett. "Will you come if I go? Even if the crowd is trashy?"

She thinks it over. "Yeah, what the hell. I owe you a party after bailing on the one last weekend."

I grin. "Sweet."

"And anyway, Lincoln peeps aren't as bad as the Lex crew." Then she offers an annoying reminder. "You're grounded, though."

"Shit. Right." I chew on my lower lip, ponder and shrug. "I'll have to sneak out, I guess." And why not? At this point, my parents can't punish me any more than they already have. What are they going to do, break down my bedroom walls?

"You're not sneaking out," Jeff says darkly.

I frown at him. "No offense, Jeff, but you can't tell me what to do. If I want to go to a party, you can't stop me. And don't you dare threaten to rat me out to my parents, because that would be a total dick move."

When he flushes, I know the thought absolutely crossed his mind. "Fine. Then I'll take you."

My eyebrows shoot up. "What?"

"If you want to go, I'll take you." He reaches for his water bottle and takes a long sip before setting it down. "At least then you'll have someone there to watch your back."

There's a stir of excitement in my belly. "You'll help me sneak out?"

Jeff grins. "No sneaking out required."

"But I'm grounded."

"Don't worry about that. I'll talk to your parents. I'm like the parent whisperer."

"I want to go, too," Macy declares, tugging on Jeff's arm.

He flashes a regretful smile. "Sorry, my car's a two-seater." Jeff drives his dad's old Audi TT, or at least he did before he left for England. "If Scarlett's going, she'll have to take her own car."

"Forget it," Scar says in a flat tone. "I'm out."

"Why?" I ask in disappointment. It's always more fun when Scarlett is around.

"I'd only be going to keep you company. So if Jeff's going, there's no reason for me to be there, too."

Her explanation makes zero sense to me. Why can't the three of us all keep each other company? But Scarlett picks up her phone and starts scrolling through it, making it obvious she doesn't want to be questioned. So I let it go.

"Meet me after school," Jeff tells me. "I'll drive you home. I've gotta meet with my guidance counselor now."

Jeff takes off, and the rest of us finish eating. Scarlett's quiet for the rest of lunch. I can tell that for whatever reason, she doesn't like the plan for tonight, so as we're putting our trays on the conveyor belt, I assure her, "Jeff's going. Nothing bad will happen to me."

"It's Jeff I'm worried about."

"Ouch."

She shrugs. "Sorry." Only I can tell she's not. "But you're really all about yourself these days."

That's also painful. And I don't think I totally deserve it, either. I might've asked Scarlett to cover for me last weekend, but I've always had her back, too. I used to cover for her all the time when she was going out with Matty.

"Jeff's a big boy," I retort. "But if you're so worried about him, then come to the party with us. You'll be able to keep an eye on him."

"I already told you, I don't want to."

Shrugging again, Scarlett heads toward the cafeteria door. She doesn't check to see if I'm following her, which tells me she's done with this conversation. Unfortunately for her, I'm not.

"Scar, come on, wait." I grab her arm just as she reaches the entrance.

Her expression is cloudy, and she flips her auburn-colored hair over one shoulder like some R & B diva. "What?" she asks tightly.

An unhappy groove digs into my forehead. "Why are you so mad?"

"I'm not mad."

"You look mad."

"Well, I'm not." She flips her hair to the other side. "I just don't like that you're dragging Jeff to this party in Lincoln when it's obvious he doesn't want to go. I know you're having a hard time with that asshole killer being back, but don't take advantage of your friends."

"I didn't ask Jeff to take me," I protest. "I wanted to go with *you*."

Scar presses her lips together. "Whatever, Lizzie. I just think you could have handled that differently."

"Beth," I say irritably.

"What?"

"It's Beth. I've told you that a million times, but you keep calling me Lizzie."

"Sorry, *Beth*."

This time when she stalks away, I let her go.

We avoid talking to each other in our afternoon classes. Chase shows up for Music History. I avoid him, too. At this rate, I'll have alienated the whole school by the end of the day.

After class, I pay a quick visit to my locker and then head outside to the parking lot to meet Jeff. He's already there, and his brown eyes sweep over me as I approach him.

"You look a bit pale," he observes. "I'm gonna have to take you to get something to eat."

"I'm not hungry."

"That's what you think now. Wait until I get a plate of Freddie's nachos in front of you."

"I'm really not hungry," I insist, but Jeff's not having it.

"We'll grab some food after we go to the hardware store so I can talk to your dad. Then I'll drop you off at home, head to my place to shower and change and come back to pick you up around seven. Party won't get hot 'til about nine or ten, but your folks will be suspicious if I pick you up that late. We can grab some ice cream or something until we're ready to go there."

He has our entire night planned. I find myself both annoyed and impressed.

"Sure," I finally say, because clearly arguing with this guy is pointless. He's going to do whatever he wants anyway.

"I honestly don't know how you're going to convince my dad of this," I say as I hop into the passenger side of his Audi. "They're still pissed at me for sneaking out last weekend."

Jeff grins. "Oh ye of little faith." He starts the engine. "I've got this."

After ten minutes at the hardware store, I have to concede— Jeff really is the parent whisperer.

"Thank you so much for the advice, sir." Jeff transfers the box of nails to his left hand so he can shake my dad's hand with his right. Under Jeff's arm is a crowbar. I'm holding two screwdrivers.

"No problem, son. It's good to hear that you're working with your hands. Not a lot of kids your age have the patience for this kind of work."

"I'm going to screw up so bad, but I know where to come if I have any questions."

Dad beams, his chest puffing out. "My door is always open."

Jeff wraps his arm around my shoulder. "And thanks for giving me a helper."

"Hard labor will be good for her," Dad declares with a hearty laugh.

I'm almost gagging at the sight of these two getting along so well. At home, Dad barely cracks a smile. Here with Jeff, he's laughing like a giddy schoolgirl. I don't get it—why can't he be like this with Mom and me? Mom is worried and hysterical half the time, but at least she can still smile. She still laughs when she's watching a funny show or if I tell a good joke. But Dad just walks around with a dead, vacant expression. It's like the mere sight of us reminds him of Rachel's death, and he completely shuts down.

As we stow away the purchases in the back trunk, I eye Jeff suspiciously. "Are you really building a garden arbor in your backyard?"

"What? You don't believe me?" He snickers. "Of course I'm not building that. Why would I?" He holds up his hands. "These babies aren't made for manual labor." As we climb back into his car, he glances over with a broad smile. "Am I good or am I good?"

"You're good, but I still have to be home by eleven," I point out.

"I'll be able to stretch it out. I mean, we worked *so* hard on the arbor that we decided to take a break before I drove you home, and then we fell asleep and woke up in the middle of the night, and I panicked but figured your dad wouldn't have wanted us to drive at night."

I roll my eyes. I think Scarlett has nothing to worry about when it comes to Jeff. He seems perfectly capable of handling himself in any situation. "That's some story. Your parents aren't going to narc on you about the unbuilt arbor?"

"Oh, there's an arbor going up. I'm just not the one building it. And my parents aren't going to talk to yours." He looks over. "No offense."

He means my parents aren't rich enough.

"Not offended." Although I slightly am, because it's not like Jeff's family is better than mine. Yes, they have loads more money, but money isn't what makes a person valuable.

At least not in my mind.

Five minutes later, Jeff pulls up in front of the Mexican place. I'm still not hungry, but I doubt he'd listen to me if I told him. I wonder if Rachel knew how domineering Jeff could be. Honestly, I think it would bother me if my boy-friend was like Jeff, making all our plans and not listening when I said something that went against what he wanted.

I quickly push aside the negative thoughts. I'm making him out to be a monster right now, and he's not. Jeff's a good guy. He's just very decisive. Decisive can be a good thing.

Besides, if it weren't for him, I'd be stuck at home tonight, sitting in a bedroom without a door and staring at the wall because my parents took my phone away.

So when Jeff turns to me and asks, "We gonna split some nachos or what?" I muster up a big smile and say, "Absolutely."

12

As planned, Jeff picks me up around seven and we grab some ice cream. He talks about England the whole time, but I'm okay with that because I don't particularly want to talk about myself. While he blabs, I send Scarlett a text asking if she's changed her mind about the party and she responds with a curt no. Okay then.

Before the party, we stop by Jeff's house.

"I've gotta trade cars. This is way too expensive to take to Lincoln," he explains as he drives past the gates and down the long driveway to his, well, there's no other way to explain it—mansion. I don't know what Jeff's dad does, but they have lots and lots of money.

He bypasses the circular drive in front of the house and pulls up along a side entrance. "Wait here," he says.

One side of Jeff's house could fit the entirety of ours. I've never been inside, but Rachel says it reminded her of a house you'd see in a magazine and that when she talked, it echoed. I mean, she *said* that. Back when she was alive.

Toward the back, there's an indoor pool with a slide and a

hot tub. Despite all the extras, Jeff never has parties here. Ra-chel says—*said* that he's very particular about who he allows in his space. I guess that's why I'm waiting outside instead of being offered a glass of water or something.

Suddenly, I experience a teeny jolt of panic. Because, what am I doing hanging out with Rachel's boyfriend? This feels weird and sort of like a betrayal and—

And he's not her boyfriend anymore, I have to remind my-self. Rachel doesn't have a boyfriend, because Rachel isn't alive. And I'm not really "hanging out" with Jeff. He's doing me a solid tonight, and I appreciate it, but I don't have any interest in starting something up with him.

Whether she's dead or not, Jeff will always be my sister's boyfriend to me.

Jeff returns, jangling a pair of keys. He changed into a loose-fitting blue button-down that's only halfway tucked into jeans. He points toward the rear of the house. "I'll be right back."

"I can walk to the car with you."

"Nah." He waves me off. The ends of his shirt flap as he jogs away.

I look down at my own jeans and tight T-shirt. I wish I was wearing a skirt, but Dad wouldn't have believed I was going to help out with building if I was dressed to go partying.

A minute later, Jeff pulls up in a nice four-door sedan. "Get in."

I climb inside and glance around the tidy interior.

"Sorry about this piece of trash," he says, "but I can't risk my baby."

Piece of trash? This car is as nice as mine. "Whose is it?"

"Debbie's son's."

"Debbie?"

"Our housekeeper." Jeff flips me a cord. "Jack in your phone and play some tunes."

I hesitate, my hand on the door handle. Maybe we should take something else? There's my perfectly good car sitting in the garage at my house. Jeff's so good at talking my dad into anything, maybe the Jeff magic would work on my car.

I open my mouth to suggest it, but Jeff presses the gas and guns the car down the driveway.

"What happens if it gets boosted?" I ask as I buckle in.

"Not my concern. They should have insurance or something," he says cavalierly.

I run a hand against the cloth interior. The car smells vaguely like lemons and the interior is spotless. Even the floor mats look like they've been recently vacuumed. Whoever the housekeeper's son is, he loves this car.

"I hope nothing happens to it."

"Don't worry about it," Jeff says. "If anything does happen, he'll probably get a new one from the insurance company."

I'm not certain that's how insurance works, but Jeff's so confident. Besides, he'd know the son better than me. I force myself to relax into the cushions. "Okay."

Jeff reaches out and squeezes my shoulder. "Look at you being all thoughtful. It's cute."

I ignore the prickle of discomfort I feel at being called "cute" by Rachel's boyfriend. Jeff's doing me a favor. If he wants to call me cute, then I'll deal.

We drive for a bit in silence. My mind drifts back to school and Chase. I wonder if it would be better if he left. This is Rachel's school. Her name is actually on a tiny "in memoriam" plaque near the music room. The reminders have to bother him, right? I wish *I* could get away from all the memories, so it must be just as bad for him.

"Do you think Chase should leave Darling?" I ask Jeff. Jeff must be haunted by Rachel, too, although he doesn't seem like it. His two years away must've helped a lot. If it was me, I would've stayed in London.

"Chase?"

"Charlie Donnelly."

"You call him Chase?"

I squirm in my seat at Jeff's incredulous tone. "He told me that was his name."

Jeff heaves a huge sigh. "Lizzie—I mean, Beth, you're a little too innocent for your own good. If you call him by a nickname, he's going to think he's forgiven for what he did."

"And you don't think he should be...forgiven, that is," I tack on at the end.

"No. He killed your sister," Jeff says, his tone flat. Unstated is the message that he shouldn't even have to remind me of this.

I slink down in the seat, guilt pressing heavy on my shoulders. Yes, Charlie ran his car into Rachel. Yes, he's responsible for her death. If I'd known that Chase was Charlie, I would've run in the opposite direction. Instead, I threw myself at him and now we both regret it.

Worse, I don't think I regret it more than him, which means I'm less worthy of forgiveness than Chase. I should hate Chase. The same amount of loathing that colors Jeff's words when he speaks about Chase should be in mine. I should've thought of the nickname Manson and I should be the one throwing spitballs at his back. I should be in the principal's office every day demanding that Charlie Donnelly be expelled from Darling High.

But I'm not doing any of that. I can't stop thinking about the party and our connection and then the *sex*. In Health, you talk about venereal diseases and other physical dangers. There's no discussion about the emotional danger. And I didn't get any talk of that at home. Mom gave me an American Girl doll book on sex ed and Rachel said that I was too young to even think about it.

"Hey, we're here," Jeff announces, breaking into my sex-crazed train of thought. "Wow, this place looks shittier than I thought it would be."

He reaches past me and opens his glove compartment. A black shiny thing glints menacingly in the dim light of the interior.

"Is that… Oh my God, do you have a *gun?*" I gape at him.

He slams the compartment shut. "It's Darling, Beth. Everyone has a gun. Your dad sells them in his hardware store."

"Yeah, but he doesn't have one in his glove compartment," I mutter as I get out of the car.

"Look at this rat hole." He joins me on the curb. "I should be bringing my piece inside."

The image of preppy Jeffrey Corsen walking around with a handgun tucked into the waistband of his three-hundred-dollar Citizens of Humanity jeans is so unintentionally hilarious I bite the inside of my cheek so I don't burst out laughing. I can't believe he called it a *piece*.

"I'm glad you aren't," I manage to say civilly.

He scowls and pushes me forward. "This place looks like it should be condemned. Are you sure you want to go in?"

"We drove all the way here—it's dumb to leave without even checking it out. And I don't think it's so bad." The house is small, but tidy. The lawn is perfectly kept and there are actually window boxes in the front.

"You're too nice." He bounds up the stairs and jabs the doorbell.

The door opens and a beautiful girl appears with amazing hair and deep, dark eyes. "Yes?" An imperious eyebrow rises.

Jeff's starstruck. He stammers. "I... We're... Us..." He jerks a thumb over his shoulder.

I peek around his arm and offer an assist. "We're here for the party."

"Oh, come on in. No drinking in the house. No drugs and you have to blow into that before you can drive home." She nods toward a small black machine sitting on a side table.

"Are you sure this is a party? There are more rules here than at the Darling Country Club," Jeff jokes. "If you want to have more fun, I could find us something. What's your name?"

"*Us* as in your friend and you? You don't need my name for that." With the flip of her glossy hair, she walks off.

"Wow, what a bitch," Jeff says loudly.

"Jeff." I tug on his arm, embarrassed. Fortunately, I don't think the gorgeous girl heard him.

"Seriously. I was being nice. They wouldn't let her into Darling Country Club if she begged."

He might be right, but not because the girl doesn't belong. Because Darling Country Club is primarily a bunch of old white men who grew up thinking segregation was the key to a successful society, at least according to Scarlett's mom, who knits pink Pussyhats in her spare time.

"Do you want to leave?" I ask, because I'm growing increasingly uncomfortable standing next to Jeff. He looks like he wants to declare war on the people who are throwing the party.

"We'll see. Maybe it's better away from her." He takes my arm and pulls me toward the hall where the noise seems to be coming from. We pass a living room and spotless kitchen and end up in the back on a deck.

There are about thirty people here and it feels like every one of them turns to stare at us when we step out of the house. Several are either in or crowded around the hot tub in the corner of the small yard. About eight guys, half of them shirtless, are playing a game of flag football. The rest are sprawled on the wooden deck or on the lawn.

"Oh fuck, it's Manson." Jeff's voice rises to an obnoxious level. "What the hell are you doing here?"

Manson?

I spin in the direction Jeff's pointing to see Chase sitting in a lounge chair in the back corner, smoking a cigarette. Another pretty girl, her hair all in braids, sits at his feet. It's dark where they're located, so that's probably why I missed them the first time around.

I can't believe he's here. One of the reasons I wanted to come to this party was for a distraction, so I'd stop obsessing over the guy. But he's *here*. How does he even know any of these Lincoln kids—

He used to live in this neighborhood, I suddenly remember. That's what someone at school said, that Chase's mom lived in Lincoln before she married the mayor of Darling. He would've spent all his summers here.

"Manson? There's no one here by that name." A tall, built boy climbs up the deck stairs. "Who're you?"

Jeff ignores the question and keeps talking. "Charles Donnelley is right over there. He killed Beth's sister three years ago and he just got out of prison. Isn't that right, Manson?"

I flush all over. If a house could fall on me right this minute, I'd be happy. Instead, I watch as everyone swivels toward Chase. Again, because of me, he's the subject of unwanted attention.

I guess this is why I can't hate him. The rest of the world does it for me.

I open my mouth to explain, but the boy on the stairs speaks first.

"Dude, we already knew that. Why do you think we're having this party in the first place? It's Chase's welcome-home bash." He finishes climbing the steps until he's practically toe-to-toe with Jeff. "And you're ruining our vibe, so why don't you and your girl here show yourselves to the door."

"Like I'd want to hang out with losers like you." Jeff grabs my arm. "We're going. It stinks in here anyway. I've crapped in toilets nicer than this place."

The boy steps closer to us.

"We're sorry," I say hurriedly. "We'll be going now."

This time it's me grabbing Jeff's arm and pulling. Jeff doesn't balk, but he does complain, "Why'd you say I was sorry? I'm not sorry. These guys are assholes. Who throws a welcome-home party for a killer? No one but a bunch of lowlifes."

"Jeff, there's like thirty of them and two of us," I hiss. "Can you shut up before we get destroyed?"

He jerks out of my grip. "Whose side are you on?"

"What are you talking about?"

We reach the sidewalk and he pins me with a glare that chills my bare arms. "I'm asking you why you're always defending Manson." His voice is low.

Guilt makes me defensive. "I'm not always defending him. I did it once and that's because you were all giving me a headache. I'm tired of hearing about him."

"Then you should go to the principal's office and get him kicked out."

"No. I don't want to do that." But hadn't I thought about

that on the ride over? About how much easier my life would be if I didn't have to deal with Chase every day?

Jeff shakes his head and walks to the driver's side. "I don't get you," he says over the roof of his car. "Manson is bad news. It's fucking disgusting to have you and him in the same school let alone the same classes. Besides—" he points to the front door of the house "—look at the trash he hangs out with. That doesn't belong at Darling. You're the only one who can get him expelled."

"That's not true."

"You're her sister." His features harden. "Rach wouldn't want her little sister going to the same school as her killer."

Hearing him use her nickname hurts my heart. "Rachel is gone," I say shakily.

Anger flashes in his eyes. "If you won't do it for your own sake, what about me?"

"I…"

"You think it's easy for *me* to see him every day? He took away the most important person in my life. Rachel was *it* for me."

His passionate declaration doesn't fully sit with me. Jeff and Rachel were sixteen when they were going out—that feels a bit too young for Jeff to know that they were *it*. And even if they were each other's soul mates, I don't know how to explain to Jeff that getting Chase kicked out of Darling feels all kinds of wrong. If it happens, I'm not going to complain, I guess, but I'm not actively going to campaign for it.

"Well?" Jeff prompts.

"It doesn't feel right," I say.

He snorts. "Fine. Maybe you need to think about it some more." He opens his car door and gets in and, before I can respond, he speeds off, leaving me choking in his exhaust.

"Jeff! Jeff!"

I sprint after him. There's a stop sign ahead. I'll catch him there. I run faster, but Jeff doesn't even stop. He guns the car around the corner and by the time I reach the intersection, his taillights are a half mile away.

"You asshole!" I scream after him.

I can't believe he left me here. I don't even have a phone!

I jab my fingers in my hair, trying not to panic. What am I supposed to do now? Is he going to come back for me? I heave a shaky sigh and sink down into a crouch.

There's something wrong with me. Clearly. Jeff is more torn up being around Chase than I am. Rachel's my sister. Jeff dated her for less than a year. But he can't stand to be around Chase. Me, I'm sticking up for him, just like Jeff accused.

And the thing is, I feel guilty that I don't defend him *more*.

I don't know what's going on with me anymore. I'm so confused. About everything. I have no direction. No career goals. No passion. No ride home.

I'm sitting on the sidewalk in another town where I don't know anyone but the guy who killed my sister. And worse, he doesn't want to have anything to do with me.

No one does. Scarlett's mad at me. Jeff's mad at me. My parents hate me.

I push to my feet. Maybe if I was more… What? More obedient? More robot-like?

Fuck that. I want to have a life. I want to have fun. All these people are choking the life out of me, telling me what I should and shouldn't do. That includes Chase. I'm done with him, too. He said he doesn't want or need my support. Then I'm not giving it to him. He doesn't deserve it.

"He leave you here?" a deep voice asks from behind me.

I turn around to see a stranger. I squint. Was this someone from Kavill's house?

"How did you know?"

The boy grins. "I saw the whole thing from my porch. Mad about Kav's party? He's kind of a straightedge, but you can come over to my place. I don't have a hot tub like Kav, but I've got some other fun party favors."

"You sound like a villain from a Stephen King novel," I tell him bluntly.

Surprisingly, the boy throws his head back and laughs. "Got a little tongue on you, do you?" he says before sticking out his hand. "I'm Jay Tanner. I go to school with Kav." He pulls out his phone. "Look, I've got his number right here. Call him and check it out."

Jay doesn't know that I'm totally abandoned. He thinks I know the kids inside of Greg Kavill's house and that we left because the party was too tame. I'm too embarrassed to admit I don't know Kav at all, so I say, "Nah, it's fine."

"Then come over. You'll have fun," he says. "I promise."

I find myself following him across the street and down the block. He didn't lie. His house is only a few addresses away from Kav's. I can hear the music as we walk up the sidewalk. There are plenty of lights on inside the house and from what I can see, there are lots of kids, as well. My spirits lift.

"I'm Beth," I tell him.

"Nice to meet you, Beth. What school do you go to?"

"Lex," I lie. If I say Darling, he'll assume things.

"I know Harvey Bassett. You have any classes with him?"

We climb the three steps of the front porch. He holds the door for me.

"Lex is a big school," I answer, because I have no clue who Bassett is.

"Yeah, that's true. How do you know Kav?"

"Friend of a friend."

Inside, the place is smaller than it appears outside. It might be the music. It's so loud it feels like a physical assault, but at least I don't have to answer any more uncomfortable questions.

Jay makes a drinking motion with his hand. I nod. He holds up one finger and disappears deeper into the house. No one stares at me. No one even really notices that I'm here. They're dancing or making out on the sofa or playing a video game. I relax and wait for Jay to come back.

He reappears with two red cups. I accept mine and take a cautious sip. A sweet rather than bitter taste hits my tongue.

"You like?" he shouts in my ear.

I shoot him a thumbs-up. If there's alcohol in here, I can't taste it. I take a big swallow. And then another. And then another until it's completely gone.

"I'll get you a refill," he yells.

I nod gratefully but have to stop as soon as his back is turned. The nodding made me dizzy. My legs feel weak. I hold an arm out to steady myself. What I really need is to sit down, I decide.

I find a set of stairs and plop down on the first one, ignoring the couple halfway up that are practically humping each other.

Jay comes back with two more glasses and a big grin. *I'm going to make this one last*, I think. But it's so good.

So good.

I guess I'll just have one more.

Or maybe two. Yeah. I'll stop at two.

13

I wake up to the sound of a jackhammer. It's the loudest, most annoying noise I've ever heard. It's so loud it actually makes me sick—my stomach turns over a few times, nausea creeping like sickly strands of ivy up my throat.

It takes me a few seconds to realize that the deafening pounding is actually in my head and not coming from outside at all. And I feel sick because I'm drunk.

Groaning softly, I try to get my bearings. When I do, my stomach churns even harder.

Jay is lying beside me.

I fight through my queasiness and try to focus. The room is dark, but there are no curtains on the window and moonlight is streaming in. We're on a double bed, with about three feet of space between us. He's snoring softly. We're both fully clothed.

I almost keel over with relief. I'm still dressed. Oh, thank God. I quickly look around the small bedroom and find no signs that at one point I may have *un*dressed. The bedspread is still on the bed, only slightly rumpled from me and Jay lying on it. There are no empty condom wrappers or pieces of underwear scattered on the floor.

Still, that doesn't mean something didn't happen. Maybe we got dressed right afterward. Maybe—I almost throw up again—maybe we didn't use protection.

Tears flood my eyes. Oh my God. At least with Chase last week, I was completely sober. I knew what I was doing. Just because I regretted it afterward doesn't mean I was coerced or forced into it. I *wanted* to have sex that night.

This time...

As panic courses through my veins, I give Jay's shoulder a violent shake. "Wake up," I beg.

He's midsnore when his eyelids pop open, and he makes a startled noise that's a cross between a snort and a whimper. "What is it? What's happening?"

It would almost be comical if I weren't two seconds from both puking and having a nervous breakdown. "What...what did we do?" I ask, imploring him with my eyes. "I don't re-member anything. Did we..." I gulp hard. "Did we fool around?"

To my surprise, he just laughs. "Uh, no."

"No?" I'm skeptical, because then why else would I be in this guy's bedroom?

"No," he assures me before rolling onto his side, facing me. His eyes fall shut as he adds, "I'm gay, Beth. Told you that like five times. You know, when you kept trying to make out with me."

Embarrassment heats my cheeks. Hazy memories begin to surface, and... Yeah, I remember him gently prying my lips off his neck and explaining that even though I'm a very pretty girl, I'm totally not his type. And then he brought me upstairs after I admitted that I didn't have any way of getting home and nowhere to spend the night.

"Now, come back to bed," he says sleepily. "I was just starting to fall asleep before you attacked me."

Just starting to fall asleep? When had we come up here? It feels like it was hours ago. Squinting, I peer at the alarm clock on the end table: 12:34 a.m. It's not even that late. And although I don't have a phone, I do have some cash. I can call a cab and go home instead of crashing at the house of some guy I don't even know.

If my parents are waiting up, which I'm sure they will be, I'll just pretend Jeff dropped me off. I'll tell them the same dumb story Jeff planned to recite, about us falling asleep after building his stupid arbor. Either way, my parents will freak, but they'll freak out more if I don't come home on a school night. Missing curfew is better than staying out all night.

At the thought of Jeff, anger mingles with the queasy knot in my belly. I cannot *believe* he left me.

"Can I use your phone?" I ask Jay.

His eyes stay closed. "Mmm-hmm. On the desk."

I climb off the mattress as quietly as possible, but the moment my body is vertical, a wave of sickness slams into me like a speeding train. Vomit races up my throat and instead of going to the desk, I run into the hall in search of a bathroom. I make it to a toilet just in time to throw up every single ounce I drank tonight, as well as the remains of the nachos I ate with Jeff earlier. I'm sure my retching noises probably woke up Jay and whoever else is in the house, but I feel a million times better once I've emptied my stomach.

Well, kind of. Physically, yes, I feel better. Emotionally, I'm a fucking mess.

Shakily, I get to my feet and wash up at the sink. When I

stare at my reflection, I see bloodshot eyes, tangled hair and a paste-white face. A few tears leak out and trickle down my cheeks. I weakly brush them away with the backs of my hands.

What the hell is wrong with me? It's like I'm not even in control of myself anymore and I hate it. I hate the person looking back at me in that mirror. I was upset and panicked about Jeff abandoning me in this unfamiliar neighborhood, and instead of reacting like a levelheaded person, I went to another strange party and tried to kiss a gay guy.

Fear flickers through me as a different scenario plays itself in my mind. What if Jay hadn't been gay? What if he hadn't been a gentleman? I drank way too much and passed out for hours. Something could've happened to me. Something really bad.

More tears fall. I wipe them away. I take a deep breath and force myself to meet my own eyes in the mirror. Pure shame flashes back at me.

"You're not this person," I whisper to myself.

I'm still not certain who I am.

I just know it's not *this* girl.

I jut out my chin, then march out of the bathroom and into Jay's bedroom. I grab his phone, step back into the hall and call the only cab company whose number I have memorized. Unfortunately, it's a tiny taxi service based in Darling, with only a couple drivers, so I'm told it'll be at least twenty minutes before someone could get me.

"That's fine," I tell the dispatcher. I guess at this point, it doesn't matter if I come home at 12:45 or 1:00 or 1:15 a.m., now does it?

I leave Jay's house trying to make as little noise as possible. There are a few kids passed out on the couches in the living room, but nobody stirs at my footsteps. My head is still throbbing as I step outside into the cool night, but at least my stomach has settled. And my breath is minty fresh thanks to the mouthwash I swished in it from Jay's bathroom.

"You sure you don't want a ride?"

The entire street is so dead that I hear the girl's voice carry even from several houses down. I jump in alarm and instinctively duck behind the row of hedges that separate Jay's house from the one beside it.

"Nah, it's okay," says a muffled male voice. "I'd rather walk."

I'm not sure what I'm afraid of. It's obviously a few kids leaving the other party at Kav's house, not some serial killer prowling the neighborhood for prey.

I peek out, but I can't really make out the shadowy figures. They're too far away. Then a car engine hums in the night, and two red streaks illuminate the darkness as a small hatchback reverses out of Greg Kavill's driveway. A few seconds later, the car whizzes past the hedgerow.

Exhaling softly, I emerge from my silly hiding spot. The taxi is picking me up in front of Jay's house. I decide to sit at the curb and wait, rather than loiter on the front porch. I threw myself at the poor guy more than once tonight—the least I could do is graciously get off his property.

A mortified groan slides out and I drop my face into my hands. How is this happening? How did this night turn to such shit?

Jeff left me. I got wasted. I tried to make out with someone.

I moan, but that small sound is not enough to release all the awful things I'm feeling. So I scream into my palms. "Argghhhhh!"

"Seriously?"

My head snaps up at the sound of his voice. "No," I whisper, more to me than him. "Just go away, Chase. Please."

"What are you doing out here? It's almost one in the morning and there's school tomorrow."

"You go to school, too," I snipe. "Why are you allowed to be out late and I'm not?"

"I can get by on no sleep. You, on the other hand, look like you're about to pass out. Are you okay?"

I ignore him by burying my face in my hands again. I can't deal with him at the moment. Nice, right? I lost my virginity to this guy and I can't even look him in the eye. And the fact that he sounds legit concerned for me only makes it worse.

"Beth," he says roughly. "Look at me."

"No," I mumble against my hands. "Just move along, Chase. Nothing to see here."

"All right. Whatever."

I hear footsteps.

My heart speeds up, because once he's gone, I'm back to being alone out here so late at night. Not that I want him to stay or anything. I just...

I don't know what I want.

The footsteps grow fainter, and I finally raise my head. He really is leaving. Just walking away. I stare at his black-clad back. He's wearing a hoodie again. His jeans aren't black, though. They're blue, and so faded they look like they've been washed a thousand times before. His tall frame gets smaller the farther away he gets. I keep watching, because what else am I going to do? I still have so much time to kill before the cab comes.

When he reaches the end of the street, he halts at the same stop sign I raced toward earlier, when Jeff sped off like a total fucking asshole.

I narrow my eyes. Chase remains still for several moments. Then, very slowly, he turns around and starts walking back in my direction. My pulse speeds up.

By the time he's in front of me again, my heart feels like it's going to burst out of my chest.

His blue eyes scan my face, and his voice is slightly hoarse as he asks, "Did anyone hurt you?"

I jerk my head no.

"Are you sure? Because it's obvious you've been crying." He drags both hands through his messy hair, trying to slick it away from his face. "Why the hell are you here, Beth? You're not friends with Kav or Maria or their crowd. And you sure as shit aren't friends with Tanner's crew."

"What's wrong with Jay?" I demand, oddly defensive of a boy I hardly know. But he was nice to me tonight, and I don't like the contempt in Chase's voice. He has no right to condemn anyone.

"Nothing's wrong with Jay. It's his brother's crew I'm talking about. Dave's a drug dealer," Chase says flatly. "But I assume you already knew that, since you were chilling at his place tonight."

I didn't meet a Dave, as far as I recall, and I'm suddenly glad Jay didn't introduce us. I feel a bit faint, though, because the revelation that someone in that house deals drugs just confirms what I already knew—I might've gotten really hurt tonight if Jay hadn't taken care of me.

"Well, nobody hurt me and I'm fine. So you can go away," I tell Chase. "I'm waiting for a cab."

He nods. But he doesn't leave.

"Just…*leave*," I spit out. "We don't have anything to say to each other. You made it clear, okay?"

His tone is wary. "Made what clear?"

"That just because we had sex doesn't mean there's some kind of bond between us. You want nothing to do with me. I want nothing to do with you." My eyes feel hot all of a sudden, stinging so badly my throat tightens.

"Do you *want* there to be a bond?" Now he sounds incredulous. "Because that's just screwed up, Beth."

Like water crashing through a broken dam, my tears pour out.

He's right. It *is* screwed up. The very fact that I can look at this guy without wanting to rip his throat out is screwed up. To want to form any kind of connection with him? That's *beyond* screwed up.

But if there's no connection, no bond, then that means what Chase and I did meant nothing.

"I get it, okay?"

His pained words draw me back to the present. "Get what?"

Chase lowers himself beside me and kicks his long legs out. In the moonlight, the scruff on his jaw looks blonder. "You were a virgin," he mutters.

I don't see the point in denying it, so I nod.

His expression grows more upset. "I should've figured it out, picked up on the signs, but I…I was too…" He trails off.

"Too what?"

"Too into it, okay?" Shame colors his voice and hangs in the droop of his broad shoulders. "I hadn't been with a chick in three years, Beth. I wasn't a virgin last weekend, but I might as well have been, considering how bad I wanted it and how eager I was."

I bend my head to mop up my tears with the sleeve of my T-shirt. The action means I can't look at him, and that's a good thing. I don't want to see his face right now.

"I get it," I murmur. I still won't look at him, though.

"But the only way to move forward is to put it behind us. It didn't mean anything, right?"

A whimper slips out. I bite hard on my bottom lip and valiantly try not to cry again.

"Beth," he says in frustration.

I stare straight ahead.

"Fucking hell, Beth. What do *you* want to do?" Chase stumbles to his feet and starts pacing the pavement. The shards of light from above emphasize the agitated crease in his forehead. "You want to start going out? Hook up again? I went to fucking jail for killing your *sister*."

My face collapses. My shoulders sag, unable to support the weight of guilt bearing down on them. "I'm a terrible person," I whisper.

His blond head snaps toward me. "What? You're not."

"Yeah. I am." I don't bother wiping my tears anymore. I let them stream down my cheeks and dribble off my chin. "I'm the slut who slept with my sister's killer."

"You didn't know," he says roughly. "And you're not a slut. No girl is for having sex or liking it."

I know this, but… I weakly meet his gaze. "Then why do I feel like one?"

He has no answer for that. He doesn't try to comfort me. Doesn't move toward me, touch me. He simply stands there, staring at me with regret in his eyes. I stare back, wondering what he sees when he looks at me. Wondering why I can look at *him* without wanting vengeance for what he did to Rachel.

Pain slices through my heart. Rachel. God, why did she have to die? I miss her. I really… I banish those thoughts to that steel-walled dungeon in the very back of my heart. Thinking about Rachel is pointless. It just hurts to do it. And missing her won't bring her back. It won't change the fact that this boy in front of me is the reason my sister isn't here.

"Are you even sorry?" I find myself blurting.

He looks startled. "What? For what happened Saturday? I—"

"No," I interrupt. "For what happened three years ago."

Stunned silence crashes over the darkened street. Chase runs a hand through his hair again, the movement quick and stilted. His gaze drops to his scuffed sneakers and I can see his chest rise and fall in a quick rhythm, as if he's breathing hard.

Still he doesn't say a word. Doesn't answer the question. A stupid question, really. Because even if he's not sorry, it's not like he's going to admit it.

The silence drags on, finally broken by the sound of an engine. Two huge spotlights point at Chase's back, blinding me. I stand up. Chase quickly moves to the side to allow the taxi to pull up to the curb.

"Beth?" the driver asks after rolling down his window.

I nod. "Yeah, that's me." Without acknowledging Chase, I open the car door and slide into the back seat.

Before I can close the door, Chase steps forward.

"Beth," he says gruffly.

I bite the inside of my cheek. "What?"

"Yes."

"Yes what?"

He visibly swallows. "Yes, I'm sorry for three years ago. More than you will ever know."

My eyes start stinging again. I tear my gaze off Chase and address the driver. "Can we please go?"

He steps on the gas and we leave Chase in the rearview mirror.

14

To my complete and total shock, Jeff is waiting on the curb when I arrive at my house.

"Where have you been?" he whispers, grabbing my arm and dragging me away from the front walk.

I jerk out of his grip, still stunned at the sight of him. "What do you mean? Where should I have been? You left me on the street!"

"I went back, and you weren't there," he accuses.

My head pounds. "I have to get inside. I don't want to talk about this anymore." I'm not sure how I'm going to sell this to my parents, but I'm going to have to try.

He grabs me again before I can leave. "You can't go inside. I already covered for you."

"What do you mean?"

"I mean I called them after I couldn't find you and told them you fell asleep in the family room and I didn't think I should wake you up." He points angrily to his Audi parked half a block down. "Come on. You're crashing at my house and I'm driving you to school in the morning. That's what I told your parents is happening."

I rub my fingers in my eyes, trying to sort out my feelings. Confusion is my default state these days. I sift through my choices, but Jeff's right—his plan is the best one, because that's the one my parents are supposedly on board with.

"Fine. Let's go."

He arches a brow. "You're not going to thank me?"

My jaw drops. "Thank you? You *left* me in Lincoln!"

"Keep your voice down," he orders sharply, but his eyes have softened. "I know I did, and I'm sorry. I really am. I just can't control my temper when it comes to that killer."

I don't entirely forgive him—I could have been seriously hurt tonight, thanks to Jeff abandoning me—but it's too late and I'm too hungover to have this argument. So I nod and mumble, "Whatever, it's fine. Let's just get out of here."

I wake up at 8:00 a.m. in an unfamiliar bed. It takes several seconds and a lot of blinking to remember where I am—Jeff's sister's room. He dragged me up here last night when we got to his house. And I think he mentioned his parents were out of town, which is a huge relief. How awkward would it have been making small talk with my dead sister's boyfriend's parents over breakfast?

But there's no breakfast in the cards. I've just finished washing up in the private bath when Jeff knocks on the door, announcing it's time to leave.

I stare down at my wrinkled, day-old clothes. "But I'm wearing the same clothes I had on yesterday," I tell the closed door.

"Raid my sister's closet" is his response. "There should be something that fits you."

In the walk-in closet, I rifle through a couple skirts and several tops in varying shades of floral and pastels. Jeff's sister must've really loved pink in her high school days.

Five minutes later, I'm dressed in a pink skirt, a white polo and a deep pink, sleeveless V-neck sweater vest. I tie my hair in a ponytail as I duck out of the bedroom. Jeff's waiting in the hallway, and he appraises my outfit with a grin.

"No offense to your sister, but I look like a golf course model," I grumble.

He furrows his brow. "You look pretty. I like that look better than what you usually wear."

"What I usually wear is T-shirts and jeans."

"Exactly. You've got a nice body, Beth. You shouldn't be afraid to dress it nicely. Not that I think you should dress like a slut like Macy does, but it'd be nice for you to wear something more girlie."

His criticism is irritating, but he did cover for me with my parents last night, so I try to keep the annoyance out of my voice. "Girlie isn't my style and Macy doesn't dress like a slut."

"I can see her bra every day," Jeff retorts.

"So what? If you don't like her bra, don't look at it." Fuck, Jeff is annoying. Was he like this with Rachel?

"Fine, but she *is* a slut. Everyone knows Macy will have sex with anyone who shows the least bit of interest. Calling Macy easy is an insult to easy girls everywhere."

I tighten my jaw. "That's rude, Jeff. And not even true. Not to mention it's a complete bullshit double standard. I don't hear you trashing Troy, and everyone talks about how he tries to bag a cheerleader from every school Darling plays against. Macy's sex life is none of your business." Why is he even harping on Macy?

"I don't like that you hang out with her. She's a bad influence." Jeff keeps talking as if I don't exist.

"I'm done talking about Macy." And her *non*slutty ways. I don't care that she's slept with a lot of guys. I wish I had her confidence. She's completely unbothered by her sexual activity. Maybe what I need to do is sleep with more guys. Like, maybe the reason I'm obsessing over Chase is because he's the only one I've been with.

"Just saying."

I refuse to speak to him for the rest of the car ride. After he parks in the school lot, I hop out of his Audi as fast as I can. "Thanks for the ride," I mutter and then dart toward the entrance.

He catches me before I get more than a car length away.

"I know you're not like Macy, Beth. From what I hear, you haven't dated at all." He pulls me toward him. His face is uncomfortably close to mine. "I like that," he says seriously. "I like that a lot."

I don't know exactly what he means by that, but it makes me super uncomfortable. Like when Gary Keller's dad chaperoned our eighth grade dance and went around telling girls that their dresses were too sexy. He was leering and judging us at the same time.

"I have to get to class," I say, prying his hand off my wrist. I rub it and wonder if I'm going to have a bruise from all the grabbing he's done there.

"We're cool about what happened last night, yeah?"

I'm still pissed off that he deserted me, but I'm not in the mood to fight, so I say, "Yeah."

"Okay, good. I'll see you at lunch, then."

"Sure." But as I run into school, I start planning different lunch options.

At AP Calc, I hurry to my desk.

"What on earth are you wearing?" Scarlett demands as I take the seat next to her.

"Don't ask," I mumble.

"How was the party?" Her voice is tight. I'm sure her expression is, too, but I don't have the energy to look over at her.

"Don't ask about that, either," I say, and then I slump in my chair, duck my head and shut out the world.

It's too humiliating to look at Chase today. I need to take a page out of his coping book and pretend no one else exists. And for the next fifty minutes, I'm able to do that. I take copious notes. I keep my eyes pinned to the whiteboard when Mrs. Russell is talking. Otherwise, I'm staring at my notebook, applying myself to all the equations. I even do the extra-credit ones at the back because I finish early.

When the bell rings, I run out of class and to my next one. I repeat this all morning, ignoring everyone around me. A few times Scarlett, Yvonne or Macy try to engage me in conversation, but I mumble something about being sick and they eventually leave me alone.

I skip lunch and head for the library, where I plan to hide until classes resume again.

"Are you not having lunch today?" Ms. Tannenhauf, our school guidance counselor and librarian, asks.

"I'm trying to get a head start on a research project," I lie, and hope she doesn't ask me what project because it doesn't exist.

She looks around and then gestures for me to come close. Reluctantly, I drag myself over to the circulation desk.

"Yes, ma'am?"

"Why don't you step inside my office for a minute?" She points to the closed door behind her.

"I don't know. I've got all this stuff to do." I jerk my thumb vaguely in the direction of the library stacks.

"You don't even have a pencil, Beth," she chides gently. "Come inside."

It's an order, not a request.

I trudge unhappily toward Ms. Tannenhauf's office. Behind me, she places a sign on her desk saying that she'll be back in fifteen minutes. At least this lecture is only for a finite period.

I drop into the chair in front of the desk and heave a huge put-upon sigh. Ms. Tannenhauf appears at the tail end of it, and the idea of repeating the childish action seems too stupid. I settle for folding my arms and glaring stonily at the guidance counselor.

Instead of taking a seat behind the desk, she drags it next to mine and sits down. Her Converse sneakers are inches away from mine. I tuck my feet under my chair. What is it with people invading my space today?

"You look unhappy, Beth," she says. "Is there something you want to get off your chest?"

"No." It's the truth. The last thing I want to do is talk about my feelings. Especially not with Ms. Tannenhauf.

"I'm worried about you."

I have nothing to say so I keep quiet.

Ms. Tannenhauf does as well, probably hoping her silence will be so uncomfortable that I'll start babbling—about how my parents suck, how I lost my virginity to the guy who killed my sister, how I drank so much last night I woke up in bed with a complete stranger, how my sister's ex-boyfriend is freaking me out and how I have weird, strange, wrong feelings for Chase.

Okay. I have a lot of things I want to get off my chest, but I don't have anyone to talk to. The last meaningful conversation I had with anyone was with Chase and look what that led to.

Ms. Tannenhauf sighs, a big gusty why-am-I-doing-this-job exhalation. She reaches across her desk and places something on my knees.

I glance down to see it's a brochure for the animal shelter where I used to work. *Used to* being the operative words.

"I got a call the other day from the shelter asking if we had anyone who was interested in volunteering because their current student up and quit on them. I thought you loved that job, Beth."

I did love that job, I seethe inwardly. It started off as a requirement—every student at Darling has to perform twenty hours of community service starting junior year. I chose the shelter because I love animals and we could never have pets at home. And once my twenty hours were done, I kept volunteering.

It wasn't my choice to quit. I have no choices left in my life. I'm always dancing to the tune of others. I have to do what my parents say. If I try to break free, I have to obey someone else, like Jeff. I fall in line or else. I'm powerless, and the helplessness I feel is like a noose around my neck that gets tighter with every breath I take.

"Like I wanted to quit! I *did* love that job. It was the best thing in my life!"

"What happened, then?" Ms. Tannenhauf is unfazed by my outburst, as if she's heard this tale countless times before.

I shut down. There's nothing she can do to help me. My parents wouldn't listen to her. They won't listen to anyone because their fear is too loud.

"Nothing." I stand up on unsteady legs. "If that's all, I'm going to go study."

Ms. Tannenhauf nods and says nothing until my hand is on the door and I'm halfway out of the room. "By the way,

Sandy Bacon at the shelter said if you ever wanted to come back, the door was open."

"Thanks," I manage to say. Any more words and the tears I've been holding back will spill out. I walk briskly to the corner of the library, choose a book off the shelf at random and sink to the floor.

I'm seventeen and it feels like my world is ending before it even gets started. It's a melodramatic response, I know, but graduation seems like an eternity away. And even after, what do I do? My parents trashed my college applications. If their plans work out, I'll be going to Darling College.

True freedom seems as far away as Paris and just as un-attainable. And all this constraint makes me want to bust windows, get drunk and have sex with as many people as possible. I don't know if it's a way to show my parents that they can't control me, or a way to experience some type of independence. I just know that I feel like screaming.

Everywhere I look, I see a closed door. A dark passage. Locked windows.

If there's a way out, I can't visualize it.

I wrap my arms around my knees and blink through the sting in my eyes. Then I stop fighting it, because who cares if I cry at school? It's not like my life can get any more pathetic.

At the sound of footsteps, my head snaps up. I don't have time to wipe my eyes before Chase rounds the corner and enters the aisle.

He stops abruptly, spots me and sighs deeply. "Fuck," he says. "You weren't kidding about the crying thing."

15

Of course. Who else would catch me bawling in the school library? Who fucking else?

But as embarrassed as I am, I'm also tired of it. Tired of feeling humiliated every time I encounter Chase Donnelly. So I don't bother wiping my eyes. I just meet his gaze head-on and say, "I told you. I can't control it."

"Who or what are you mad at?"

I wrinkle my forehead. "What?"

"You said you cry when you're mad and everyone thinks you're sad. So what pissed you off?"

"I'm not pissed off. I'm sad," I admit. "I cry when I'm mad and I cry when I'm sad and I laugh when I'm supposed to cry. I suck."

He sighs again. "Why aren't you at lunch?"

"Why aren't you?"

"Wanted to get a head start on that Music History essay." He takes an awkward step forward. Then he takes a step back, as if he's just remembered who he's talking to and knows he shouldn't come near me.

"Yeah, that's what I'm doing, too," I lie.

His gaze drops to the book on the floor. Even from five feet away, I know he can clearly read the title. *Climate Change: A Global Epidemic.*

"You might want to use a different book as a reference," he says helpfully.

I scowl at him.

For half a second, it looks like he's going to smile. But then his eyes go shuttered and he shuffles backward some more.

"What? Afraid to be seen with me?" I taunt.

Chase shrugs. "No. I'm thinking about you right now."

"What does that mean?"

"It means you probably shouldn't be seen talking to me."

"Why not?" I challenge, even though the answer to that question is stupidly obvious.

Chase confirms that. "For obvious reasons, Beth." And then he adds a curveball. "But also because of Corsen's crusade."

"Jeff?" I say blankly. "What crusade?"

"The petition he's passing around." Chase's expression is cloudy, but I can tell he's more uneasy than angry.

He props one broad shoulder against the bookshelf and avoids my gaze. The long fingers of one hand splay on the top of his jeans, the thumb hooked in his belt loop. I remember how those fingers felt on my bare skin and I want to start crying again.

Am I ever going to *not* think about that night? I get it— most people never forget their first. But my first is someone I shouldn't be allowed to remember. Someone I can't even be seen talking to.

"What petition?" I ask.

Another indifferent shrug. Except I know he's not indifferent to any of this at all. His unhappiness is written in every tense line of his body. "Your buddy Jeff—"

"He's not my buddy," I cut in. "He just dated my sister."

We both blanch at the reminder of Rachel. She'll always be between us. Always.

"Whatever," Chase says. "He's been passing around his little petition all morning, trying to get signatures from everyone at school. Guess he's hoping that if enough people join him, Principal Geary will have no choice but to kick me out of school."

I swallow. "They're trying to get you kicked out?"

"Like you didn't already know that," he says quietly. "I know Corsen's parents spoke to the school board." He gives me a pointed look. "Yours, too."

Guilt weighs low in my belly. I swallow again. "Obviously the school board ignored them, since you're still here."

"Yeah. My stepdad took a stand. Not because he gives a shit about where I go to school. Brian just doesn't like being pushed around by anyone. As long as he says I'm going to this school, then make no mistake, I'll be going to this school. He said it's a matter of principle."

"Brian...as in, the mayor? Your mom married him, right?" I voice the questions before I can stop myself. Why, though? Why am I trying to get to know him?

"Yeah, this spring." Sarcasm drips from his next words. "I totally would've made it, but I was *indisposed* at the time." Chase chuckles darkly. "That's the line Mom gave everyone, like all those fuckers didn't already know exactly where I was and why I couldn't attend."

Discomfort tickles my throat. Oh God. I don't know about this can of worms I just opened. I'd wanted a glimpse into Chase's home life, and now I have it and it's so...sad.

"Sounds like you don't like your stepdad much," I say carefully.

"Nah, I'm indifferent to him. He's an all right guy, I guess. We just don't have much to say to each other." Chase shoves a hand through his hair and exhales in a rush. "Fuck, I need a smoke."

"You shouldn't smoke," I say immediately, because that's what I always say to anyone who smokes. "It's an awful habit."

Rather than respond, he sweeps his gaze over me, a thoughtful expression filling his face.

Under his long, studious examination, my cheeks grow warm. "What?" I mumble.

"I can't figure you out, Beth." His voice is low, wary.

"I can't figure me out, either," I quip, but my tone is weak and so is the smile I try to muster.

Chase slowly moves toward me, and my heartbeat quickens. Not from lust, but because his presence itself is intimidating. He's tall and broad. His jaw is covered with scruff. His jeans are ripped and his black T-shirt stretches across his big chest.

"I was never a crier before. I didn't even cry at…" I wave my hand. He knows what I'm talking about.

"Maybe that's why you keep crying now."

I narrow my eyes at him. "Spare me the pop psychology."

"Fine." He starts to walk away.

I don't want to be alone. I may have thought that was a great idea at first, but now, faced with his back, I realize I don't like that at all. I grab for the bottom of his jeans.

"What?"

"Don't…" I swallow and force my request out. "Will you sit down? It's hurting my neck to keep looking at you."

"I'm going back to study." He gently shakes his leg, trying to loosen my grip.

"No." God, is he going to make me beg? I shutter my eyes and plead, "Please."

He makes a small sound, halfway between surrender and frustration. The former wins out. The air shifts as he drops to the ground beside me.

I drop my head to my knees, but I don't let go of his jeans. He doesn't shake me loose, either. The silence that was so uncomfortable at first becomes a comfort. Or maybe it's Chase who's the comfort.

"Who are you hiding from?" he asks quietly.

"Who am I not?" I twist my head, resting my cheek on my knee. He looks beautiful even from this angle.

"But why? You're Ra—" He cuts himself off. "You're Elizabeth Jones. Why would you have to hide?"

"Because I'm Rachel Jones's sister," I say bluntly. Both of us have been skirting around her, but there's no point. "Because her name is on a plaque on the wall. Because her bedroom looks the same way it did when she died. Because every part of my life is dictated by her death."

His face tightens. "I'm sorry. That's why I shouldn't be here." He waves to my hand still latched onto the hem of his jeans. "I'm a bad reminder of her."

"No. Not really. When I look at you, I don't see her." I close one eye and then the other. He remains the same no matter what view I have. The same straight nose. The same sharp jawline. The same oval-shaped deep blue eyes. "I guess that makes me wrong."

I sit up, resting against the spines of the books. The denim between my fingers is soft, worn down from all the times it's been tumbled in the dryer. I wonder if he'd be okay if I cut off a piece. It seems to bring me comfort. Of course, my parents would find it and demand to know why I brought contraband into my prison cell.

I snort.

"What are we laughing about?" he asks wryly.

I tell him, because why not. He already thinks I'm a sicko for seeking out his company. "I was thinking about asking for a piece of your jeans but my parents would confiscate it. They're my wardens, you know." I glance over to see if he has a smile on his perfect face. He doesn't.

Instead, he frowns. "Your wardens? You think you live in a prison?"

"Yeah," I say unthinkingly. "They dictate where I go and when. Who I see. Where I'm going to college. I don't have access to my car. They made me quit my volunteer job at the animal shelter and my real job at the Ice Cream Shoppe. They took the door off my bedroom." I whisper the last part because it's so frickin' humiliating.

"They took your bedroom door off?" Chase's mouth drops open and his eyebrows shoot up.

"Yes!" I semi shout. Worried, I check to see if anyone heard me. "Yes," I repeat in much quieter tones. "See, wardens."

"Not to downplay your misery, but that's not what a real prison is like."

"Close enough," I mumble.

"No. Not even close. Granted, the door thing is fucked-up, but prison is literally being locked inside a tiny cell with a drain in the corner where you have to piss. You get three meals a day and you eat them in a cafeteria full of punks who are probably thinking about stabbing you with their forks. There's no freedom to move between classes. You don't get the sun on your face whenever you feel like it. Anytime they want, they can ask you to strip off your jumpsuit and bend over to make sure you're not hiding real-life contraband in your ass."

My cheeks are red-hot with embarrassment. I keep forgetting that Chase was in actual prison.

"They don't even call you by your name. You're a number. 'Number Three-Ten, get your white ass out here and mop up the shit on the floor.'" He mimics a high-pitched, nasally tone that must've belonged to one of his guards. "I get that you think life is terrible, but your life isn't a prison. Not like a real one, at least."

"Sorry," I say with my eyes pinned to the carpet. I'm too ashamed to look at him.

"Don't be." He sighs. "I didn't mean to go off on you. The fucked-up thing is that I thought the same as you before… before prison. My dad was always on me to go to basketball practice. I wanted to screw around, go to the skate park or hang out with my buddies or lie on the sofa and play video games. I didn't want to go to the gym and practice my fifteen-foot jump shot for two hours. And that was during the year. You think I got a break in the summers? Yeah, right. Dad made sure I went to basketball camp in Lincoln when I came to visit my mom."

"You didn't like basketball?"

"No, I did. But I didn't *love* it. I mostly played because my dad used to play, and I had friends on the team. But I sure as hell didn't want to spend my whole summer stuck inside some gym. That last summer…" He visibly swallows. "I couldn't take it anymore. So instead of going to practice, I stole my coach's car and went for a spin. You know the rest. The best thing to come out of it was that my dad was done with me. He washed his hands of me the day I pleaded guilty. Told me that since I was done listening to him, he was done talking. That's the last time we spoke."

It's so matter-of-fact how he describes his father's abandonment.

"Have you talked to him since?"

"Nope." Chase shakes his head. "Like I said, it was for the best. He's an asshole. I was ten when they got divorced, and I was honestly happy about that. He was constantly running down my mom, telling her she wasn't pretty or smart. When she hooked the mayor, he couldn't believe it. He told Brian—" Chase cuts himself off. "Rotten, shitty stuff. That's what he said to Brian. So it's better for all of us that he's out of our lives."

I wrinkle my forehead. "Why did you live with him, then?"

"Had no choice. He sued for full custody and won," Chase says darkly. "He gave a whole speech about how boys need their fathers, yada yada. Mom bawled her eyes out in court, but the judge ruled in favor of Dad. So he got me during the year, and Mom got me for the summers."

Chase's home life before the accident sounds terrible, but prison had to be worse. I try to imagine what it was like. I put myself in my room, and instead of the open space where the door is supposed to go, there are bars. I cross my ankles and hug my knees tight to my chest. I wouldn't be able to survive. I wonder how Chase managed.

"How did you cope in juvie?" I ask.

"By thinking about tomorrow. Each day that passed was one day closer to my release. No cage is forever, Beth. I tried to find one small thing that I could be grateful for each day, like the extra ten minutes of free time outside or a work release picking up trash or ice cream for dessert. That's how I kept my sanity—I focused on one good thing instead of all the fucked-up stuff."

One small thing.

Chase gets to his feet. "Lunch is almost over. We should get going."

I stand up, too, but I'm not ready to go yet. Tentatively, I reach out and place my palm on his forearm. His breath hitches. After a long, long moment, he shifts his own hand so that his thumb is pressed against my wrist.

"Chase," I start hoarsely.

"Is he bothering you?"

Scarlett's high-pitched voice has me jumping in surprise. I swivel my head to find my best friend, hands on hips, at the other end of the aisle. I realize that from where she's standing, it looks like Chase is gripping my wrist.

Apprehension darts through me. I could fess up and say I was the one who touched *him*. I was the one talking to *him*.

But the horror in Scar's eyes triggers that shame I've been plagued with since the second I found out Chase was Charles Donnelly. Everybody hates him. *I'm* supposed to hate him. Jeff is handing out petitions. My parents are trying to get him kicked out.

The more contact he has with me, the bigger the target is on his back, which means the one small thing that gets him through this day and all the rest of the days before he graduates will be harder to find.

The best course of action I can take for both of us is to keep my distance from Chase.

His vivid blue eyes lock with mine. Clean, bright and full of permission, he gets what I'm about to do. It doesn't make me feel better, though.

I mouth, *I'm sorry.*

Then I wrench my hand away. "I told you, I *don't* want to talk to you," I snap.

Scarlett rushes over and puts a protective arm around my shoulders. She glowers at Chase. She was so mad and prickly yesterday, so the solidarity she shows toward me now is touching. Like she'd actually fight him to protect me.

"Leave Beth alone," she orders, and I'm touched again because she called me Beth. "It's bad enough that she has to see you every day. Don't you dare try to talk to her."

One corner of Chase's mouth lifts wryly.

Scarlett gasps. "Are you laughing at me? Oh my God! Leave Beth alone, you hear me?"

He lets out a breath and that almost smile fades. Then he walks away without a word.

The moment he's gone, Scarlett frantically searches my face. "What did he want from you?"

"I don't know," I lie.

"Are you okay?"

I am not okay. I am truly awful. Chase just made me feel so much better about everything. He comforted me. He listened to me. And I repaid him by acting like he was a leper the moment someone saw us together.

"No," I say, and it's not a lie.

16

Even though Chase gave me silent permission, I still feel terrible about what went down in the library. I can't stop obsessing over it, and my guilt is made worse during Music History when Troy Kendall goes in on Chase. For the entire class, the Manson comments come hard and fast, but Chase merely keeps his head down and stoically endures.

When Ms. Dvořák has her back to the class, Troy turns to me. "You sign Jeff's petition yet?"

I ignore him.

"Hey, Lizzie, did you hear me?"

"Shut up, Troy," Scar says. "Leave her alone. Can't you tell she wants you to shut up?"

Thank you, Scarlett. I throw her a grateful look. She smiles and reaches over to squeeze my hand. Yesterday's annoyance is gone, our misunderstanding obviously set aside.

"Thanks for helping me out," I tell her after class.

"Of course. I'm your best friend." She smooths my hair down. "I haven't been a very good one, though."

"No. It's me who hasn't been the good friend," I protest.

"I was a total bitch to you yesterday," she counters, looking genuinely remorseful. "I'm sorry I snapped at you about the party."

"What was that about anyway?" I have to ask. "One second you wanted to go, and the next you were all mad that Jeff was going."

Scarlett sighs. "I'm gonna blame it on PMS. I'm supposed to get my period this week and I'm feeling so cranky." She changes the subject by staring pointedly at my outfit. "You still haven't explained the country-club look you're rocking today. Whose clothes are those?"

"Jeff's sister," I admit. "The party ended up being a total disaster and I had to crash at Jeff's house." When her eyebrows soar, I say, "Long story. I'll tell you later. But let's just say that I don't plan on going to another party with Jeff ever again."

For some reason, she perks at that. But her tone is sympathetic as she says, "Aw, I'm sorry it sucked." She eyes me hopefully. "We're good, though, right?"

I haul her in for a hug. "Of course we are," I whisper into her shiny hair.

"Are you two gonna start making out? If not, move your hot asses out of the doorway," Troy says.

"Screw you," I tell Troy, peeling myself away from Scar.

"I'm open. What time and when?" He waggles his eyebrows. "I'll take you both. My dick is long enough to satisfy both of you."

God, Troy is gross. "That'd be half past never," I reply.

Scarlett laughs behind her hand.

"I'll see you at five. I'll supply the condoms—" He breaks off as someone brushes by his shoulder hard, knocking him off balance. "Hey, fucker, don't touch me."

It's Chase who bumped him. And Chase, in very Chase-like fashion, merely ignores the mouthy football player. I hastily step in front of Troy when it looks like he's going to run Chase down.

"Five o'clock isn't a good time. You have football practice," I remind him.

He peers down at me, trying hard to catch a glimpse of my cleavage. Again, he's gross. "Yeah, okay, but we can get together after. I know you girls like it when I'm sweaty." He raises his arms and flexes.

How is it that Troy can be so unsexy, while Chase, who doesn't even try, makes me tremble?

"Let's go." I grab Scar's hand.

"What're you doing tonight?" she asks as we leave a protesting Troy in our wake.

"Home," I say glumly. "My parents expect me home every day after school."

"Do you want a ride?"

"It's out of your way."

"So?"

"So…yes."

We exchange smiles, but mine fades away faster than hers. The conversation I had with Chase in the library is still haunting me. I know that prison is supposed to be a punishment, but hearing him speak about it in such stark terms makes my heart ache.

I don't believe Rachel would want everyone to be sad and suffering because of her death. She hated it when people were angry or upset. She was such a positive, peppy person, and she went out of her way to try to make people happy.

So I need to apologize to Chase, because even though shunning him is what he wants, it doesn't feel right.

As Scarlett drives me home, I make a real effort to find

out how she's been. She's going to visit Northwestern, even though she doesn't think she'll get in.

"It's Dad's dream school for me," she confesses. "I don't have the grades for it, but I know just visiting will make him happy. What about you? Still on for one of those beach schools? Have you resent those applications? You still have a couple weeks before the deadlines."

"I'm mailing everything out on Monday."

"Make sure you physically hand the envelopes to the mailman this time," she advises.

"Trust me, that's the plan. My parents don't get to screw up my college prospects twice in one month." Though if I do get accepted to any of those colleges, I'm not sure how I'll ever convince Mom and Dad to let me go.

"Am I selfish for not wanting you to go away to a coast?" she gripes. "If you do, I'll never see you."

"Sure you will. We'll come visit each other. And we can plan epic holiday reunions."

"Oooh, or we can go away for the holidays. Girls' trip to the Bahamas or Aruba or wherever, really. As long as it's hot."

"Deal."

When she drops me off at home, she's smiling, and I'm glad for that. Her PMS story isn't entirely believable to me, but as long as we're not bickering anymore, I don't care what was up her butt yesterday. I'm just happy it's not there today. Maybe today's one small thing will be reconnecting with Scarlett.

Actually, no. My one small thing today is going to be apologizing to Chase. That's going to make me feel better.

At my front door, I take a deep breath and start thinking of excuses. I'm going for a long walk. Like a really long, two-hour walk. I have a study group with… Not with Scarlett. I don't want to use her. I don't want to use anyone.

I walk into the house. It feels empty. "Mom?"

No one responds.

I wander through each room. "Mom? Dad?" My heart rate picks up. It's eerily silent in here. I quicken my pace. In the kitchen, I find a note on the counter.

Dad has to make a special delivery of lumber to Prairie Hill tonight. He won't be home until eight p.m. I'm heading back to the office to handle a work emergency. Back around seven thirty. We're trusting you to stay inside.

I crumple the paper.

Good. I don't need an excuse. I check the clock. It's nearing four. I have four hours to get across town to the mayor's house, which is five miles away. I should be able to make that in an hour. I run upstairs and change into a T-shirt, shorts and running shoes.

I'm going for a run, I jot on a new piece of paper, just in case one of my parents comes home earlier than scheduled. *Be back soon.*

This probably falls outside of my list of approved activities, but I'm not in prison, am I?

17

The mayor lives on a sprawling estate in Grove Heights, Darling's richest neighborhood. The streets here are wide and lined with majestic oaks. All the driveways are set super far back from the road, and every house is considered a mansion. Jeff's family lives only a couple of blocks away, so I make sure to avoid their street as I slow from a run to a jog.

I'm out of breath and red faced as I trot up the long, tree-lined drive. I thought I was in better shape than this, but I started feeling out of breath thirty minutes into my run. I make a mental note to use our treadmill more often.

The house has a pillared entrance and a huge wraparound porch. I'm nervous as I ring the bell, because what if Chase's mom or the mayor answer the door? I don't think either of them would recognize me as Rachel Jones's little sister, but if I introduce myself with my real name, there's a huge chance they'll contact my parents.

My worst fear comes true when the door swings open to reveal a woman who can only be Chase's mom. Her hair is the same shade of blond as his, and they have the exact same eyes, a dark, vivid blue.

"Hello there." Her words are nice enough, but there's wariness in her voice. She takes in my running gear and the disheveled hair that's come loose from my ponytail.

"Hi. Um. Mrs. Donnelly?"

Her gaze instantly cools. "It's Mrs. Stanton," she corrects.

Right. Of course she took Mayor Stanton's name after they got married. Already I'm off to a bad start.

"I'm…Katie," I lie. "A friend of your son's. I'm in his Music History class at school."

Her eyebrows soar to her forehead.

I hurry on. "I lent him some, um, notes and he forgot to give them back to me earlier. So I came by to pick them up. Is he home?"

"Charlie?" she says.

Does she have another son I don't know about? And why is she staring at me like my nose has grown two sizes? My face heats up, because obviously she knows I'm lying about who I am and why I'm here.

"Y-yes," I stammer.

"You're a friend of my son's," she says slowly. "From school."

It takes me a second to realize that she's amazed, not suspicious. Those blue eyes do a careful sweep of me from head to toe. She blinks a few times. It's like she can't believe there's actually someone, on her porch, who wants to see Chase.

Without another word, she pivots and calls, "Charlie! You have a visitor!"

Footsteps sound from the interior of the house, and then Chase appears. When he spots me, he does a double take.

I see his surprised mouth forming my name. "B—"

But his mother, fortunately, cuts him off. "Your friend Katie is here to pick up some notes?"

A wry glint lights his eyes. "Katie," he says, sounding resigned. "Hey."

"Hey," I answer. I shift from one foot to the other. "Um, yeah… I came by for those Music History notes I gave you."

Another nod. "Yup. Got them in my room."

"Come in," Mrs. Stanton urges, and her tone is far more gracious than when she first opened the front door. "Would you like something to drink?"

"No, thank you. I won't be long. Just gotta get…those notes," I say lamely.

"This way," Chase mutters, gesturing for me to follow him.

"Are you sure I can't bring you down any snacks?" his mother calls after us.

"We're fine, Mom."

I wince at his sharp tone. I kinda feel bad for his mom. From the way he described her in the library earlier—the excuses she made to her wedding guests about her son's whereabouts— he made her sound a bit crappy. But she seems decent. Yes, she was cold at first, but once she realized I was a friend of Chase's, she instantly warmed up. She was so…*eager* for him to have a friend.

I give Mrs. Stanton a grateful smile and wave but keep following Chase. I'm startled when he bypasses the spiral staircase in the foyer and walks right past it. I thought he said we were going to his room.

Instead, we walk down the hallway, past the kitchen and a gorgeous sunroom that overlooks a massive property in the back. We turn, pass a laundry room and then reach a door that Chase quickly opens.

"Down here," he says.

I follow him downstairs to what I deduce is the basement. His big shoulders are set in a tight, tense line, and his steps are brisk. Is he pissed off? I'm starting to think he is, and my pulse quickens. Maybe coming here was a bad idea.

The air becomes musty when we reach the bottom of the stairs. I expected a finished basement, those awesome ones that have game rooms and soft carpeting and maybe even a fireplace.

Instead, I find cinder-block walls and scuffed laminate floors. And it's freezing down here. I shiver in my shorts and T-shirt as I follow Chase deeper into the huge space.

His bedroom is off to the left, down another corridor. When we walk in, I'm appalled. He has a bed and a desk and that's it. Like, that's *it*.

"This is your room?" I exclaim before I can stop myself. "There's hardly any furniture."

He glances over. "There's a bed. What else do I need?"

"Does your stepdad make you sleep down here?" It's like I stumbled into a bad fairy tale.

"That's quite the imagination." He rolls his eyes. "I picked it out. I like this place."

Liar. He likes the open air and lots of space. He told me that first night that he'd rather sit out in the pouring rain than be inside. I stare at the barren white walls, then the stack of books on the desk. Does he just sit in this empty, lonely room every night and read? There's no TV, no gaming systems. He has a phone, though. Maybe he plays games on that? All I know is that I expected Chase to be living it up in the land of luxury over at Mayor Stanton's house, and instead he's like Cinderella, banished to the basement where he probably has to scrub the floors.

When I shift my gaze from the desk to Chase, I find him scowling at me.

"What are you doing here?" he asks.

I gulp. "I…"

"Seriously," he says flatly. "Why are you here, *Katie*?"

I blush. "Sorry about that. I just thought it would be better if she didn't know who I was."

He gives a quick nod. "I agree. But that doesn't answer the question."

I inhale deeply, ordering myself to be brave. "I came to apologize for what I did earlier. When Scarlett found us in the library, I mean."

Chase shrugs. "No apology necessary. I didn't care at the time and I don't care now."

He's lying. He *has* to be. Because I know that if I spent my entire lunch period comforting someone, and then they turned around and shunned me, I'd be devastated.

"I'm sorry," I repeat, firmer this time.

"Nothing to be sorry for."

"Oh my God, Chase. Will you please accept my apology?" I growl. "I ran all the fucking way across fucking town to give this fucking apology."

He bursts out laughing.

Then his mouth slams closed, and a startled silence crashes over the room. He looks like he can't believe he laughed in my presence. Truthfully, *I* can't believe he laughed in my presence.

I sink onto the edge of his bed and play with the sleeve of my T-shirt. "Why is it always so awkward between us?"

That gets me another laugh, this one more of an incredulous bark. "Why do you think?"

I sigh. "I know why, Chase. I just mean…the night we met, it wasn't awkward at all."

"We had sex," he says bluntly. "That's pretty awkward."

"It wasn't for us," I argue. "But my friend Macy said her first time was the most embarrassing thing on the planet. And my other friend had weird, uncomfortable moments in bed with her boyfriend all the time."

With me and Chase, it wasn't like that at all, not even when he undressed me. I'd never been naked in front of a boy before. I should've been mortified. But I wasn't. Yes, I was nervous. Yes, my heart was beating so fast I thought it would explode in my chest. But when Chase's strong hands gripped my hips and his warm lips covered mine, discomfort was the last thing I was feeling.

"I don't know why it wasn't awkward that night, then," he says, leaning against his desk. "But I can tell you why it is now. You shouldn't be here, Beth."

"Your mom didn't seem to mind."

"My mom is probably upstairs crying with joy that her ex-con son has a girlfriend."

My gaze flies to his. "I'm not your girlfriend."

"No shit. But she probably thinks you are. And perfect timing, too." Sarcasm creeps into his tone. "At dinner last night, Mayor Brian warned me it might be tough to meet women because I've got a record."

"He really said that?"

"Yeah. Mom pointed out that since I was sentenced as a minor, my record is sealed. But Brian said everyone knows who I am anyway, so it doesn't matter if there's an official record or not." Chase's eyes soften. "Mom got really upset by that. So, yeah, maybe it's a good thing you stopped by, actually."

I offer a dry smile. "Glad I could help." I pause for a beat. "Your stepdad sounds like an ass."

"He can be. Most of the time I don't think he realizes he's being an ass, though. He really thinks he's being helpful."

"Why'd your mom marry him?"

"Because he's not an ass to her," Chase says, and he sounds reluctant to admit it. "He treats her like a queen." Even more reluctantly, he goes on. "Some of the nastier people in Darling think he just wanted a trophy wife, but he doesn't treat her like one. He's good to her."

"But he's not good to her son," I accuse, waving my hand around the barren room.

"I told you, I picked this place. The mayor isn't going to stash his stepson in the basement. Bad for the image." Chase shrugs. "I'm not some tortured character in a bad soap opera. He treats me fine. Feeds me, clothes me, puts a roof over my head. That's more than what my own father was willing to do. In exchange, I stay out of Brian's way."

If this is really Chase's choice, his guilt runs deeper than I ever imagined. That he would imprison himself down here in the basement of this huge mansion isn't normal, but I don't think he'd listen to me if I told him that. "At least you have some privacy." A wave of annoyance washes over me. "I got home from school to find this stupid note from my mother." I mimic her higher-pitched voice. *"We're trusting you to stay inside."*

Rather than the laugh I was hoping for, Chase's blue eyes darken.

"What?" I say defensively.

He gives another shrug.

"No, tell me. What?" I stand up and cross my arms. "You think I'm overreacting that my parents won't let me step foot outside the house?"

Chase shakes his head, but I don't think he's shaking his head no. It's more a gesture of disapproval.

"Ugh, would you please say something?" I demand.

"Nah."

"Why the hell not?" I stomp toward him and poke him in the chest.

He doesn't even flinch. "Because you're not going to like what I have to say."

"Try me," I challenge.

"Fine." He snatches my index finger, gently twists my hand around and presses my own finger against *my* chest. "There you go, Beth. That's your problem."

"What do you mean?"

"You," he says simply. "You're the problem."

My jaw drops. "Excuse me? I am *not* the problem!"

Chase lets go of my finger. "I told you, you wouldn't like it."

I fold my arms again. "I just don't understand how you can possibly say I'm the problem in my house. There's protective, there's overprotective, and then there's my parents," I say angrily. "They took away my bedroom door!"

"Why?"

"Why what?"

"Why'd they remove your door? What happened before they did it?"

I hollow my cheeks in frustration. "I snuck out to that party in Lex Heights."

Chase's smug little shrug makes me glare at him.

"Are you saying I deserved to lose my door?"

"Nope." He's quiet for a moment before hopping up on the desk and resting his forearms on his thighs. "This kid in juvie, Darren, used to have this saying—you teach people how to treat you."

Although I'm still irritated by his accusations, I find myself sitting back down to listen to him.

"There was this other guy—Russ, a punk-ass dealer who always antagonized the guards, talked back to them, caused trouble. He got knocked around on a daily basis, and he'd get punished for doing the same shit that other guys never even got a slap on the wrist for doing. And Russ would constantly bitch about it on the basketball court. So one day Darren got fed up of hearing it and told him to shut the fuck up. 'You teach people how to treat you,' Darren said. If you keep causing trouble and stirring up shit, then they'll treat you like a troublemaker and shit disturber."

My anger slowly ebbs, replaced with a rush of remorse when I understand what he's getting at.

"If you act like a stupid, reckless kid, then your parents are gonna treat you like one," Chase says bluntly. "End of story, Beth."

He's right. But… "I didn't act like a stupid, reckless kid after Rachel died. Or the year after, or the year after that. It's only these last few months that I've been doing dumb shit," I admit. "They've just… They've gone too far. What they're doing lately is beyond inappropriate. It's insane."

"Yeah? And has acting out shown them the light? Has it changed their behavior?"

"No," I say reluctantly.

"Exactly, because you can't control or change how your parents act. You can only control and change how you respond."

"I can't stand their overprotectiveness anymore, Chase. I just *can't*."

His face conveys zero sympathy. "Guess what, Beth, there's tons of crap you're not going to be able to stand in your life. Are you going to sneak out to parties and get drunk or do some crazy rebellious thing every time you find yourself in a crappy situation?"

I swallow.

"You want my advice?"

I want to say no, but several seconds tick by and I can't get that one syllable out.

So he takes my silence as a yes and keeps talking. "Stop focusing on all the stuff you can't do and start focusing on what you *can* do. Start thinking about something other than partying and having fun or whatever it is you're thinking about." His tone is gruff. "Because that's not what being an adult is about."

"What if I don't want to be an adult?" I whisper.

"Nobody does, doll."

Doll. Did he really just use an endearment? My cheeks feel hot all of a sudden. I hate this so much. I hate that I feel these stupid things for the one person I shouldn't be feeling them for.

"I have to go," I say abruptly, shooting to my feet.

"You're pissed."

I force myself to look at him. "I'm not," I say honestly. "I… You…you've just given me a lot to think about, okay? Plus, I actually do need to go. I snuck out of the house to come see you, remember?"

He walks me back upstairs. Mrs. Stanton isn't lurking behind a chair or potted plant, thank God. It's a good thing, too, because when we reach the front door, Chase touches me.

All right, he touches my *hair*, which is part of me. Therefore, he touches me. His hand thrusts forward and his fingers tuck some loose strands behind my ear.

I freeze.

"Your ponytail's a mess," he says roughly. "You should retie it or you'll have a bitch of a time running home."

Somehow I manage to find my voice. "Yeah. I'll fix it. Thanks."

He takes a step back. "See you at school."

"Um, sure. See you."

I dart out the door as if my butt is on fire. My cheeks feel like they are. But my stomach feels like there's an ocean current of queasiness down there.

You can't like this guy, I plead with myself. *You can't. Rachel is gone because of him—*

But as always, I push all thoughts of my sister out of my mind. I can't think about Rachel. It's too hard. It's been this way since her funeral. Everyone tried to get me to talk about her. Everyone wanted to share all these stories about her and talk about how amazing she was. Me, I shut down.

I just…can't. Talk about her, think about her, look at pictures of her. That's probably why I feel like throwing up every time I see the pristine condition of her bedroom, because it forces me to remember.

So does Chase, but it's easier to be around him than in the shrine that used to be Rachel's room. It's easier to think about the virginity I gave him than about what he took from me.

I'm breathing hard the entire run back home, and this time, I don't think it's because I'm out of shape. My throat feels tight. My stomach, my shoulders, my heart, they all feel tight. Plus, there's a tremor of dread inside me. I'm terrified that I'll come home and one of my parents will be there, and they'll tell me they got home two hours ago and where was I for two hours and how could I be so irresponsible. And then they'll find a new way to punish me.

I'm relieved to find the driveway empty. I race into the

house and hurry upstairs to shower and change. Afterward, I wander down to the kitchen to grab a bite to eat—and that's when I get an idea.

Teach people how to treat you.

Chase's words buzz around in my mind. I don't know if *everything* he said was right, but I can't deny that I haven't given my parents many reasons to have faith in me lately. First, I threw a tantrum after I found those college applications Mom took. I mean, I think I had every right to be angry, but I can concede that maybe screaming about my dead sister wasn't the smartest thing to do.

Then I lied about my plans with Scarlett and went to a party in a sketchy neighborhood. Granted, I don't think it's right of them to read my text messages, but I had been lying to them a lot lately.

What I told Chase was the truth, though. I've been a good girl for years. I've followed their rules, I've worked hard at school, at the clinic. But these past three years, the walls just kept closing in on me more and more, the noose around my neck kept getting tighter and tighter, until finally I snapped. I know every person is responsible for their own actions, but my parents' behavior absolutely drove me to do some of the things I've done.

But…Chase is right. Losing my temper and acting out isn't helping me. It's not helping me get my car or phone back, not helping me go back to the shelter, not helping me regain their trust.

I'm going to cook them dinner.

This brilliant idea hits me as I stand in front of the fridge. Fine, so it's not the grandest gesture in the world, but it's something. It's a start. It shows that I'm willing to sit down and eat with them and be part of the family that I've been running away from all summer. And maybe if it goes well, if they appreciate my efforts, I might be able to convince them to let me go back to the animal shelter. Even once a month would be amazing.

Happy with myself, I start yanking ingredients out of the fridge and setting them on the cedar island. I figure I'll make pasta, grilled chicken and salad. That's easy enough and won't take long to prepare. It's seven, and they'll both be home around eight. I'll have dinner ready and on the table when they walk through the door. They'll have to appreciate that, right?

I'm just placing a pot of water on the stove when I hear the front door open. My heart sinks. Dammit. They're home early!

"Lizzie?" Mom calls.

"In the kitchen!"

Footsteps echo in the hallway. It sounds like more than one set.

"Is Dad with you?" I call back. "I was just making us some dinner."

"You were?" Mom enters the kitchen and looks at the counter in happy surprise. "What a lovely treat!"

I turn back to the stove so she can't see my smile of satisfaction.

"Your father's just parking the car. He finished his delivery earlier than scheduled. But dinner will have to wait, I'm afraid. We have something to discuss first."

I tamp down my uneasiness and turn around to face her again. That's when I see a flash of movement from the doorway. A second later, someone else appears.

It's a police officer.

18

Dad is right behind him. The three adults stand in the kitchen, all of them staring at me.

A bolt of terror pins my feet to the ground. Am I getting arrested for going to see Chase? Can disobeying your parents be a crime? I swing my head toward Mom, wondering if I can get some mercy from her corner.

Dad gestures me forward. "Lizzie, come meet Nick Malloy. Officer Malloy, this is my daughter Elizabeth."

I still don't move, but I manage a weak "Hi."

Mom brushes by me. "Can I get you something to drink, Officer Malloy?"

"No, thank you, and it's Nick, remember?"

I swear he winks at her. Okay, he wouldn't be winking at her if he meant to throw me in the slammer. Right?

Is this how Chase felt when the police arrived at his house the night he ran over Rachel? Or did he get arrested at the scene? I suddenly realize I have no idea how it all went down. I only remember the police showing up at *our* door to give us the devastating news. My mom falling to her knees and wailing in anguish. My dad clutching his chest as if someone had just torn his heart out of it.

Chase did that to us. He made my mother cry and he hurt my father. And I sat in his bedroom today and talked to him like we were best friends. I had *sex* with him.

Oh God, I feel like I'm going to faint. Or throw up. Or both.

"Elizabeth, Officer Malloy is here to help us with your school problem," Mom says. She makes a face at me, one that says for me to get my ass into the living room.

I trudge over and tip my chin in Malloy's direction.

Mom grows impatient and drags me to the couch, then forces me to sit down beside her. My unreasonable panic begins to recede. There's no way that an arrest is going down this slow and easy. Since I don't have a school problem, this must be about someone else.

Officer Malloy takes a seat next to me and places a file folder on the coffee table. He flips it open and pulls out a form. I read it sideways. *Temporary Restraining Order.*

"What's happening right now?" I ask slowly.

Mom takes my hand. "This is for you."

"But I don't have any problems at school."

Officer Malloy frowns and taps his cheap ballpoint against the folder. "No problems?"

"Oh, Lizzie would never complain," Mom says. "That's why we need to do this."

"This? What's this?" I'm confused.

"So you aren't being harassed at school?" Malloy asks.

"No, not at all." The panic returns in a flood as I finally grasp what's going on.

My parents want me to fill out police paperwork against Chase.

I bolt to my feet. "There's nothing wrong at school. School's fine."

"Wrong," Dad says rudely. "As long as Charles Donnelly is there, my daughter will never be safe."

"Sit down, Lizzie," Mom chides.

I do, but only because my legs are unsteady at the moment.

"Have you tried talking to the principal?" the officer inquires.

"Of course we have. We've been all the way up to the board of supervisors. Your boss, Mayor Stanton, is shouting about discrimination and lawsuits if we try to get him kicked out again." Dad's features are pinched. "Until he causes physical harm, damage to school property or anything that would warrant an expulsion, he stays."

Good. I send a mutinous look at Officer Malloy. "And since he's not bothering me, there's no need for that." I jab a finger at the form.

"Your parents said he intimidated you in the library," the cop prompts. "Are you scared of him? Is that why you don't want to report what happened? These restraining orders are here to protect you."

I'm numb with shock. How do they know about the library thing? It happened today. Are they spying on me at school?

"Scarlett's mother called me at work," Mom explains, reading my confusion. "Scarlett told her he was harassing you in the library."

Dammit. My lie is coming back to haunt me. I sink into the cushions and cover my face with my hands. "He wasn't bothering me," I say, but no one believes me.

"Obviously I called Principal Geary right away, but he said even if you came in and filed a complaint, it'll be just a suspension because it's Donnelly's first bullying offense."

I want to scream. Chase didn't do anything wrong.

Except kill your sister.

Bile creeps up my throat. Over my fingers, I can see my

parents staring at me. I sink deeper into the cushions, trying to find a way out of this.

But Mom takes my silence for distress. "Are you all right?" She frets. "I knew he was harassing you!" In a shrill voice, she addresses the cop. "We can't wait until something dangerous happens. I've already lost one daughter." Her hand flies to her throat.

Dad comes over and places a hand on her shoulder. "We're not waiting, Marnie. We're filing the restraining order."

"I can certainly assist you with that," Officer Malloy says gently. He turns to me. "Why don't you describe what happened so that we can put this paperwork in front of the right judge?"

I feel even sicker. "No. I don't want to do this."

"Lizzie," Mom says.

"It's Beth."

"Beth. It's for your own protection."

"He's a menace to this town," Dad says. "He's reckless and—"

"It was an accident," I interrupt and then glance at Malloy with imploring eyes. "You know about the case?"

He nods, because of course, he knows. Everyone in Darling does. It's what my fucking family is known for.

"It was ruled an accident," I remind him.

He nods again.

"This isn't a crazed maniac roaming free. And trust me, I hate him, too." The lie burns my throat on its way out. "But I don't feel right saying I feel physically threatened, because I don't."

Dad looks on in disapproval.

I turn to my mother and grab her hand. "Please. I'm not in any danger. I was sitting in the corner of the library feeling sick because I skipped lunch. Chase was there and I was embarrassed that he saw me crying. I snapped at him. He…" I apologize mentally for my next lie. "He snapped back, and then Scarlett showed up. It was nothing."

"It's not nothing," Dad thunders.

Mom, though, searches my face. I squeeze her hand and plead, "Please."

"You really don't feel in danger from him?"

"I don't." My tone is clear and even. "If that changes, I promise to let you know."

She examines me for a few moments longer before coming to some internal determination. She nods and looks at Officer Malloy. "I'm sorry to have wasted your time, but we do appreciate the information you provided us with. I assume we can contact you again if we decide to go forward with the TRO?"

"Of course." There's a hint of relief in his voice.

We all get to our feet. For once, I don't feel like a stupid kid. I told the truth, or most of it. Mom listened, and the outrageous injustice toward Chase was averted. All without crying, throwing a tantrum or freaking out. *Act like an adult and maybe they'll treat you like one* was Chase's advice.

To my surprise, it's actually worked.

Dad walks Officer Malloy to the door while Mom stays with me in the living room.

"That was very mature of you." She shakes her head slowly. "But he's not a good boy." Her voice catches. "I'm afraid."

"Don't be." I've never felt the least bit endangered by him, but I can't explain to Mom all the times that Chase has had opportunity to hurt me and hasn't, because that would be grounds for locking me in the basement.

Dad comes back and doesn't even look at us. He's pissed.

"I'm going out," he mutters. "Don't wait up."

Before either of us can object, he storms out of the house.

I always thought Mom was the one who couldn't move on. After all, she keeps Rachel's locker empty in the mudroom.

She leaves Rachel's bedroom completely untouched. She won't let me have a dog because Rachel was allergic.

But Dad is the one who's still clinging to his anger and hurt. He was the first one to cry for Chase's blood after the accident. He pressed for a murder charge and raged for weeks when it was pleaded down to reckless homicide. It doesn't matter that Rachel had run into the street without checking for cars. Chase had taken his baby.

Dad will never forgive him.

Mom and I eat dinner by ourselves. She makes grilled cheese sandwiches. I heat up tomato soup.

"How's Scarlett doing? I haven't seen her in a while. You two are still friends, right?"

"Yes. We're good." But I'm still worried about the way she snapped at me after Jeff offered to take me to the party. I don't want our friendship to be on shaky ground; it's one of the best things in my life right now. Scar and I have been best friends since kindergarten. I don't know what I'd do if I lost her.

"Hey, can we go shopping this weekend?" I ask my mother. "I want to see if I can find something for Scar."

"Is it her birthday? I thought that wasn't until January."

"No. It's just an…'I appreciate you' gift." Over the years, Scar and I have bought each other a ton of little friendship gifts, but it's been a while since I've done it. It's definitely way overdue.

"Oh, that's so nice. Of course we can go this weekend. Tomorrow morning?" she suggests.

"Sure." It's not like I have anything on my calendar. Since I have nothing but school, my schedule is surprisingly free. All my other classmates are busy with extracurricular stuff, but I gave that up years ago. The reasons escape me.

After dinner, Mom goes to do laundry, and I retreat to my bedroom. I sit at my desk, but I don't have any homework. I flip open my laptop and check my friends' social media feeds. A message bubble pops up. The sender is Jeff.

I scratch my neck. The idea of chatting with Jeff ranks very low on my scale of fun things to do. I'm still mad at him for abandoning me at the party.

I slam my laptop shut and grab a book off the shelf. I've read this one before, but I enjoyed it, so maybe I can lose myself in the words again. After ten minutes of reading the same paragraph repeatedly, I snap the book closed and throw it on my desk.

Mom passes by my room with a laundry basket.

"Do you need me to fold that?" I ask, rushing to the doorway.

She looks up at me in surprise. "No. It's all done."

I glance down and see a stack of folded towels. "I'll put it away, then."

"All right." She backs away slowly, as if my offer of assistance is so bizarre that I might not be in my right mind. "Thank you."

With that, she disappears down the stairs. It takes me only a minute to stow the towels in the closet.

"Do you need any other help?" I yell down the stairs.

"No. I'm fine. I'm going to watch some television and knit."

I return to my bedroom. There's nothing to do in here. I run a hand over the door frame. If I had a door, would I feel differently?

I twist around to look at the door across from mine. Slowly, I cross the hall. The knob turns effortlessly and the door swings on silent, well-oiled hinges. I leave it slightly ajar.

The room smells fresh, as if someone had the window open. I walk over and peer into the backyard. The corner of the house, where the swing hangs, is dark. A small yellow pool of light splashes across the patio. The Palmers' labradoodle three houses down barks as she's let out into her yard to poop and pee.

It's an ordinary night. I pull back and survey the room. Rachel's trophies and medals from five years of club volleyball decorate a shelf next to her bed. On the mirror above her desk, the pictures of her and her friends hang neatly along the edges. I pull out her white desk chair with the fluffy cushion and take a seat.

On the left side are several photographs of her volleyball team. Arms are slung around each other. Rachel's closest friend, Aimee, is making rabbit ears behind Rachel's head in all of them. It must be an inside joke. There are a lot of things about Rachel's life that I don't know. We were close, but she was still two years older. I'm sure she had her secrets.

On the right side of the desk are two family photographs. One features all of us, taken at my cousin Randy's wedding the year before Rachel died. Mom bought me heels to wear and I was over the moon. The other is of Rachel and me. It was taken after one of her school volleyball meets. Rachel is sweaty and smiling. I'm holding the volleyball and staring up at her like she's the center of my world.

A choked sob flies out of my throat, and suddenly I'm on my feet and racing out of Rachel's bedroom and down the stairs. It hurts too much to see pictures of us together. It hurts to see me looking at her like she hung the moon and the stars. I idolized her, and now she's gone.

I burst onto the back patio and suck in a gulpful of fresh air. It helps ease the tightness of my throat, but not the ache in my heart. I charge toward the swing, but it reminds me of Rachel so I bypass it and head for the fence instead, where I sink onto the grass and lean against the wooden slats.

The sun has already set, but the sky isn't pitch-black yet. I stare at the clouds and pick out one that looks like a dragon. Then I wrench my gaze downward, because that's another thing that reminds me of Rachel. When we were kids we'd throw a picnic blanket on the grass, lie down on our backs and try to find animal shapes in the clouds.

The back of my throat grows scratchy and heat pricks my eyelids, but instead of tears pouring out of my eyes, laughter trickles from my mouth. I try to choke it back. Then I give up and let it come. It's like Rachel's funeral all over again. I couldn't cry, so I laughed. I don't want to cry right now, so I'm laughing.

"Arf."

A yip cuts through my hysterical giggles. "Hey, pupster." I chuckle at Morgan, whose head appears through the slats. "How's it going?"

He doesn't answer, but he does stick his tongue out and lick my shoulder.

It's just what I need. "I missed you, too."

He licks the side of my neck now, then my cheek. I welcome the doggy slobber, because it's way better than salty tears.

"Not as much as I miss Rachel, though," I whisper.

Lick. Lick.

"She'd probably be disappointed in me if she was here right now," I tell Morgan. "Rachel was so focused. Especially with volleyball."

I played volleyball back in the day, too. I joined the same club Rachel belonged to. I was a setter, like her. Our weekends were always full as we went from one tournament to another.

It all ended when Rachel died. It was like all my ambitions and dreams were really Rachel's and when she was gone, my passion for anything dried up like ash and blew away.

"She had choir, too. Oh, and honors club." Plus, she had

Jeff, the golden boy. Rachel was going places. I have no doubt she would've gotten into whatever Ivy League college she applied to and rocked it there.

Me, I have nothing to do with my time. Working at the shelter was the only thing I really enjoyed, but other than that, I tried to fill my time with parties and boys. I didn't sleep with Chase to piss off my parents. If that was the case, I would've told them. I slept with him because something was missing in my life and I felt like I could fill it with him.

But I only feel emptier now.

I've become directionless. Or I've been directionless for a while and just came to the realization today. I've been so busy blaming everyone else for my unhappiness that I didn't take a look at myself.

I don't like what I see.

Frowning, I force myself to get to my feet, even though it means no more doggy kisses from Morgan. "I'm sorry, pupster, but I've gotta go. Time to make some changes."

Upstairs, I sit on my bed and open my laptop. With a sense of determination, I pull up Darling High's webpage. Wow. There are a ton of different electives and clubs, so many it's hard to scroll through them all.

I start reading and taking notes. A shadow pauses by the doorway but moves on without interrupting. I keep scrolling. I do some additional researching.

"Bingo," I say, staring at my round letters on my notepad.

I start typing. It takes me several hours, but when I'm done, I'm pretty darn pleased.

As of this moment, I'm no longer the girl without direction. I'm the girl with a plan.

19

"What's this?" Mom asks the next morning as I slide the printed page toward her.

"It's a contract," I say proudly. I reach across the kitchen table to give Dad his copy.

He squints at it, unable to read without his glasses. "A contract for what?"

"It's a..." My mom trails off as she keeps reading.

"It's a family contract," I declare. There were other titles, like Contract for Good Behavior and Contract for Responsibility, but they all sounded so demeaning and one-sided. "I promise to abide by rules that you believe will keep me safe, and in exchange you allow me to visit the school of my choice."

"You are not going to USC," Dad says, slapping the paper down.

I have to bite back an angry response. "It's not USC or UCLA or Miami. It's Iowa State."

That stuns them into silence. Mom picks up her coffee cup and takes a quick sip. Dad narrows his eyes at me.

"Iowa State," he echoes suspiciously.

I lean back in my chair and cross my arms. "Yes."

Mom finally finds her voice. "Why Iowa State? This is the first time you've mentioned it."

"It's the first time I've thought of it," I admit. "But it's the one school that came up over and over again in my research last night."

Mom looks curious. "What research?"

Her receptiveness has me barreling forward. "I want to be a vet. I'm going to have to change a few classes next semester, although I don't think my high school credits matter much. But it's always a good thing to have extra sciences under your belt if you're going the medicine route, even doggy medicine. Iowa State is one of the top vet schools in the country, and it's close by so that you can visit often." But far enough away that I can have some feeling of independence. I don't explain this point to my parents, though. No sense in scaring them away.

Mom purses her lips in thought.

Dad still looks skeptical.

"It's only six hours away from here," I tell them. "And I'm not even asking to attend there. I'm asking for a school visit."

Dad glances down at the contract again. "It also says that we'll give you back your phone if you've been compliant with all our rules."

"Yes. It's hard to contact you if I have a problem at school or on the way home."

"And you want to go back to the animal shelter."

"Yes."

"Since when do you want to be a vet?" Dad asks.

"Since last night," I confess. "It was an epiphany."

Mom's lips twitch as if she's trying not to smile, but then she can't fight it anymore, and a huge grin spreads across her face.

My heart squeezes, because it's been so long since I've gotten such a big smile from her. And her eyes are shining with pride.

"You know how much I love animals. If it was up to me, we'd adopt every stray that showed up on our doorstep." From the moment I saw my very first dog at the age of three, I'd begged my parents for a pet. A dog, cat, fish, hamster, anything. But our house has always been staunchly pet-free.

"So last night I sat down and really thought about what I want to do after high school and what I love most in the world, and I kept coming back to animals. I want to work with animals." I shrug. "And I'm good at sciences, so I think I'd do really well at vet school."

"I think you would, too," Mom says, and my heart nearly explodes with happiness.

Dad is slowly coming around, too. He scratches the bridge of his nose and studies me carefully. "If we agree to this—" he gestures to the contract "—we have your word that you'll follow the rules? That means no lying about your whereabouts, no parties unless we give you permission, none of that nonsense."

"None of it," I promise. Then I hesitate. "Also, I didn't put this in the contract, but I'd really like my door back."

There's another brief silence.

Mom, still smiling, picks up the pen that Dad was using to fill out his Saturday crossword. She scribbles something on the contract and slides it my way.

"Initial here," she says solemnly.

My face feels like it's going to crack in half, I'm smiling so hard. Under the list of privileges I'm asking to get back, she's written DOOR.

Next to it, I scribble EJ. Mom initials it, too. And then all three of us sign the contract.

"I'm going to make a copy," Dad announces, scraping back his chair.

I can't contain my laughter. "What, in case I destroy the one and only copy and you need to hold me to it?"

"Yes," he says tartly, but his eyes are dancing with laughter. For one amazing moment, he's the father I had before Rachel died. The father who made cringeworthy puns and couldn't go five seconds without busting out in a huge smile.

Once he's gone, Mom reaches for my hand and gives it a squeeze. "You've surprised us this morning."

"I surprised myself."

"I'm proud of you for doing some soul-searching and coming up with these decisions."

My throat squeezes. "Thank you." I pick up my glass of orange juice and take a huge gulp, hoping she didn't hear how choked up I sounded.

But I think she did, because her gaze softens even more. "Did you still want to find a present for Scarlett today?"

I nod eagerly while drinking my OJ.

"Okay then, tell you what. Go upstairs and get dressed and we'll leave whenever you're ready."

The mall is super busy for a Saturday morning. Then again, I can't remember the last time I woke up before noon on Saturday morning, so maybe this is how the mall always is at 10:00 a.m.

Mom and I wander around aimlessly for a couple of hours. She buys me a hoodie from American Eagle, and I buy Scarlett a pretty scarf from Forever 21. Scar's obsessed with scarves. She's got like a hundred of them, and I know she's going to love this pink-and-gold one with its tiny skulls with flowers for mouths.

It's around one o'clock when my stomach starts growling. "Oh my God, if I don't eat something, I'm gonna pass out," I declare.

Mom rolls her eyes at me. "Aren't we melodramatic?"

"Nope, we're hungry, Mom. *Famished.*" I grin and point in the direction of the food court. "Can we eat something before we head home?"

She thinks it over, then shakes her head. "I have a better idea."

Intrigued, I follow her in the direction opposite the food court. We pass a block of jewelry stores, a Foot Locker and a Guess, and eventually come to a stop at the other end of the huge complex in front of one of my favorite restaurants. My friends and I always grab lunch here when we come to the mall. They have the best ham-and-cheese omelet on the planet.

"Eggcellent?" I say happily. "You rock, Mom." I hold up my hand for a high five.

She slaps it with her palm, and my spirits soar even higher. I can't deny this is one of the best days I've had in a long while, and I'm shocked that it's with my mother. We haven't seen eye to eye for so long that it feels almost foreign now to actually enjoy each other's company.

"Let's get a table," I say, but Mom doesn't follow me to the front doors. "Hurry up, slowpoke."

"Actually, I think I'll leave you to it."

I stare at her in confusion. "What?"

She winks at me, then checks her watch and says, "Your friends should be here any minute. Why don't you grab a table while you wait?"

My jaw drops to the shiny tiled floor. "Are you serious?"

"I called Lisa when you were in Forever 21 and suggested

that maybe Scarlett would like to meet you here at the mall for lunch. She's picking up Macy and Yvonne on the way."

I practically bounce with excitement. Lisa is Scar's mom, and Scar is on her way here with our other friends. And I can't believe this was my mother's idea. I can't wait to tell—

I try to shut my brain down before it can finish that thought.

I can't wait to tell Chase.

How sick is it that that's the first thought I had? That I want to tell Chase that his advice worked. That acting like an adult resulted in my parents loosening the reins a bit. That my dad smiled at me today. That my mom is actually *encouraging* me to see my friends when mere days ago she was forbidding me from leaving the house.

"This is amazing. You're amazing." I lunge forward and throw my arms around her.

She hugs me back tightly and then releases me. "Have fun, Beth. Lisa said Scarlett will be able to drive you home."

The moment Mom's gone, I let out a squeal of joy. Several passersby turn their heads in my direction, but I don't care if they think I'm a crazy person. I have a life again! I'm getting my phone back soon. I'm allowed to volunteer again. I get my door back. I'm about to see my friends.

This fucking rocks.

Inside the restaurant, I order a chocolate milkshake while I wait for my girls. The first sip of chocolaty goodness tastes phenomenal. Or maybe it's the flavor of freedom that's making my taste buds dance.

"Ahhhhh!"

That's Macy's opening line when my three friends hurry up to my booth.

"You're freeeeee!" Yvonne chimes in, while Scarlett slides onto the bench beside me and smacks kisses on my cheek.

I giggle and try to bat her off me. "Chillax, Love Machine. You'll ruin my makeup."

"You don't wear makeup," she retorts, rolling her eyes.

"Which we should totally hate you for," Yvonne chides as she and Macy sit across from us. "Nobody is allowed to have skin that smooth and flawless without the use of BB cream."

The waitress comes over and takes their drink order. We all take a break from chatting to study our menus and figure out what we're going to eat. I decide on a burger and fries to go with my milkshake. While Macy and Yvonne are still deciding, I discreetly slide Scarlett's gift onto her knee under the booth.

"What's this?" she whispers.

"Just a bestie present," I whisper back. "Open it when you get home."

She beams. "You da best, Beth."

I mock gasp. "You called me Beth!"

"Did I? Nah, you're imagining it."

I poke her in the ribs. "You totally did."

The four of us joke around and gossip until our lunch arrives, and then we keep joking and gossiping even as we're eating, not caring that our mouths are full and everyone's probably staring at us in disapproval. It's been a long time since I've felt this relaxed around my friends. At school, the tension that Chase's presence creates is always looming like a dark cloud over our heads. At home, I don't have a phone or a door or any privacy to talk to my friends.

This is the best day ever.

Or at least it is until Yvonne brings up Chase.

"Okay, so I know we're not allowed to talk about Charlie Donnelly," she starts.

"Who said we're not allowed to talk about him?" I interject.

Her gaze darts in Scarlett's direction before returning to me.

Sighing, I glance at my best friend. "You're telling people not to talk to me about him?"

"Of course I am," she says hotly. "Every time anyone brings up his name, your face goes white like a ghost and you look like you're going to throw up."

"Actually, you *did* throw up," Macy reminds me.

"Yeah, from shock." I shrug. "But now that I know he's at Darling and there's not much I can do about it, I can't let him affect me anymore." Except he does affect me, more than my friends will ever know. I think about him constantly.

I turn to Yvonne. "What were you going to say about him?"

She takes a long sip of her soda before speaking. "My sister's home from college this weekend and she was out with her friends last night and all this stuff about Charlie came up."

I frown. "What kind of stuff?"

"Well, okay, you know how Taylor's friends with some girls from Lincoln, right?"

Taylor is Yvonne's older sister, and I have no idea who her friends are, but I nod in spite of that.

"They're two years older than us, like Taylor, and one of them knew Charlie back in the day," Yvonne goes on. "Her name's Maria—I don't know if you guys ever met her."

"Why would we have met her?" Scarlett says. "You just said they're two years older than us."

"True. Whatever. Anyway, Maria lives in Lincoln and she

was friends with Charlie. They hung out in the summers, and I guess they hung out the other night. Thursday night," Yvonne says, giving me a meaningful look. "She was at Karl's party."

"Kav," I correct.

"Whatever." She takes another sip. "Charlie went to that party, too. Did you know that?"

Macy gasps. "Oh my God, did you see him when you were there?"

"No," I lie. "But I didn't stay very long at all."

"Well, that's a relief," Scarlett says, reaching over to squeeze my shoulder. "Imagine he tried hanging out with you at a party?"

"Or if he made a move on you?" Macy adds with a gasp.

I swallow a lump of guilt. Been there, done that. Except it was me who wanted to hang out with *him* at that first party, and me who made the move on *him*. The truth sits on the tip of my tongue, and I'm so tempted, *so tempted*, to spill all the dirty, horrible, wonderful details.

I want to tell my friends that I had sex for the first time. I want to tell them how confused I am about Chase, how I think I might have feelings for him but I don't know if it's because the sex bonded us or if I actually like him.

But I can't say a word. I'm terrified they'll judge me. Or worse, that they'll judge me, hate me for it and then tell the entire school what I did. Or even worse than that, tell my parents.

So I keep quiet and listen to the rest of Yvonne's story.

"So Charlie was there hanging out with Maria—"

Is Maria the gorgeous girl who Jeff was rude to? I wonder. Suddenly I hope not, because the idea of Chase spending time with such a beautiful girl brings a spark of unwanted jealousy to my belly.

Argh. I have to *stop* this.

"—and he told her that he was at another party last weekend, he didn't say where, and that he met a really cool girl there and—"

"*What?*" I exclaim. My cheeks begin to scorch. Chase brought me up to his friends? He said I was *cool*?

He might not have been talking about you, a voice in my head warns.

That triggers another jolt of jealousy.

"Seriously?" Scarlett says angrily. "He's been out of jail for, what, a *second*, and he's already making friends and hooking up and acting like he didn't do anything wrong? He's a killer!"

Her outburst sends several heads swinging in our direction.

"Sorry," she whispers sheepishly.

"No, I'm with you," Yvonne says. "I thought the same thing when I heard that. Also, according to Maria, Charlie used to be a player before he got arrested. He was always the life of the party, and he hooked up with a ton of girls and apparently he was a sweet-talker. Like super smooth."

I have to stifle a laugh, because whatever Chase used to be back then, he sure as heck isn't now. A sweet-talker? Hardly. He has no problem being painfully blunt and telling me things I don't want to hear. Life of the party? Yeah, that's why he's always holed up in some corner at every party he's at.

Being locked up obviously changed him. It turned him from a boy who wanted to hook up and have fun to a guy who's now appreciative of everything he has. A guy who can find one small thing every day and be eternally grateful for it.

The Chase that Maria knew three years ago is gone. I didn't know that Chase. I know the quiet Chase. The serious one. The one who smiles so rarely that when it happens, it's like witnessing a solar eclipse. And it's beautiful. I love it when he smiles. I—

Misery wells up in my throat. Argghhhhhhh. This. Needs. To. Stop.

"Are you okay?" Scarlett demands.

I bite my lip, wondering what on earth my expression is conveying that's put so much urgency in Scar's voice. "I'm fine," I assure her. I take a breath. "But…you're right…maybe I don't like talking about him."

"See," Scarlett says, turning to glower at Yvonne. "I told you it's a sensitive subject. We are *not* talking about that creep anymore."

I pick up my milkshake and drain the rest of it, but the cold, sweet liquid can't wash away the lump of unhappiness still lodged in my throat. Not talking about Chase is easy.

Not thinking about him? A whole other story.

20

I wake up the following morning with the biggest smile on my face. Last night, Dad knocked on my door—my *door!*—and informed me that he and Mom decided I could drive myself to the shelter today. In my own car.

I swear, my life is getting so much brighter I'm scared it might all be a dream. But I'm wide-awake as I get dressed, as I scarf down a quick breakfast, as I hop in my car—my *car!*—and plug my phone—my *phone!*—into the car charger to load some tunes.

Today is going to be a good day. I veered off course these last few months, but I finally feel like I'm back on track.

When I arrive at the shelter, however, I'm faced with a dose of disappointment. After hugging me tightly and saying how happy she is to have me back, Sandy informs me that I can't interact with the animals today.

"No doggy love?" I say glumly. "Why not?"

"We have these new insurance and liability forms that all volunteers are required to sign. In your case, we need your parents' signatures since you're a minor. I would've emailed them to you when we got them last week, but—" she shrugs "—I didn't think you were coming back. Your father was pretty firm on the phone that you wouldn't be."

"Luckily, he changed his mind," I say with a happy smile. "And it's fine—I'll give everyone extra pats and kisses next weekend." I tuck the set of papers inside my messenger bag. "I'll bring these home and have my mom sign them."

"Great. Then today you get to pick up dog poop." Sandy grins. "Probably not how anyone would want to spend their weekends, huh? Especially in senior year."

"Actually, it sounds awesome," I tell Sandy. "I've decided I want to be a vet, so the more I'm around animals, the better. Even if it's just picking up poop."

A big grin spreads across her face. "Yeah, picking up dog poop for free is exactly how I spent my senior weekends, too. Every party ends up being the same, right? The same couples hooking up. The same fights breaking out. Everyone acting like high school is their last moment on earth."

She could be talking about my empty life.

"Anyway, we're building a new dog kennel in the back, but we need to clear the brush and get rid of all the trash and poop out there. Since you're wearing pants and a sweatshirt, you should be well protected."

I look down at my old leggings that are starting to pill after repeated washings and the oversize Darling High hoodie that's faded so much it's hard to make out half the letters. "Sounds like a plan."

Sandy hustles me down the hall to the storage room, where long metal shelves filled with shovels and boxes and bags line the walls. She arrows to the back, grabs something and returns. "Here, you'll need these." She hands me a pair of blue-and-black work gloves.

I slip them over my fingers. They're a little long, but I don't want to complain. I'm lucky they gave me my job back after my father quit on my behalf without warning.

We head out the back door and then down a rock path toward the edge of a wooded area. There's already a worker there moving dirt and debris from one pile to another. His long-limbed, easy gait reminds me of Chase. But then everything does these days.

"So are you seriously considering vet school?" Sandy asks.

"Yes. You know how much I love animals. I really wish I could have a pet at home but, you know, allergies." I don't say *my dead sister's allergies*, because that sounds utterly insane, and I don't want Sandy to think my parents are nutjobs.

"That's too bad. There are hairless cats and stuff, but they're pretty expensive. Plus, you already know we encourage adoption rather than buying from breeders. Last year, there was, like, a million unwanted pets put down."

I gasp. "A million?"

"Yeah, tragic, right?" We reach the construction site, and Sandy waves a hand over it. "We just bought this property last week and as you can see it's kind of an actual dump. We need to clear the land. Metal, compost and trash are all being separated. If you have any questions, give Chase a holler. He just started a couple days ago. Hey, Chase!" Sandy waves as the male worker slows the wheelbarrow to a stop near us.

Shock gives way to pleasure.

Seriously? I get to see Chase *and* be free of my parents for a few hours every weekend?

I don't care how much poop I have to shovel. It's worth it.

"Hey, Sandy. What do you need—" The grin on Chase's face immediately disappears when he recognizes me.

"This is Beth Jones. She's our new volunteer. Well, techni-

cally, she's an old volunteer who's going to be rejoining us."
Sandy knocks shoulders with him.

I stiffen. Are they dating or something? He looked so happy
to see her before he spotted me, and she's acting like they're
old friends. Did he cheat on Sandy with me at the party? Or
is this something new? Sandy's pretty, but she's older. Like, I
swear she's in her mid to late twenties.

I stare at Chase, who stares back grimly.

"Nice to meet you," he replies in a tone that says it's anything but nice for him.

Sandy gives him a curious glance, but Chase is saved from
explaining his abrupt mood change when someone from the
shelter hails Sandy.

"You two going to be okay?" she asks, clearly hesitant to
leave us alone.

"Sandy," the guy at the back door calls again.

"We'll be fine, thank you," I say, because I *want* her to
leave us alone.

"Yeah, go on, Sandy. I got this." Chase gives his coworker
a chin nod.

The Chase standing in front of me seems so much more
confident than the one at school. In the hallways, his head
is always down. In the classroom, he stares straight ahead.
Here, he meets your eyes full on. His shoulders are straight.
He even looks taller—and hotter.

The minute that Sandy is out of earshot, Chase leans toward me.

My heart starts beating so hard, I swear I can feel it knocking against my rib cage. I gulp. The air between us thins. As
his mouth gets closer to my face, my breath catches in my
throat. Is he… Is he going to…?

"Are you following me?" he whispers in my ear.

I jerk back. "What?"

"Why are you here? Did you follow me?"

Any warm feelings I was experiencing are washed away by outrage. "Of course not. I've been volunteering here for two years!"

His eyes narrow, as if he doesn't quite believe me.

"It's true," I insist. "Didn't you hear what Sandy said about me being an old volunteer? This was *my* place long before you showed up here."

To punctuate that, I push past him and grab a tree branch. Of course, it's larger than I anticipated and gets stuck under some other object, so I don't get to stomp away like I wanted. My plans are always being thwarted.

A big hand curls around mine and the branch comes loose. "I'm sorry," he says roughly. "Can we start again?"

Wouldn't that be great? "From where?"

"From the beginning?" He slowly lowers his end of the branch and then sticks out his hand. "I'm Chase Donnelly."

I reach for his hand and shake it. His long fingers curl around mine, shooting shocks of electricity throughout my body. Ignoring them, I say, "I'm Beth Jones. I'm volunteering here again after a short hiatus."

"This is part of my probation."

I drop his hand. "Seriously, Chase. You can't lead with that." So much for starting over. I reach for the branch and start dragging it.

"Why not?" he says, grabbing the heavy end and hoisting it in the air. "It's the truth."

"So? There's a ton of other truths you could lead with. Like, the mayor is your stepdad. Lead with that."

"That makes me sound like a pretentious asshat," he grumbles.

"And saying you're on probation makes you sound like a…a…" I search for the right word.

"Criminal?" he offers.

"…delinquent. And you're not," I add.

"But I am."

"I thought we were starting over."

"I'm not going to mislead anyone."

Impatiently, I toss my end of the branch into the woodpile. Talking to Chase is like making a speech to the pile of logs. It's worthless and the words get swallowed by the denseness.

"Look, I'm not trying to be stupid here," he says, appearing over my right shoulder. "It just doesn't feel right not to let people know I'm on probation. Like I'm operating under false pretenses."

"It's not false pretenses to let people get to know you before you tell them something like that. It's called putting your best foot forward. In an interview, you don't tell them that you have a hard time getting up in the morning. You tell them you're eager to start work at any time." I cross my arms. "Let's try again—why'd you get a job here and not somewhere else?"

"The shelter has a deal with the state's juvie rehab program."

I throw up my hands in disgust. "Forget it. You should just get *Chase Donnelly, Felon* tattooed on your forehead."

"My forehead? Nah, I was thinking my neck."

"What?" I spin around to see Chase grinning at me. He was joking, thank God.

"Okay, how about this?" He strides forward, grabs my right hand and says, "I'm Chase Donnelly. I go to Darling High. I think we have some classes together."

The electric shocks happen again, but I pretend that his mere closeness isn't making my insides go crazy. "I'm Beth

Jones. I've seen you in AP Calc and Music History. Do you play an instrument?"

"No, I can't play an instrument to save my life. I can't sing and I can't even draw stick figures, but I had to fulfill that Fine Arts requirement so I picked Music History."

"Same." I smile sympathetically. "Plus, I heard that Dvořák lets us listen to pop music during class and I unironically enjoy pop music."

To my surprise, he doesn't make fun of me for that. Instead, he says, "The One Direction guys are lit now."

"Harry Styles all the way."

"I'm more of a hip-hop head. Gucci Mane, Post Malone."

"I like that, too."

We stare at each other, hands clasped, smiles on our faces. It feels like I'm being baked in the sun. Finally, we both realize we've held hands for way too long to constitute a normal handshake. I let go first. It seems like he's reluctant to release me. Or it might be my imagination.

"You like animals, huh?" he asks as we walk back to the trash pile.

"I always wanted a pet, but we can't have one because Ra—because my mom's super allergic to them," I lie. "Do you like them?"

"Yeah. They're pretty nonjudgmental. That's a big plus."

"I don't know about that. There's a new pit bull inside who glares at everyone."

"Rocco? No way. He's a sweetheart. The worst he'll do is slobber all over you. Someone brought him in a few days ago and I sneak him treats every chance I get."

"Who else is new?" I ask curiously. "I've been gone, so I'm behind on intakes. And has Opie been taking his meds?"

"Not without a fight," Chase answers with a wry smile. "It takes like three people to get him to swallow those pills."

"Not when I'm here," I say smugly, remembering how easily the grumpy rottie responds to me.

"Well, good thing you're back, then."

Chase adds in a few more tidbits about some of the new arrivals I've yet to meet. Mittens, an unoriginal name for a cat if I ever heard one, looks haughty but if you give her a little milk, she'll be your friend forever. Sylvester is a parrot that speaks in French. No one knows why, but the assumption is that she had a French-speaking owner despite Darling never having had a French family for as long as anyone can remember.

"My favorite is Boots, though," Chase tells me. "He's a tough old dog. His owner died last week and the family didn't want Boots. I don't think anyone's going to adopt him, so I'm hoping I can get permission to take him home."

"That's good." I think of Chase's empty bedroom in the basement, and my heart clenches. He could use a friend.

"Yeah, but he's got some kind of stomach problem and he's always puking. Mom would kill—" He halts and clears his throat. "Mom wouldn't be happy if I brought home a dog that would ruin the mayor's thousand-dollar rugs."

"It's okay. You can say things like *kill* or *murder* and I'm not going to hold it against you." I hate that he has to watch what he says around me.

His blue eyes meet mine. "Nah, I really can't say those things," he admits. "Because even if you don't hold it against me, I would still feel guilty. I've lost a lot of sleep feeling guilty over you." It's not an accusation; it's a sad, sorrowful admission.

Without another word, Chase bends down and picks up

a huge hunk of white-painted metal and lugs it toward the metal pile.

We work quietly until closing time.

"Can I give you a ride home?" I offer as we wash up.

Chase shakes his head no, drying his hands. "The mayor is coming to pick me up."

"Do you call him that to his face? Hey, Mayor, what's for dinner? Nice tie, Mayor. See you later, Mayor." I wave my hand.

Chase smirks. "Nah, I call him Brian."

"Did someone mention me?" A trim figure steps into the back room.

I recognize Mayor Stanton's handsome, clean-shaven face from his campaign posters, but he's much shorter in real life.

He holds his hand out to me. "I heard my name and, like any good politician, raced to see what was being said."

"Sir," Chase says formally.

He calls him Brian, my ass. I shake Mayor Stanton's hand firmly. "Only good things."

"You're my favorite kind of voter." Chase's stepdad smiles and it feels genuine—not a show he's putting on in front of the public. "So you must be Chase's friend Katie?"

Oh God. I shoot Chase a wild glance. I'd forgotten I'd lied to his mother about my name.

"She goes by Beth now," Chase jumps in. "She used to go by Katie when she was younger but felt it was too cutesy, so she prefers to be called Beth."

That sounded so dumb. Is that what my friends think when I keep insisting they stop using Lizzie?

"Well, Beth it is. Although I think Katie is a lovely name. Are you visiting any colleges these days? Chase's mom and I have been begging him to apply to some schools in Arizona so we have somewhere warm to visit."

"I wish, but no, my parents want me to go to Darling College."

Mayor Stanton's a smooth politician, but even he can't completely hide his surprise over this. "Well, Darling has some good classes, which I'm sure will help you get a head start on whatever it is you want to do. You ready, Chase?"

"Yup. See ya later, Beth."

"Bye." I watch him go, noticing the way his dark blond hair shines gold under the rosy tones of the sunset. How ironic that Chase's parents want him to get away, but he's determined to stay here and beat himself up every day, whereas I can't wait to escape the stranglehold of my parents.

But Chase feels like he can't start over or, at least, doesn't deserve to. And for me, no matter how many times I tell people I'm Beth, I'm still going to be Lizzie to them. No matter where Chase goes, he'll always have a record. It's a juvenile record and it's sealed, but it's there.

Those truths float around inside me and sink like rocks thrown into a pond. Chase's light gait has disappeared, replaced by a heavier one, as if an invisible weight is bearing down on him. Only, it's not invisible. It's me. I'm the weight. I'm the flesh-and-bone manifestation of his guilt.

Even if I were okay with the past, I don't think Chase will ever be.

21

"You're in a good mood today," Scarlett says as we hit our lockers before Calc class.

"Am I?" I glance at myself in the mirror. I don't look any different than I did yesterday. I pinch my cheek. "I put some lip gloss on this morning."

She rolls her eyes. "I'm pretty sure it's not the lip gloss. Come on, spill. Why are you all smiley?"

I turn toward her. "I signed a contract thing with my parents that says I promise to be a good girl and in exchange I get some of my privileges back," I confess.

Scar's eyes widen. "Holy shit. Is that why your mom invited us to lunch this weekend?"

"I think so. And they gave me back my phone, car and door."

She snickers. "That's the first time I've ever heard anyone say they're getting their *door* back."

"I know, right?"

She checks her reflection in the mirror, dabbing at the corner of her mouth to fix her lipstick. "Is it, like, a legal contract?"

I snort. "Um, doubtful. If they go back on their word, I

don't think Judge Judy is going to order them to fulfill the terms or pay some fine."

"Imagine you took it to court," Scar says, starting to laugh. "That would be both badass and insane." Before I can blink, she throws her arms around my neck. "But whatever, I'm so happy for you! I'm glad they're not being total tools anymore."

"God, me, too."

A commotion at the end of the hall breaks up our hug. We both turn to see Troy and his pals circling Chase.

My shoulders tense. Why can't those assholes just leave Chase alone? He's as tall and built as any of the football guys, but everyone knows Chase won't fight back if they knock him around. He can't afford to get in trouble at school, and he tries hard not to draw attention to himself.

"Want to come to the game on Friday?" Scarlett chirps, shifting her gaze away from the group of guys.

I glare at the football players. "No." I'd rather poke my eyeballs out than cheer for those bullies.

Across the hall, Chase keeps a steady forward movement, not looking to the right or the left. How he maintains that bubble, I will never know.

"Please. I don't want to go alone," Scar is saying.

I tear my gaze off Chase and refocus on my friend.

"Yvonne is going away on a school visit and Macy's got a club volleyball tournament."

I narrow my eyes. "You hate football," I remind her.

"It's not about the football."

That makes me grin. "Ah, okay. So who's the guy?"

Her eyes instantly slide away. Since when does Scarlett hide what boy she's interested in? I'm not sure I like that.

"Really? He's that shady that you can't tell me about him?"

Then I shut up because who am I to talk.

"Just come, okay?" she asks quietly.

"Okay." I capitulate, because if I go to the game she'll have no choice but to confess who she's crushing on.

"Yes," she says happily. "You're the best!"

She hugs me again, just as Troy and his buddies approach us.

"If you two are going to make out, can I take some pictures?" Troy leers as he walks by.

"You're so gross." I move to the side. "You're sure you want to go to the game?" I ask Scar loudly.

She wrinkles her nose. "It's not like we're going to cheer for them. We don't like losers."

Troy scowls and takes a step toward us. Chase's hard frame appears, cutting off Troy's line of sight. I grab Scarlett's hand and we book it to class.

"It's Jeff," she blurts out when we reach the door.

I look around. "Where?"

"No. Jeff. Jeff is the guy I want to see at the game."

I'm dumbstruck for a moment. "Jeff? Rachel's Jeff?" And then immediately regret my thoughtless words when Scar visibly shrinks. "No, wait. He's not Rachel's Jeff anymore. I was just…" Wow, I'm kind of like my parents, still keeping Rachel alive in my head. "Jeff doesn't belong to anyone. Definitely not to anyone with the last name Jones," I finish.

She peeks at me under long eyelashes. "You're not mad?"

"No. Gosh no."

"I thought you might be interested in him, but he said that you weren't. Like, he was really forceful about it." She still sounds worried, though.

"He's right. I'm not interested." Especially not after he abandoned me at the party.

The thought makes me hesitate. I should tell Scarlett about that, but how? If I say anything now, she might chalk it up to jealousy. Or she may feel even guiltier. Either way, I'll have to keep it to myself until a better opportunity arises.

"If it's Jeff you want, Jeff it will be," I declare, hopefully as forcefully as Jeff denounced me.

Scarlett squeals. "Yay! It'll be fun. We'll get dinner at Mixed and then head to the game. We can all meet up at my house afterward. I'll have my parents call yours."

"Sounds good." I try to be cheerful for Scar's sake, but I don't know how thrilled I am about her liking Jeff.

When he was dating Rachel, I thought he was the greatest guy in the world. But truth is, I didn't know him too well. Since he's come back to Darling, I've gotten to know him better, particularly the night of the Lincoln party, and—I have to be honest again—the more I know of him, the less I like.

But I can't say that to Scarlett, because she looks so excited about this Friday night plan. Also, because Jeff is sauntering our way.

"Hey, hotties," he says with a wink.

Jeff joins us, slings an arm around both of our shoulders. "Let's skip out and go to Starbucks for a midmorning snack."

"We're not supposed to leave campus unless it's for lunch," I remind him.

"Today no one will care," Jeff promises.

"What a great idea, Jeff," Scarlett says enthusiastically. A little too enthusiastically for someone who's agreed to spend too much money for a box lunch with three apple slices, eight grapes and a pita bread the size of your palm. But Scar's beaming. True love never gets hungry. "Come with us." She tugs on my arm.

I give in again. "Sure. Why not?"

"Okay. Meet me after Calc. I'm skipping." He bends over with a hand to his stomach. "Stomach flu."

He scampers off to the nurse's station, high-fiving Troy on the way.

"Isn't he funny?" Scar coos.

True love doesn't need a good sense of humor.

"Hilarious," I say and then hurry to the classroom before Scar's crush requires more lies from me.

We're ten minutes into AP Calc when the classroom phone rings. Mrs. Russell throws down the dry-erase marker and stomps over to answer. She's not happy with the interruption. Troy uses the time to throw wadded-up notebook paper at Chase's back.

"Mr. Donnelly. You need to go to the principal's office. Your probation officer is on the phone."

Troy and his friends erupt in jeering laughter.

My stomach drops. How does Chase stand it? My fingers curl into a fist, but I keep my eyes pinned to my desk because if I see even the smallest hint of pain in his face, I'm going to lose it.

Chase leaves, his gait stiffer than normal but his head still high.

"He's tough," Scarlett admits in a whisper. "I couldn't stand this abuse."

I'm startled. Scarlett's been pretty vocal with her anti-Chase sentiments—Jeff's rubbing off on her, I guess. But she sounds genuinely sympathetic right now.

"I wouldn't be able to stand it, either," I whisper back.

Minutes elapse. Mrs. Russell scribbles a formula on the board. I jot it down carefully just in case Chase needs it later.

Troy and his cronies are whispering about something. I try to tune them out, but *Manson* catches my attention. I lean back as nonchalantly as possible.

"...catch him...kick out...finally."

Worried, I glance at the clock. It's been nearly ten minutes. I raise my hand.

"Yes, Ms. Jones?"

"I need a bathroom pass."

"Come and get it." The teacher nods to the key on the desk.

Scarlett shoots me a questioning glance.

I'll tell you later, I mouth. Although what I'll tell her, I haven't decided.

I grab the key and hurry down the hall. Halfway toward the principal's office, I see Chase returning to the classroom.

"Hey." I give him a little wave. "What was that all about?"

He shrugs and keeps walking.

I fall in step beside him, wishing he'd say something. What did his probation officer want? Is he going to be taken away?

My distress must be written on my face, because he lets out a quick breath and says, "You can chill, Beth. There was no probation officer, okay? The caller hung up the second I said hello."

I flash back to the chortling boys at the back of the classroom. "Probably Troy and his stupid crew."

"Probably. It's no big deal." Which I think means that he wants me to stop talking about it.

I pause in the middle of the hall, shifting awkwardly. "Are you going to the game Friday night?"

His incredulous expression tells me what a stupid question that was. Like he'd ever cheer for anything but for Troy to fall into a lake.

I hope he doesn't notice me blushing. "I'm going to take that as a no."

"Good call." He starts walking again.

I dash forward to keep up with him. "I gave my parents a

contract where I promise to be good in exchange for them allowing me some freedom," I blurt out.

This time, he's the one who halts. "And?" he says, looking interested.

"And it worked. They agreed. I got my phone and my bedroom door back. And my car, but only to go to school and work."

"That's great." He sounds genuinely enthused for me.

"I'm pretty happy. Plus, I'm wearing new lip gloss so today's a good day." I make a pretty pout with my lips.

A small smile tugs at his lips. "Lip gloss is all it takes to make you happy, huh?"

"You said to focus on one small thing at a time. Today it's new lip gloss. It tastes like strawberries." I nudge his arm with my shoulder. "What's your thing today?"

He gazes down at me. I swear his eyes linger on my lips. "I was thinking of how much I like the color rose."

I rub my lips together. His gaze tracks the movement. I remember how my mouth tingled when his lips were pressed against mine.

"And how much I like strawberries," he adds, and I swear I can see his pulse hammering in his throat.

Is he going to kiss me?

He inches a bit closer.

My own pulse careens wildly. If he kisses me, I don't know what I'd do. Probably push him away.

Chase's calloused hand cups my cheek, and I don't push him away.

"Such a bad idea," he whispers as his mouth dips closer.

"Terrible idea," I whisper back.

My breath gets stuck in my lungs. His lips are soft and warm as they brush mine in a kiss that lasts barely a second, because the screech of a fire alarm has us jumping away from each other.

Just in time, too, because without warning, students start bursting out into the hallway.

Scarlett comes running and grabs my arm. She doesn't even notice Chase; she's too excited. "It's a fire alarm!" she squeals. "Let's go get Jeff. Starbucks, here we come."

I try hard not to look at him. *Don't look, don't look.* If I do, my expression will give something away. Scarlett will know something just went down between us. Hell, I'm surprised she can't hear my deafening heartbeat over the fire alarm.

Don't look, I order as Scarlett starts dragging me away.

I can't help it—I take one quick peek over my shoulder. Chase's blue eyes convey understanding as they lock with mine. In fact, his lips even quirk in a smile, as if to say *what can ya do?*

Not kiss my sister's killer in the middle of the hallway at school—*that's* what I can do.

I'm breathing hard by the time we make it outside, and it's not just from the trek it took to get out here. Chase's kiss stole the oxygen from my body, along with my common sense. I can still taste him on my lips.

Jeff's waiting on the curb when we reach the front doors. Scarlett flies down the stairs, laughing. She looks like she wants to jump into Jeff's arms.

"Hurry or we'll have to wait in line," she urges.

As I notice other students stream across the street, I see we're not the only ones with the bright idea to sneak in a caffeine fix.

"Not to worry." Jeff brandishes his phone. "I already ordered using the app."

"Oh, you're so prepared!" Scarlett gushes.

Almost too prepared…

Suspicion builds inside me, but I try to ignore it as we head over to the Starbucks. I ignore it when we're standing at the counter to get our drinks, and I ignore it as we leave the coffeehouse.

I'm just being paranoid. So what if Jeff was already outside and all prepped with a coffee order for us, as if he'd known we'd be running out of the school at that exact moment? So what if—

"Did you pull the fire alarm?" I blurt out, unable to stop myself.

Scarlett gasps midsip of her Frappuccino.

Unfazed, Jeff licks the whipped frothing off the top of his drink. "Maybe I did, maybe I didn't."

I gape at him. "Why would you ever—" The demand dies in my throat when we near the school.

There are two cop cars and a fire truck parked out front.

"Oh no," Scarlett says, clutching the sleeve of Jeff's navy-and-white-striped shirt. "You're going to get in trouble."

"No, I won't." His handsome face sports a smug grin. "I'm not the criminal in school."

And sure enough, the crowd parts and two men in blue uniforms lead a familiar figure to the back of the last cop car.

I thrust my cup in Scarlett's direction and start running.

22

"Beth! Are you nuts? Come back here!"

I've made it only ten or so yards before Scarlett catches up to me and yanks me backward. She's on the school track team, so she's fast when she wants to be. And right now she's determined to keep me from racing to Chase's rescue.

"What are you doing?" she demands. "The cops are dealing with him. You'll just get in their way."

Wait, she doesn't think I want to help him. She thinks I want to help the cops.

All around us, the kids waiting out the fire alarm whisper and gossip among themselves. Pointing at Chase, snickering behind their hands, spreading a wave of poison through the crowd.

"Of course it was him."

"He was the first one I thought of when I heard it was a fake alarm."

"I hope he's gone after this. He's ruining this school."

"I knew he pulled the alarm the moment I heard it. I have

a sixth sense about these things." This is from Macy, who rushes up to me and Scarlett with Yvonne in tow.

Her stupid comment has me whirling on her. "Seriously, Mace? You believed that a blind person could drive as long as a seeing-eye dog was in the car at the time."

She gasps. "Yvonne swore it was true. Why wouldn't I believe my best friend?" She crosses her arms over her chest in indignation.

"Macy's gullible, but it doesn't mean she's a bad judge of character," Yvonne chimes in.

"Yeah, what she said."

The two of them stand in solidarity against me. Actually, make that the four of them, because Jeff marches up to join the group. He thrusts Scarlett's Frappuccino in her hand, while white-knuckling his own drink.

"Why were you running over there?" Jeff asks in a low voice.

"Because he didn't do it and somebody needs to tell the cops that," I announce frostily.

A stunned silence falls.

Then they all attack.

"You're standing up for him?" Scarlett, incredulous.

"Are you fucking stupid?" Jeff, repulsed.

"Why are you standing up for him?" Macy, horrified.

"He killed your sister." Yvonne, disappointed.

None of them are being quiet about it, which means everyone around us can hear what's being said. And my other classmates have no problems voicing their unwanted opinions, too, until all I hear are whispers and accusations again.

"You're sick," says another student.

"I heard she never even cried at her sister's funeral."

"Cried? I swear, she was laughing."

The insults start flying. My friends don't defend me.

"So it's going to be like this," I say to them, shaking my head.

I don't wait for an answer. Chase needs my help, and I'll be damned if I let him get punished for something he didn't do.

I push through the crowd, ignoring the jeers.

"Stop. Stop." I wave my hands toward the cops. "I'm a witness," I call out. "He didn't do it."

"Beth, don't," Chase murmurs. His hands are shackled behind his back. There's a dull flush highlighting the tops of his cheekbones.

One of the cops has a hand around Chase's upper arm. The other is opening the back of the police cruiser. I catch a glimpse of a dirty interior and the cage separating the front seats from the back.

Ignoring Chase, I turn to the officer nearest me, a stocky guy with a thick middle and a round face.

"Sir. Please. Chase—Charlie didn't do it. He was with me when the alarm went off." *He was kissing me.* Oh God, what if I have to say that out loud, in front of everyone? I ignore the queasy knot in my gut and insist, "He couldn't have pulled it."

"Did you see him not pull the alarm?"

I pause, not quite understanding the question.

"Go to class," Chase says in a voice that is more tired than confrontational.

"You heard your boyfriend. Go back inside." The officer jerks his head toward the brick building. "Kids these days. No sense at all," he mutters to his coworker. "Come on. In you go." He jerks Chase forward.

I try to intervene and am met with a hard arm.

"Go inside," the cop orders.

"He's not my boyfriend. And I'm telling you the truth. He didn't do this."

"You can make a statement at the station."

"But—"

"Don't" is Chase's urgent whisper.

The look of pain on his face wounds me. Without another word, I spin on my heel and run in the opposite direction toward the school. Screw this. The cops obviously don't want to hear what I have to say. Chase doesn't even want me to say what I have to say.

But there's no way I'm letting this happen.

There are more whispers as I sprint past groups of students. Words pelting me like sharp sleet.

"Isn't that Beth Jones?"

"What was she doing with him?"

"You'd think she had better taste."

I burst into the principal's office to find it thick with adults. I search for Principal Geary, standing up on my tiptoes to see over the heads of people crowded in the administration hallway. I give up and arrow to the front desk.

"Where's Principal Geary?" I ask our receptionist.

"He's busy, dear." She barely looks up from her computer.

"I know, but—" I spot him out of the corner of my eye, huddling with a few other teachers. "Mr. Geary!"

"Beth—" the receptionist intervenes.

I ignore her. "Mr. Geary." I wave my hand in the air.

He walks over. "What is it, Elizabeth?"

"It's about Chase—I mean, Charlie. Donnelly. It's about him. I know— I saw— He's not." I can't get the words straight.

"It's all right." He pats me on the shoulder. "This should be enough to get him expelled."

"But he didn't do it," I cry, throwing up my hands in frustration.

"You don't need to stand up for him. It's admirable that you want him to get a fair shot here and we gave him one. Now it's time for him to get his education in a place that doesn't disrupt the rest of you." Geary smiles with encouragement and turns away.

I could scream. No one is listening to me. Absolutely no one. I feel the tears coming and I blink through the stinging sensation. I don't care how mad I am right now. I *cannot* cry. Everyone is already not taking me seriously. Tears will just make me look hysterical.

I scan the room frantically, looking for someone—anyone who will take me seriously.

When I spot my guidance counselor, I hustle over and tug on her sleeve. "Ms. Tannenhauf, please listen to me."

"What is it?" she asks, turning in my direction.

I launch into my defense. "Charlie didn't do it. I was with him—um, walking right beside him when the alarm sounded. He got called to the principal's office because his probation officer was on the phone, but the probation officer wasn't on the line. You can call the officer. There have to be records, right?"

Ms. T squeezes my shoulder. "I'm sure they'll check all those details out at the station."

Will they? Why would they? They have their target, and I'm afraid Chase won't speak up for himself. He doesn't want to cause trouble.

"Take me there," I beg.

"Where?" She smiles, not comprehending my request at all.

"To the station. I need to go there. Nobody is listening to me here."

Enlightenment dawns, and with it a frown of disapproval. "You should go back to class, Beth."

That's when I lose it. With a dark glare, I plant my hands on my hips and face off with the guidance counselor. "All my life you teachers have said that we need to stand up and do the right thing. That if we see someone being bullied, we need to say something. If there's something bad going down, we don't turn away. That it takes one voice to make a difference. Well, *I'm* that voice." I jab my thumb in my chest.

Around me the room has fallen silent. The teachers and administrators are staring at me. I might've been shouting, but I force myself to lift my chin and not avert my eyes. I'm doing the right thing here. I'm not going to be embarrassed.

"Please." I direct one last plea in my guidance counselor's direction.

She sighs, but nods. "Okay. I'll take you down."

"Emma, do you think that's wise?" Mr. Geary interjects.

"Yes, I do. It's the police station, Jim. What could happen there?"

I hope exoneration.

The ride to the police station is quiet. Ms. Tannenhauf doesn't play any music, so the car is filled with road noise and the engine of her white Toyota Camry. I twist my fingers in my lap, wishing that the drive wasn't taking so long.

Ms. T keeps glancing at me, questions in her eyes. I don't want to talk about Chase, though.

Before she can ask, I blurt out, "I signed a contract with my parents."

I hope this small morsel will distract her from Chase. I don't know how to answer her questions anyway. He's not my boyfriend. He's a guy I hooked up with. He's a guy who occupies my thoughts at an alarming rate. He's a guy who makes my heart beat faster. He's a guy who killed my sister.

Would anyone have answers to that?

"A contract? Like a behavioral contract?" Ms. T sounds excited.

"I found it on the internet," I tell her. "Actually, I copied one word for word. I'll probably be kicked out for plagiarizing."

She smiles. "I think we can let it pass in this instance."

"I hope so. It's working so far. I'm back at the shelter and my parents agreed to let me apply to Iowa State."

"Well, that's encouraging."

"Yup." I fall silent. I've exhausted my topics of conversation.

Ms. Tannenhauf starts up. "Beth, if there's ever anything you need to talk about, my door is open. I'm just here to listen."

The police station comes into view, and I think comically that I've never been so glad to see one.

"Thanks, Ms. T," I say and tumble out of the car almost before she can come to a complete stop.

Inside, the Darling station is surprisingly quiet. I guess we don't have much crime here. Over in the corner, I spot Chase's mom. She stands when she sees me, recognizing me from that one time I came to the house.

"Katie!" she says in alarm. "What are you doing here?"

I feel sick. I know I need to tell her the truth about who I am, but I can't get the words out. I'm rooted in place for several seconds, guilt churning in my stomach as I wonder how to respond.

In the end, I just say, "Where's Chase?"

"He's being held until my husband's lawyer gets here." Her fingers look red like mine, as if she's been rubbing them nervously together, too.

Her answer isn't good enough for me. There's no reason for Chase to be "held." No reason for him to be here at all.

Without another word, I hurry to the front desk. "I'm Elizabeth Jones—"

A loud gasp sounds from behind me.

Cringing, I do my best to ignore Mrs. Stanton and keep talking. "I need to make a statement about the incident at Darling High today."

The male officer blinks at me. He's so young I wonder if he's a high school student. "Ah, okay." He bends down and rummages in a drawer. He pulls out a piece of paper and slaps it on the counter. "Fill this out."

"I need a pen." I came here without my purse or bag or anything.

"Here's one." A quick hand slaps a pen on the counter.

I find the courage to glance over. Chase's mom is at my side, but the hurt and betrayal I expect to see in her eyes isn't there. She seems more confused than angry about my deception.

I grab the black pen and start filling out the form, scrawling my name and address, along with my age. The statement section is a box with about twenty lines. I gnaw on my bottom lip. What can I say to convince them that Chase is innocent? The officer didn't seem to believe me. I guess I need specifics. Should I tell them about the kiss? God, I don't want to, especially with Chase's mom here. Will they check Jeff's phone? I'd bet my college fund that he was the one who called pretending to be the probation officer. And he's definitely the one who pulled the fire alarm.

I know these things are true, but how do I prove them? Luckily, I don't have to.

A buzz sounds and I look up to see Chase coming through the heavy metal door.

"I didn't give my statement yet," I blurt out.

He shrugs. "You didn't have to. My probation officer agreed that he never called me. The officer said someone played a prank."

I'm hit with a flood of relief. "So you're free to go?"

He nods, a brief, tight movement. I've never seen him this tense. Even when Troy's been at his worst, leaning over and calling him Manson, Chase has been able to keep an aura of controlled calm.

I want to wrap my arms around him and hug him. But of course, I don't. Instead, it's his mom who steps past me to grab Chase. She doesn't exactly hug him, but she squeezes his shoulders so tight that her knuckles turn white.

"Charlie," she says in a choked voice.

"I'm sorry," he murmurs, his head hanging so low I can almost see the back of his neck. "I'm sorry."

My heart cracks. I reach forward, but Ms. Tannenhauf pulls me back. I didn't even realize she was in the station with us. That's how focused I was on Chase.

"Let's go," Ms. T whispers.

Reluctantly, I let her lead me away, but the scene of Chase's mother standing at arm's length while Chase is bent over in apology is all I can see for the rest of the day.

23

There's a strange beep when I step inside the house. I check my phone, but the screen is off, so I dismiss it. My head's too full of the day's activities to actively care about strange sounds coming from my phone. I probably imagined it anyway.

I'm starting to get paranoid. Every whisper and glance in my direction, I read as an indictment of my actions. Once I got back to school, my classmates alternated between whispering about how Chase got off because his dad was the mayor and how they couldn't believe I stood up for him. Even Scarlett kept casting me dark looks.

Jeff tried to talk to me, probably to make sure I wouldn't snitch, which made Scar madder for some reason. And the one person I wanted to show up never did. Chase must've gone home with his mom. Good call. I should've gone home, too. Ms. T offered to write me a pass, but I wanted to be at school—in case Chase showed up.

Not that he wants my support.

I hang up my jacket and notice my bag is slightly over into Rachel's space. "Sorry, sis," I whisper and nudge my bag over.

Behind me, I hear the chirp again. I glance up to see Mom walking through the back door.

"What's with the sound? Is the microwave broken?"

Her eyes don't meet mine. "Oh, that? Just a new security system your Dad installed today." Her voice is high-pitched and anxious.

"Huh. So we hear this sound every time a door opens? That's not annoying."

"I'll let your dad explain it." She stands in the mudroom doorway, blocking the view of the kitchen. "What are you doing home so early?"

"School's out." Is she acting weirder than normal or is it just me? "Why are *you* home so early?" She usually gets off at five. It's only three now.

Instead of answering me, she says, "Can you run to the store for me?"

"Right now? I just got home." A couple of days ago, I would've celebrated a chance to escape the house and run an errand. Today, my head's pounding and I just want to go to my room, shut my door and empty my mind.

"I need a few things for dinner."

"Can I change first?"

"I really need an onion or I won't be able to make dinner." She is adamant.

I huff out a breath but stop arguing. When I open the door, I hear the beep again. There's another faint echo that pings somewhere in the kitchen. I spot the red light above the door and roll my eyes. This seems like overkill, frankly.

We live in a safe neighborhood. There's no reason for extra security measures. Besides, it's not like we have anything of value to steal. Out of curiosity, I open and shut the door again.

Each time, there's a sound. And unlike the first time when I entered, there's an echo.

Suspicious, I spin around and march to the kitchen. Mom's on her phone, a pinched expression on her face.

"Do you get an alert on your phone every time a window or door is opened or closed?"

Guiltily, she drops her phone on the counter. "What did you say?"

Jaw dropping, I rush over and grab the phone. Sure enough, there's a notification on her screen.

Mudroom door open, it says. And there's a time stamp.

"Beth, let me explain—" she starts, but a loud knocking from upstairs catches our attention.

I glance up at the ceiling, then slowly back at her. "What's going on up there? Is Dad home from work?" Like her, there's no reason for him to be back this early.

"Yes, he took a half day," she says hastily. "He probably just dropped something up there."

That didn't sound like an item being dropped. "Mom." I take a calming breath. "Why did you want me to go to the store?"

"Because we need onions for—"

I'm done listening. I race upstairs. Out of the corner of my eye, I see a tiny blinking light on every window I pass. My concern over the lights is wiped out when I reach my room.

Dad is walking out of it, and for one split second, our gazes meet and hold. Then I brush past him and gasp.

My room's a mess. There's stuff everywhere. The bed is rumpled. Pillows are on the floor. Drawers are dumped out. On my dresser is an old romance book I forgot I borrowed from Scar what seems like a decade ago and a box of condoms.

Dread is replaced by anger. So much for having my parents back. They've gone right back to their old overprotective tricks.

I whirl and see Mom at the doorway and notice for the first time that my door is gone. Again!

"What is this?" I yell. "Did you search my room? Why?"

"Beth…"

"Answer me!"

"Don't yell at me," she shouts back.

"Don't yell at your mother!" Dad roars.

"Why did you search my room?" I'm so furious I can barely breathe. My eyes are stinging, throat so tight it's difficult to talk. "What's wrong with you guys?"

Mom hedges in. "We did this because we're concerned about you being on drugs—"

"Drugs!" I screech. Oh my God, they're certifiable. They're fucking *nuts*.

"You went to the police station to protect that boy!" Dad thunders at me. His face is as red as I'm sure mine is. We're both breathing hard, absolutely livid with each other. "Principal Geary called me at work to let me know that Donnelly pulled the fire alarm today—"

"He didn't do it!" I clench my fists at my sides. Tears of impotence are threatening to fall.

"You're defending him again!" Mom shakes her finger at me. "You are defending the boy that killed your sister! What's wrong with *us*? What's wrong with *you*, Elizabeth? What is wrong with you?" she repeats in an anguished tone.

"You! You're what's wrong with me!"

I push past her, leaving the contents of my life exposed and scattered. I hear Dad's shouts and Mom's sobs on my way, but I don't give a damn. I race outside, climb into my car and start driving.

When I stop, I find myself parked in front of Chase's house. I don't know how I got here or why. I don't know what I'm planning to do. The doors are shut and so are the windows. I see no movement.

Are there slamming doors and shouting going on inside? No, Chase doesn't seem like the type of guy to lose his temper. It's probably icy silence.

Meanwhile, my parents are going overboard, wondering if I'm taking drugs because I'm not picketing in front of the school and demanding that Chase be kicked out.

"Oh, Rachel, what should I do?" I moan miserably.

I press the latch for the sunglass compartment and pull out the photo I have hidden inside. Laying my head on the steering wheel, I stare at the image of Rachel and me. We're leaning against each other, wearing our Lady Hawks club volleyball jerseys. A few of Rachel's hairs have escaped her tight ponytail and, because of the sweat and humidity of the gym, she has tiny baby curls forming at her forehead.

She's not smiling, but I can tell she's happy. I don't remember this day. I don't remember what I felt like. I don't remember what she may have said. The last really clear memory I have of her is the day before she died.

She wasn't smiling then, either. Something was bothering her. I could hear her sighs through the walls. I sat outside her door, debating whether I should knock, but I was afraid of getting my head bitten off, so I didn't.

And the next day she was dead.

I regret not knocking. I regret not taking the chance to speak to her one last time.

A tap on my window startles me. The picture falls from my fingers. I see Chase standing next to the car. He's wearing the same clothes from school—a pair of dark cargo pants and an equally dark T-shirt. He's thrown a long-sleeved green-and-blue flannel over the top. A black beanie covers his dirty-blond hair.

Eagerly, I roll down my window.

He opens his mouth to say something, but then his expression darkens. "What's wrong?"

"Nothing. Why?"

He brushes a finger under my eye and holds it up. I see a dot of wetness there.

"I cry all the time," I say, swiping the backs of my hands over my face. "It's a flaw. I don't even want to cry and the tears fall. I think I have overlarge tear ducts or something. Rachel was the exact opposite. She never cried."

Silence falls between us when I say her name.

"Sorry," I mutter.

"For saying Rachel's name? Don't be. I'm sorry you don't feel comfortable talking to me about your sister. But I know why and I don't blame you." He shoves his hands in his pockets. "I saw your car from the living room window. You staking me out?"

Somehow, despite the anger I'm still feeling inside toward my parents, I actually laugh. "You wish." The humor dies fast, though. "Did you come out here to ask me to leave? Did your mom see me? Is she mad?"

"No. Disappointed, which is even worse." He tries to smile, but he can't. He's too upset at himself. "It'd be better if she was like my dad, who pretends his son doesn't exist. But instead, she keeps loving me and I keep…" He sighs heavily. "Screwing up," he finishes. "Anyway, I came out to thank you for standing up for me today."

"Really? I thought you'd be pissed because I'm making it worse."

"No. I was wrong to say that before. Those guys want to flex on someone and I'm an easy target. I'd probably be doing the same thing if I were in their shoes."

"No, you wouldn't." I know this.

The side of his mouth quirks up. "Yeah, you're probably right. I wouldn't." He ducks his head for a moment. When he looks up again, his smile is gone, but there's something warm in his eyes that makes me tingle all over. "It feels good to not be alone."

Those tingles turn electric. I curl my fingers around the steering wheel so I don't do something dumb with them. "No one should be alone."

We endure another uncomfortable silence. He shoves his hands in his pockets and scuffs the toe of his boot against the asphalt. I squeeze the fake leather steering wheel so hard I'll have a permanent indent on my palms from the stitching.

"How are things at home?" he finally asks.

"Fine," I lie, because I can't tell him that my parents are going nuts over the fire alarm situation. I can't tell him that they took away my door again, and that I fled like a fugitive after one of the worst arguments we've ever had. He'll feel guilty and then never talk to me again. And that's a loss I'm not ready to accept. "You?"

"There've been better days," he admits. "The mayor isn't happy. This incident is a mark on my school record, and if I get three of them, I'll be out."

"What? That's ridiculous!" I'm outraged again. "You were innocent!"

"They don't know that for sure. The cops don't have enough evidence to arrest me, but the school operates on a different level." He shrugs, his hands still stuffed in his pockets.

"That's bullshit."

"Let it go," he advises. "I'll keep my nose clean and it won't matter in the end."

"What about Troy and Jeff?"

He shrugs again. "I stay out of their way."

"You've stayed out of their way since school started. They're the ones who are pushing themselves into your path."

"Maybe so, but ignoring bullies is the best way to get rid of them. I know this from *personal* experience." He emphasizes the word *personal* so I get the message that he's referring to his time in juvie.

Rachel was always a person who believed in fairness. As long as a referee called a game fairly, she was okay with the outcome, even if the ref sucked. "He called it bad both ways," she told me once after a game. "Can't ask for more than that."

I think she would've said that Chase had been punished and that we should all move on. I wonder if that can happen, though. For any of us.

I ask him, "Do you think that we—you and me—or my parents or your parents or the kids at school… Do you think any of us can put what happened to Rachel behind us?"

Chase takes a deep breath and ponders this. I like that he doesn't answer immediately.

"Part of me would like that, but part of me believes it would be wrong. I don't think I should ever forget my actions. If that means the bullies target me at school or I can't get certain jobs or my future is somehow limited, I'm okay with that. I took someone's life. Rachel can't get a job or go to prom or sit in a class again." He pauses and looks away.

Tears flood my eyes and I blink like crazy to keep them from falling. When Chase's gaze returns to mine, his eyes are wet, too.

"If it means we can't be friends, it's a harder pill to swallow."

He gives me that killer half smile and slaps his hand on the roof of my car. "You should probably go home. I'll catch you later."

And with that, he leaves. He says those words—those thoughtful, heavy words—and then runs into his house!

I can't believe it.

"Coward," I mutter under my breath.

I start the engine and drive home. Not that I remember the drive. All I can think of are his words and how he mixed the bitter with the sweet.

At the side entrance, I stop and rest my forehead against the door. I don't know what I'm going to find inside. I'm a bit scared, actually. It doesn't sound like my parents are yelling at each other, but maybe they're saving the yelling for my return. Maybe they're standing behind this door, arms crossed, feet planted firmly on the ground, ready to go to battle.

But I don't want to fight. I really don't. Ten minutes with Chase and his impenetrable composure succeeded in relaxing me, in making me see reason. My parents crossed the line today, there's no doubt about that. But screaming like a maniac and speeding off like an even bigger maniac isn't going to win me any points.

We have to make peace. I know this. I just… I'm too tired to deal with the loud, angry words I know will come before the peace part.

When I walk inside, however, I'm not greeted with anything even remotely loud. I'm welcomed by grim silence and a staredown from my father.

He looms in the kitchen doorway, his dark, expressionless eyes making my knees feel weak. He holds his phone up, and even from five feet away, I can make out what he's showing me. The screen shows a map and a green dot.

"Dad," I start shakily.

He holds up his hand to silence me.

I shut up.

Barely restrained fury echoes in my father's voice when he finally speaks.

"Stay away from Charles Donnelly or I'll have him thrown back in prison."

24

The next morning, Scarlett corners me at my locker before I can spin the combination lock.

"I don't have the energy to fight right now" is the first thing I say, and we can both hear the fatigue in my voice.

I didn't get a wink of sleep last night. I just lay in bed, thinking about Chase and my dad's threat to send him back to jail. I don't know how he'd ever even accomplish that, but my father is resourceful when he needs to be.

"I don't want to fight," Scarlett answers flatly.

"Good."

"Good," she shoots back.

I gently nudge her out of the way so I can open my locker. With my back to her, I grab my calculus textbook from the top shelf. "Go ahead. Say it."

"Say what?"

"What a horrible person I am for defending him yesterday." My back remains staunchly turned.

I hear a soft sigh, then feel a small cool hand on my shoulder. I stiffen, but Scarlett's touch is soothing, not aggressive.

"I get why you did it, okay?"

I quickly face her. "You do?"

She smooths her reddish-brown hair, moving all of it so it hangs over one shoulder. She flat-ironed it today. I'm not sure how I feel about it. I love her big bouncy curls. For that matter, so does she. Scar always says how much she prefers curls to straight hair.

"Yeah," she says, nodding. "He's a rescue to you. Like those dogs you love so much at the animal shelter. You try to act like you're all tough, but I know deep down you're just a big softy. I mean, you cry at the drop of a hat. But..."

I knew there was a but.

"He's *not* an animal. He's not some abused dog who just needs some love in order to be cool with humans again, or some bitch-ass cat who hisses at you when you walk up but purrs once you start patting it. He's a *delinquent*. He stole a car and ran someone over. You can't forget that, Li—Beth."

"You think I've forgotten?" I ask in disbelief. "God, I think about it at least twenty times a day, that I'm going to school with the guy who hit Rachel."

That I lost my virginity to the guy who hit Rachel.

That I have feelings for that guy.

That I think about *him* way more often than I think about what he did.

"Good," Scarlett says firmly. "You have to think about it. The next time you think he needs rescuing, remember who he is."

I nod weakly. I know what she's saying. I know why she's saying it. But I also know that if Chase ever needs rescuing again, I'd be the first person running to save him.

What is wrong with me?

"Anyway, Macy's still pissed at you—"

"Seriously?" I frown, because Macy's not the type to hold grudges.

Scar sighs. "She thinks you think she's stupid."

Guilt pricks my heart as I remember accusing Macy of being gullible and flaky. I mean, she is, but I didn't have to be nasty to her about it. "I'll talk to her after class," I murmur. "What about Yvonne?"

My best friend waves a hand. "You know her. She gets over shit fast. And Jeff's cool with you, too. He came over last night and I calmed him down."

Jeff's cool with *me*? She calmed *him* down? Fuck that. I'm not cool with *him*, and someone should be calming *me* down. He and Troy tried to frame Chase for the fire alarm stunt. Good guys don't do stuff like that.

I open my mouth to point all this out to Scarlett, but, speak of the devil, Jeff strides up to us with a big grin on his face. It's like déjà vu. This exact same thing happened yesterday— me and Scar at my locker, Jeff sauntering over like Mr. Big Man on Campus and then all hell breaking loose.

"Nice. You two worked everything out," he says with a nod. He glances my way. "Scarlett told me about the whole savior complex you've got going on, yeah? I get it, but I don't think Manson is someone you need to save, Beth."

First of all, his fake British accent is stupid and annoying, *yeah*? I don't know why all the girls in the senior class think it's so sexy. It's not.

Second, savior complex? Okay, Scarlett *really* tried to paint a picture of me as some kind of bleeding heart who hates injustice and stands up for the little guy. On one hand, I appreciate her trying to help. On the other, I don't get why she's making excuses for me.

Maybe she wants me and Jeff to get along so that her relationship with him is smoother sailing? But I've got nothing to do with them as a couple, if they even are a couple. Jeff doesn't seem at all interested in her.

"I think the best thing for everyone is if you stay away from that asshole," Jeff informs me. "I know you agree."

I do, do I?

I'm about to retort when Scarlett gives me a pleading look.

Argh. This is bullshit. Jeff is being a condescending jerk right now.

But is there any point in arguing with him? Probably not. So I swallow the comeback and close my locker.

"Scarlett is having people over tonight," Jeff says. "Did she tell you?"

I arch a brow at her. Is he her mouthpiece now?

"I was just about to mention it," she says quickly. "My parents have this banquet thing to go to and they won't be home 'til super late. You can come, right, Beth?"

"Nope," I say glumly. Though honestly, I'm not too glum about it. I don't want to hang out with Jeff at all. "I'm grounded again."

Jeff's eyes glitter in disapproval. "It was the police station stunt, wasn't it? Of course Dave and Marnie wouldn't be happy about that, Lizzie."

Don't call my parents by their first names, I fume inwardly. God. Was Jeff always this pretentious or did he become that way in London?

"If you were my daughter, I'd punish you, too," he says, his tone cavalier.

"Good thing I'm not your daughter," I snipe.

Scarlett's mouth tightens. "Beth."

I tamp down my annoyance. Seriously? He can throw out shitty comments but I can't respond to them?

"Anyway," I say stiffly, "they informed me this morning that I'm not allowed to see any friends unless you guys come over to my house. And I lost my car again, but not my phone."

"Then we'll go to your house tonight," Jeff announces.

Scarlett and I both turn to stare at him. Excuse me? He's inviting himself and other people to my house now?

Scar doesn't like that idea, either, judging by her deep frown. "I'd rather stick to the original plan," she tells Jeff.

He spares her a quick look. "Why? Beth has the bigger backyard, and it's supposed to be a nice night. We can start a fire in the fire pit. We'll all sit around it and roast some marshmallows. It'll be a good time."

Scarlett's unhappiness is written on her face. I've known her long enough to be able to read her mind. If everyone comes over to my place and hangs in the backyard, she and Jeff obviously won't be able to sneak off to her bedroom and make out.

"No," she says firmly. "I'd rather chill at my place tonight."

Jeff's expression clouds with annoyance. I expect him to dig in and be an ass about it, but after a long beat, he relaxes and beams at her.

"Okay. Beth will just have to miss out. We'll chill at her place another time."

"Gee, thanks for including me in plans involving my own house," I say sarcastically.

He ignores that and leans closer to rumple Scarlett's hair. "*This* looks great, by the way," he drawls, his approving gaze sweeping over her stick-straight hair. "Real sleek."

Her eyes turn brighter than the fluorescent lights over our heads. I get it now. Jeff likes straight hair. Scarlett straightens her hair. Oh brother.

"I'll see you guys at lunch," he adds before strolling off.

Scarlett is blushing as she watches him go. I haven't seen

her look at anyone like that since Matty Wesser moved away, and it brings both a pang of joy and a jolt of panic.

A part of me understands why she's so drawn to Jeff. I've seen his charming side—I know what that dimpled grin and laid-back manner can do to a girl. But I've also seen his mean side. I've listened to him berate me outside a party and then watched him drive off, leaving me alone on a dark, unfamiliar street.

I wish I knew which Jeff is the real one. I wonder if Rachel knew. She had never said a bad word about him. Ever. But she also didn't talk about their relationship much.

"You really like him," I say slowly, trying not to sigh.

"I really do," Scarlett says, her cheeks turning even redder.

"Are you guys a couple now?"

"I don't know. I hope so."

Crap. It's on the tip of my tongue to tell her my doubts, to share my uneasiness about Jeff, but I don't have the heart to ruin her good mood.

"C'mon, let's go to Calc," I finally say.

We reach the classroom just as the bell rings, and I'm disappointed because I was hoping I might get a chance to talk to Chase in the hall before we went in. But he's already at his desk when Scar and I walk in. His blond head is down, but it rises slightly at my approach.

Hooded blue eyes meet mine, just briefly. I swear I see a hint of a smile before he ducks his head. It's his way of saying *hello* or *good morning*, and I wish so badly I could say it out loud to him. I can't, though. Not after what happened yesterday. Standing up for Chase resulted in all my classmates turning against me. In my friends getting mad at me. In my parents searching my room and grounding me for life.

A public stand for Chase right now would probably send me into exile.

So I offer a ghost of a smile in return, and then we both duck our heads and pretend we don't know each other.

But when Mrs. Russell is at the whiteboard and everyone is bent over their notebooks trying to solve the problem she just gave us, I take a chance and pass a note to Chase.

My heart beats wildly as the tiny folded-up square lands on his desk. I hold my breath, but nobody notices what I've done. Nobody but Chase, whose long fingers unfold to drag the note toward him.

I bite my lip anxiously as I wait for him to read the three words I scribbled on that paper.

Come over tonight.

He doesn't look my way to acknowledge the note or offer a reply. But he tucks the paper in his pocket, and that's all the answer I need.

25

"I shouldn't be here," Chase says for what seems like the hundredth time.

"If you say it again, I'm going to kick you out." It's an empty threat, though. I still can't believe he even came over. Last thing I want him to do is *leave*.

He stares intently at the blue television light that's flickering in my family room window. Mom and Dad are watching *Gold Rush* reruns. Dad enjoys instructing the television how the crew is screwing up, while Mom makes a lot of disappointed sounds in the back of her throat along with the occasional "Do they have to curse so much?" exclamations.

Satisfied that they're not coming outside, he rests his elbows on the plaid blanket I stowed behind the tree earlier. Ten feet away, Rachel's swing sits motionless, shrouded in darkness. During the ten o'clock news, the meteorologist said it'd be a chilly night, but he must've been mistaken because I'm warm inside and out.

"You can't kick me out. We're not inside." He gestures toward the night sky.

A dog barks in the distance. Another answers. The light over the Rennicks' back porch flicks on.

"Fine. I'll set Morgan on you and he'll chase you off," I suggest.

"Nah, dogs love me."

Mrs. Rennick calls for her mutt to stop barking and come inside.

"This is true." From what I've seen, the shelter dogs all pant after Chase. "I feel betrayed."

"Don't. Whenever you leave, they whine. They miss you."

I study him from under my eyelashes. If it was the middle of the day, his broad shoulders would block the sun. Instead, the moonlight halos his form, making him look otherworldly. "Aww. Okay. You can stay."

"Sweet. I was planning on it anyway."

I'm glad it's dark and he can't see the stupid grin on my face. To be safe, I tuck my legs closer to my chest and rest my chin on my knees. This way I can hide my face and stare at him at the same time.

"I know how they feel." He sticks a blade of grass in the corner of his mouth. I watch his mouth and jaw move with way too much interest. "Because it's a lot more fun when you're around."

"I'll have to increase my hours."

"I work Monday, Wednesday and Sunday," he volunteers. That deadly half smile makes an appearance.

"Good. I'll ask for Tuesday, Thursday and Saturday."

I don't see him coming. He moves like a blur, and suddenly I'm on my back with him looming over me. I shriek and then clap a hand over my mouth. Chase's head jerks up and he eyes the back door. His whole body is tense, as if he's ready to flee into the night at a moment's notice.

But no sound comes. Not from my mom or dad. Not even a bark from a neighborhood dog. Chase hovers over me in a vague reenactment of how we were our first night. Him above me. Except that time there wasn't so much space. And I had my arms around his neck. And there were a lot fewer layers of clothing between us.

I hold my breath. I think he does, too. I want him to kiss me. I want him to brush aside the wisps of grass and replace them with his hand or arm or chest. I want to feel the heat of him against me.

"What do your parents think you're doing?" he says finally.

"That I'm thinking about Rachel," I say tactlessly. "That's her swing."

Immediately, he rolls off me to lie on the ground, putting distance between us.

I swallow a sigh of disappointment and curse myself for bringing her up. He already has a hard time managing his guilt. In his head, it's okay for him to be my friend. It's not okay to be my *boy*friend. It's not okay to want to hold my hand or kiss me.

I gesture to the wooden seat dangling in the air. "Dad built the swing for Rachel, and when I was old enough we fought over who would get to use it. We'd race out here and she'd always beat me. I'd have to push her until my arms were spaghetti noodles, and then she'd climb off and say, in a super tired voice, 'I'll push you until I have to go to practice,' which, by that time, was about all of five minutes."

"How much would you give to argue with her again?"

"So much." Chase makes me talk about Rachel more than anyone else. Even my mom doesn't like talking about her, because it means that she's gone.

"What else did you argue about?" He rolls over onto his side and braces his head on a bent arm.

"What didn't we? She'd get mad when I borrowed her stuff without asking. She had this super cute powder blue bomber jacket from Forever 21. I swiped it from her closet and wore it to a Darling football game."

"And she didn't find out?"

"Oh no. She found out. I was dumb enough to think I could avoid her the whole time, but I ran into her at the concession stand before the first half was over. She let me wear it but warned me that if I got so much as a raindrop on it, she'd beat me into tomorrow."

"And?"

"I escaped punishment. The Forever 21 jacket was returned and she ended up spilling a red slushie on it in the spring. Mom couldn't get the stain out, so Rachel threw it at me and said it was mine now."

He chuckles. "Do you still have it?"

"No. I was mad and threw it away. I wish I kept it. I also got in trouble for using her lipstick brush in her eyeliner pot. They look really similar, if you were wondering."

"I wouldn't be able to focus in school tomorrow if you hadn't told me," he confirms solemnly.

I laugh. He doesn't make any observation about how all the memories I've mentioned have to do with fighting with my sister. It's just that those moments, when she was imperfect, seem the most real to me.

"I really loved her," I whisper.

"I know."

"I miss her every day."

"I'm sorry, Beth." He's returned to lying on his back. An

arm is thrown over his eyes, as if he can't bear to look at me or feels like he doesn't deserve to. Either way, it sucks.

I swallow the lump in my throat. "I know you are."

We fall silent again. I'm caught between the past and the present. Looking at the swing, I can almost see Rachel there, pumping her legs furiously and going higher and higher and higher until she was nearly a blot in the sky next to the glaring sun. Yet, there's Chase at my side. A real live human being who listens to me, scolds me and makes me laugh.

I choose Chase, I tell the shadow. Rachel nods and keeps swinging.

"She had the most amazing serve," I say quietly. "Even when she was young, like sixth grade, she could put this weird spin on it. Her serves were real flat, like you were always surprised they cleared the net, but once the ball was on the other side, it would curve to the corner. And she was really good at serving it in that sweet spot along the line."

"How come you don't play anymore?"

"It wasn't any fun. Without her, it wasn't fun." I hadn't realized how much I'd looked up to Rachel until she died. "We fought a lot, so I didn't realize I'd miss her this much." I stop talking because my throat's too tight. It hurts to even look at the moon so I shut my eyes. Hot liquid seeps out the corners.

A big warm hand covers mine, and then I hear a muffled curse. Chase slides an arm under my head and pushes my face against his sweatshirt-clad chest.

"I'm sorry," he murmurs over and over.

I want to stop crying, because I know it's painful for him, but I can't control the tears. Memories that I've pushed down deep bubble to the surface. Rachel showing me how to shave my legs. Rachel French-braiding my hair. Rachel giving me one of her favorite T-shirts when I tried out for the A team at the club. Rachel holding me just like this when my name was not on the final roster.

"I miss her," I sob, curling into Chase's arms. "I miss her so much."

Under the tree with the shadow of Rachel's legs flying overhead, I let the buried hurt spring out of its hidden place. The pain stretches its tendrils, traveling through my veins until every part of my body aches and shudders under its burden.

This is why I held it in for so long—because it's too much to deal with. Snot bubbles in my nose. Tears stream out of my eyes like a raging river. Hoarse, ugly sounds growl up through my throat.

When Rachel died, I was scared that tomorrow my life might be snuffed out, too, so I fought my parents. I fought every boundary, every restriction as if it were a noose.

"She was my big sister," I whisper against Chase's neck. "She was supposed to protect me forever."

"I know. I know. I'm sorry." He buries his head next to mine.

One hand cups my head to his chest, muffling my sobs while the other moves in wide swaths up and down my back. I lean into him, borrow his strength, because now that the seal is off, I can't stuff any of this back inside the bottle.

I keep crying. I'm not sure how much time even passes. But he doesn't ever tell me to hush. He doesn't pull away. The rhythm of his comforting hand never skips a beat. Underneath my ear, I make out the steady beat of his heart.

He's alive. I'm alive.

Rachel's gone.

And I have to let my broken heart heal instead of pretending I've been fine.

"Shhh," Chase whispers in my ear. "I've got you."

Warm breath hits the outer shell of my earlobe, travels down my spine, spreads like a virus, fast and heated throughout my body. I raise my face and see wetness in his eyes.

I'm not the only one in need of comfort. I unfurl my fingers from his sweatshirt and run my thumb across his damp cheek. My fingertips skate along the sharp jaw to land around his neck.

A little pressure, only the tiniest bit of force, dips his face toward mine.

"Chase," I breathe.

His eyelids flutter shut. So do mine. And I wait. And wait. And wait.

The next thing I know, I'm on my back and Chase is five feet from me, dragging an agitated hand through his hair.

"Chase?"

"I need to go," he says. He shoves his hands into his pockets. His shoulders cave in as he withdraws from me.

"But…" I'm lost. He was going to kiss me. I know he was.

"I can't." He looks toward the house as he says this. "I can't."

He can't what? Kiss me? Hold me any longer? "What? You can't what?"

"All of it," he says quietly, this time shifting his gaze to the ground.

I sit up on my knees and extend a hand. "Come back. Talk to me. Please."

His eyes finally meet mine and I'm nearly knocked backward by the anguish in them. "Your sister never left you, Beth. I took her from you. I don't deserve to be holding you, let alone standing in this yard. Your dad is right. I need to be kept away."

"No. Please." I shake my head. I can't form coherent sentences right now. I've got no rational thoughts at this point. I'm just emotion and feeling.

"I need to go. I'm sorry, Beth. For everything." He turns on his heel and slips into the shadows.

Stunned, I remain paralyzed on the ground. The chilly earth turning my leggings damp and cold. His goodbye sounded so final, as if he's never going to meet me again, never even going to acknowledge the connection we have. And we have one, dammit.

I jump to my feet and race after him. "Chase. Chase," I yell, uncaring that I'm waking the neighborhood. I trample over a leaf pile on the Rennicks' lawn and then nearly run into the corner of the Palmers' shed.

"Holy crap, Beth, you're making more noise than Godzilla in a forest." Chase appears in front of me, shaking his head in irritation.

"Then stop running away," I snap.

"You're mad?" He sounds astonished. The stupid boy.

"Yeah, I'm mad. I just poured my heart out to you and in response, you run away."

He sighs. "I'm not running away. I just don't belong with you."

"Says who?" I push his chest. "And don't say my parents, because they don't count."

"How can they not count?"

"No one counts, Chase. No one but you and me. If you tell me you don't care about me, I'll cry but I'll get over it. That's your choice. But if you're pushing me away because guilt is your current girlfriend and you don't want to leave her, then that's bullshit. If you feel so wrong about being let out of prison, go back there. Violate your probation and get sent back in."

His expression turns bleak. "It's hard to live with myself, so, yeah, I tolerate the stuff at school because it feels right. Because I don't want to go back to prison, but I feel guilty about that, too. Maybe the punishment should be endless."

"And that's going to bring her back?"

"Nothing's going to bring her back. That's the point," he insists, but this time he doesn't move away.

I poke him in the chest again. "Are you ever going to let me forgive you?"

"I…"

I take a different tack. "If you're so desperate to make it right for Rachel, don't you think she'd want me to be happy?"

He narrows his eyes. "You're trying to manipulate me."

"I'm trying to make you understand that what happened with Rachel was an accident. I've forgiven you. Your response is to walk away and leave me." My finger stabs him in the chest for a third time.

He captures it, probably trying to prevent me from drilling a hole through his sweatshirt. "There are a dozen other guys at Darling who would be better for you than me."

"Name one."

He opens his mouth. Then closes it. Then opens it again. Then closes it.

"Ha," I declare. I close the distance between us and loop my arms around his waist. "There's no one out there that would listen to me like you do."

He relaxes a tad and wraps his arms around me. "You have low standards, doll."

"Not really. You were my first and I'm a senior, so I'd say I have high standards. You have a low opinion of yourself."

"Is this where you tell me to climb down off the cross?"

"Do I need to?"

He exhales heavily. "No."

We stand there for a long time next to the Palmers' shed. Finally, I let him go. "I need to go in," I say reluctantly.

"Yes." He makes no move to leave.

I walk backward, afraid that he'll retreat into his guilt-ridden shell if I take my eyes off of him.

"What's your small thing for today?" I ask as I cross the neighbors' lawn to my own.

"You."

26

On a Friday morning, I find a wildflower in my locker. An ear-to-ear grin spreads across my face, but I keep my back turned so nobody walking down the hall can see how giddy I am.

"Who's that from?" Scarlett demands, peeking over my shoulder.

I roll the single stem between my fingers. "I picked it at the bus stop," I lie, because whatever is going on between Chase and me has to remain a secret for it to survive.

Scar makes a sympathetic face. "That sucks you still haven't gotten your car back. You seem okay about it, though. Like you're smiling more these days."

I tap the bloom against my cheek. "I'm trying to focus on the good instead of the bad."

This one small thing concept of Chase's isn't bad. It's been two weeks since the fire alarm incident. My car hasn't been returned, but my door has. I'm not sure why, but it was put back up the day after I broke down in the yard with Chase. The alarms are still on the doors and windows, but I'm hopeful that as long as I toe the line, those will come off soon.

As for being grounded, it doesn't matter much, since Chase sneaks into my backyard almost every night. I have no desire to go out. Scarlett's always busy with Jeff—they're officially together now—and Chase is the only person I want to see anyway. He's the one I want to snuggle up with on a blanket in the dark and talk to.

Sadly, talking is the extent of it. I'm dying for more, but Chase is stubborn. He still insists we're just "friends."

Because friends leave *flowers* in each other's lockers.

Ha.

"Cute top," I say, redirecting the conversation. Scarlett's wearing a sheer rose-colored shirt over a camisole. Two rhinestones dot the tips of an overlarge collar. She's paired it with a slim gray skirt and gray flats.

Scar beams. "It's Chanel," she squeals.

"Shut up. For real?"

"Yes." She lifts the corner of the shirt so I can see the tiny gold square with the interlocking Cs. "I bought it off an online consignment shop. I was so worried it was going to sell to someone else before I had enough money saved up and then I was worried it wouldn't fit. I got it on Sat—"

"Where have you been?" Jeff interrupts.

Startled, Scar drops her shirt and spins around to face her angry boyfriend. "Um, talking to Beth."

"I told you to wait at the front door for me." His hand falls on her shirt at the nape of her neck. The delicate fabric wrinkles around the edges of his palm.

"I—I—I just came to say hi to Beth," she stammers.

I glance from his hand to her face, pale and unhappy. The dynamic here is weird. Scar's acting guilty—like talking to me is somehow inappropriate.

"Don't," he replies flatly. "If I tell you to be somewhere,

be there. I waited out there for ten minutes, looking like a fool. If you don't want to be with me, then be up-front about it instead of leaving me hanging. That's rude."

"Come on, Jeff. We were just talking." I eye his hand. It doesn't look right on her neck, and it's not just because the green-and-black plaid of his shirt clashes with the rose of hers. It's that his hand looks punishing instead of playful.

"You guys can talk on your own time. Before school is mine."

Scarlett's face is now emotionless while Jeff's is flushed with something I don't fully understand.

"Jeff, let her go," I order with a scowl. "You're leaving a red mark on her skin, for Pete's sake."

He ignores me. "Should I let you go, Scar? Is that what you want? To break up with me?"

"I didn't say break up with her. I said let her go." I gesture toward his hand clamped around her neck.

"Scarlett?" he prompts.

We both look at her. She's staring at the tips of her gray flats.

"No. I don't want to break up with you, and I don't want you to let me go," she replies dully.

"There you go, Lizzie. Scar likes my hand right where it is."

He squeezes her nape, and I swear I see her wince. Or maybe I imagine it. Maybe because I'd wince if Jeff was touching me like that.

"Ready to go to Calc?" I ask my friend.

Jeff answers for her. "She'll be there soon. You go on ahead." He directs a smile at me that isn't friendly at all. It makes me take a step back.

"Scar?" I say uncertainly.

"I'm fine."

She doesn't sound fine. She sounds down—a muted version of herself. I hesitate, not entirely sure what to do. Students start filing out of the hall. Calc is starting in less than five minutes. Finally, I tuck the wildflower in my notebook and say, "I'll see you in class."

I walk six feet and then bend down to tie my nonexistent shoelace.

Behind me, I hear Jeff ask, "What are you wearing?"

"It's Chanel," Scarlett responds. "I got it—"

"This is so slutty, babe. I thought we talked about your wardrobe choices. Are you so insecure that you need to give all the guys boners? Is that when you'll start feeling good about yourself? At this point, why bother even wearing a shirt? All the ones you own are fucking see-through anyway."

I wait for her to blow up at him. To tell him to take his disgusting opinions and shove them where the sun doesn't shine.

"I'm sorry. I'll change," she says instead.

My jaw drops.

"When?" he demands.

"After class."

"You better." There's an *or else* implied.

I don't like the tone he's using with her. She's his girlfriend, not his puppet. Straightening my shoulders, I stand up and confront him. "Leave Scar alone."

But it's not Jeff who responds. It's Scarlett, and in a way I didn't expect.

"Why are you sticking your nose in our business?" she bites out. "I know your home life sucks right now, but maybe stop hanging out with drug dealers and murderers. I don't do that. Jeff doesn't do that. But I guess that's why we have doors on our rooms and you don't."

I stare in dismay at how she just threw out my secret for

everyone to hear. A few of our classmates start whispering. A couple laugh.

I tighten my jaw. "Whatever, Scar."

I can't believe she just blabbed something I told her in confidence. I was sticking up for her! I stomp to class, steam blowing out my ears. I slam my books on my desk and scrape the chair against the tile. Hard.

Chase, already in his seat, arches an eyebrow. I want to vent to him, but I can't. We're not allowed to have a friendship. I'm supposed to hate the sight of him.

That makes me even angrier. I'm going to tell Scarlett off when she shows up to class. Best friends do not say shit like that in front of other people. Best friends do not... My thoughts dry up in my throat as Scar walks in wearing an oversize green polo. Her cute sheer top is nowhere to be seen.

Jeff's behind her. His plaid shirt is no longer hanging open. He made her put his polo on. What a jackass.

Another burst of alarm hits me when Scar walks right by the empty desk next to mine and stops in front of Chris Levin's desk.

"Scar's going to sit here," Jeff announces.

"What?" Chris's perfectly groomed eyebrows crowd together in confusion. "This is my desk."

"Did Mrs. Russell assign seats when the semester started?"

Chris continues to look confused. "No."

"Then move." Jeff says it with a smile—the same unfriendly one he used on me.

I sigh. "Scarlett, just sit down."

"Butt out, Beth." Jeff points to Chris. "Move."

"Please," Scar adds, putting her hands together in prayer. "Just for today."

"I get it, I wouldn't want to sit near Manson, either," Troy says snidely. "Sight of him's been making me ill for weeks."

"Is that why you sucked so bad last Friday?" I interject. Troy and his defense allowed five touchdowns in their last game.

"Screw you, Jones."

"Not if you paid me a million dollars."

"Right, because you're only going to screw guys who kill your sister."

I almost fall out of my chair. Inside me, ice-cold rage battles with red-hot embarrassment.

Someone gasps.

Chairs scrape and I find myself shooting to my feet to stand next to Chase.

"That's enough." His tone is low, rough and dangerous.

Troy leans away and folds his arms defensively across his chest. "Or what?"

"You don't want to know."

Jeff's entire face turns into a thundercloud as he turns toward me. "You're screwing Manson?" he hisses.

The deadly glint in his eyes sends a shiver up my spine. Meanwhile, Scar looks horrified, and everyone else is hanging on our every word in greedy interest.

My gaze meets Chase's, briefly, and he gives an imperceptible shake of the head that only I see. I know what he's telling me to do. And as much as I don't want to, this Jeff bomb needs to be defused, ASAP.

"Of course not," I say flatly. "Troy's just talking out of his ass, as usual."

Jeff relaxes. Barely.

Troy smirks at me. "Sorry, I forgot—you screw drug dealers, not killers."

I frown, because what the heck is up with this drug dealer

thing? Scar accused me of the same thing out in the hall. I don't know any dealers, except for that kid Jay's brother, whom I never even met.

But Troy's remark takes the heat off Chase and causes Jeff to relax, so I force myself not to argue.

At the front of the room, Mrs. Russell taps her pen against the desk.

"Everyone take their seats."

"Mrs. Russell, the class felon is in my space," Troy calls out, suddenly brave again.

"I heard. Mr. Kendall, you can either respect your classmates or leave. Mr. Donnelly, sit down or you'll get another mark in your record. Ms. Holmes, you can argue about desks with Ms. Levin after class. As for you, Ms. Jones, can you stop disrupting my classroom?"

We all take our seats. Jeff scowls. Scar stares at her desk. Chris spreads her things to every corner of the desktop, as if she's staking the boundaries of her claim. Troy's giggling behind me about some Manson shit again. Out of the corner of my eye, I see Chase shake his head in warning again. He's probably upset I challenged Troy at all.

One small thing, I tell myself. *Concentrate on one small, good thing.*

I make a T with my fingers and after a moment, Chase gives me a brief nod. He'll meet me tonight at the swing.

One small thing.

"Do you think Ms. Dvořák is the worst or Mrs. Russell? And don't say that they're not bad and that they're just doing their jobs, because I'll hit you."

"I'm not a fan of Ms. Dvořák. Mostly because she doesn't

play enough pop music. I think her playlist is stuck in the sixties. Not that 'Mashed Potato Time' isn't a fire song."

The laughter flies out before I can stop it. I slap a hand over my mouth and we both send worried glances toward the house.

"Sorry," I whisper to Chase.

He gives me one of his half smiles and leans back against the tree. We're both clad in jeans and hoodies tonight, and I almost wish I'd worn a jacket, too. It's October—the weather's getting chillier. Soon it'll be too cold to meet out here, so I'm already thinking up ways to sneak Chase into my bedroom. I'd go to his house if I could, but my parents get an alert every time a door or window is opened. Jerks.

"What are you going to do when you're out of school?" I ask.

"Dunno. I haven't given it much thought. I need to get my record expunged, but I can't do that until my probation ends."

"Which is when?"

"Next May."

"Graduation will be a good time for you, then."

"Yeah."

"Are you thinking of college?"

"Community college, maybe." He throws a pinecone toward his feet. There's a pile of about six of them.

"Is the mayor refusing to help out?"

"I'm not taking money from him."

This guy is way too proud for his own good. "What about your dad?"

Chase snorts softly. "What about him? I told you, we don't speak."

I rest my hand on his forearm and play with the frayed edge of his sleeve. "Have you thought about reaching out to him?"

"No way" is the immediate response.

I raise both eyebrows. "Aren't you the one who's always telling me to make peace with my parents?"

"Yes, because your parents are good people," he says wryly. "My dad isn't. He was verbally abusive to my mom. He bullied me into making basketball my entire life. And after I got arrested, he cut me out of his life. His own *son*. I don't want someone like him in my life, Beth. And there's no reason why he should be. Why? So he can pay for me to go to college? Even if he did, the money would come with strings. I'm not interested in his strings."

I nod slowly. "I get it."

"Anyway, I was thinking of learning a trade. I heard welding pays pretty good."

"Isn't that dangerous?" I conjure up images of torches and masks.

"I don't think so."

"Maybe you should look at schools near Ames. I bet there are good trade schools there." I say it lightly, but my intentions are so obvious I should probably just make up a sign that says Go to College with Me.

"I don't think that's a good idea," he says, tossing another pinecone.

I want to pick it up and throw it at his head. "Why not?"

"Because your parents might stop paying your tuition, and then how will you get a good job and support me?" He tugs playfully on my ponytail.

If people glowed, I would be as bright as the moon on a cloudless night right now.

"Okay, fine. But you'll have to visit."

"When I get a car."

"Good point."

Chase doesn't have wheels, and even if he did, he isn't allowed to drive one as part of his probation terms, which I think is completely unfair. How is he supposed to have a job without a car?

"The system isn't set up to rehabilitate a chicken, let alone a person," he told me once during our meetings by the tree. "And I have it easy compared to lots of other guys because they end up in juvie for fighting and when they get out, there's no one there to help them. At least I had my mom and Brian."

But because of that, Chase bikes here. It's a five-mile trek that he makes at least three times a week.

"I better go," he says ruefully.

We keep our time together short. Chase says it's to make sure we can keep meeting. If my parents find out that my nightly treks to the swing are really to see him, I'll be locked in my room. But I also think the longer he stays, the more tempted we are to stop communicating with words. I'd be okay with that, but he's not. It's comical that he's saying no, but I want to respect him and his wishes, just as he would respect mine.

"I'll see you at the shelter tomorrow."

I want a kiss goodbye, but I settle for a hug. That's progress. A week ago, I got a hand squeeze. Maybe by Christmas, he'll kiss my cheek.

27

At the shelter on Saturday, Rocco the pit bull is resisting a bath. Laughing, I march over to Sandy and roll up my sleeves. "Want me to do that?" I offer.

She wipes a forearm across her face. "I would be so happy if you would. He's being extra cantankerous today. In fact, since you're going to get wet, can you do the rest of these critters? Ask Chase to help you."

"Okay." I'm happy to do anything that involves Chase. I think Sandy knows that and takes advantage of it, but I don't care.

I find Chase outside, picking up poop. "Hey, glamour boy, come and perform in a wet T-shirt contest for me," I call out.

"I thought we agreed you wouldn't objectify me." He spins the garbage bag's neck tight and then swiftly ties a knot.

"Not only do I not remember us discussing that, but if we did, I never would've agreed to such nonsense."

He tosses the poop bag into a trash receptacle and shakes his head sadly. "The trials I have to suffer here."

"Drag the pity party inside before Rocco convinces all the other dogs that baths are terrible."

We're too late. The dogs are feisty, having been told by Rocco that we're there to torture them. The water is cold. The dogs are slippery. The soap gets everywhere. I can't remember the last time I had so much fun.

"You're really good with animals," Chase tells me after we corral the last dog back into his kennel. "You'll make a good vet."

"Thanks. Like you said, they're not judgmental." I toss the hose in Chase's direction and pick up the overturned washtub. Rocco kicked it as he was jumping out, splashing water all over our tennis shoes. Sandy came back while Boots was barking his head off and left almost immediately, not wanting to get drenched with dirty water and wet fur.

"Dunno about that. Rocco looks pissed off."

"I think I might've got soap in his eyes."

"Nah. He's just mad because I was the one scrubbing him down instead of you." He winks and reaches for the water shutoff. The motion causes his T-shirt to stretch across his abs—his very nice, very firm set of abs.

"Helloooo! Where you at, Beth? It's me," a cheery voice yells from the outer room.

It's Scarlett.

Chase looks up in panic. He drops the hose before he can turn the shutoff valve, and it sprays me, twisting around like an angry snake. I yelp and try to jump out of the way, but I'm not fast enough.

"Shit. Sorry." Chase manages to corral the hose and then thrusts it into my hands, turning his back just as the outer door swings open. He walks, almost runs down the hall.

"Hey… Oh my God, what happened to you?" Scarlett laughs when she spots me.

I look down at my drenched Darling High T-shirt. "I was washing the dogs."

Behind her is Jeff. He gives me a brief examination before looking over my shoulder. Uneasy, I glance back in time to see Chase's head disappear around a corner.

When Jeff takes a step forward, I "accidentally" lose the hose and spray him. Jeff curses loudly.

"Sorry." I raise a soapy hand. "It's slippery."

His eyes narrow in suspicion. "Was that Manson?" he asks.

"Who?" I play dumb.

"He means Charlie Donnelly." Scarlett rolls her eyes. She sounds as tired with the stupid nickname as I am.

I decide not to answer her. Instead, I spray a line of water close to their feet. "Careful. It's dirty over here," I warn.

Jeff meets my eyes. He knows it was Chase and that I'm protecting him. I lift my chin. Chase needs someone on his side. Jeff's got the whole school. Hell, he has the whole town. Chase has no one.

"We should go," Jeff announces. "I just remembered I needed to do something for my dad."

"But we just got here," Scar protests. "I wanted to hang with Beth and pet the doggies."

"Walk home, then, if you're going to be rude about it." With that, he turns on his heel.

Scar looks over at me in a panic. "It's fine," I say with a shrug. "Go."

That's all she needs to scamper after him. "I'm sorry, Jeff. I was just excited about the dogs."

"You always have a choice, Scar. If you don't want to be with me, say the word."

She falls silent. I'm torn between wanting to protect Chase and wanting to run after Scarlett and ask her what the hell she's doing with Jeff. Every time I see them, he's running her down for not doing exactly what he wants.

Was he like this with Rachel? Or did he develop this bad attitude in England? He better not have treated Rachel like this.

I rush over, turn off the water and then hurry to the window to watch them leave. When Jeff's Audi pulls out of the parking lot, I call out to Chase. "It's safe to come out."

His shoes thump on the floor. He joins me at the window, bracing an arm next to my head.

"I'm worried about Scarlett," I tell him.

Chase offers a knowing look. "Because Jeff demands more obedience from her than we do from Rocco?"

"Something like that."

He leans closer, peering out the window. "He's a bully. There're plenty like him in juvie, only without the clothes and fancy cars, but underneath he's the same as them. All he wants to do is control people. He gets off on the power trips."

"Do you think he was like that with Rachel?" I gnaw on my lip.

"I don't know. It's been three years. People can change a lot in three years. Look at me." I twist my head to see his a scant few inches from mine. He gives me a self-deprecating smile. "I was a self-absorbed, immature asshole know-it-all who thought that stealing his coach's car was the height of coolness. I wouldn't do that now if you paid me a million dollars."

"Jeff went to England, not prison," I remind him.

"I know, but it could've felt like a prison."

I flush. That was the same sentiment I thoughtlessly flung at Chase before.

"Hey." His finger tips my chin upward. "I didn't mean it like that. You're nothing like Jeff."

"You're saying there's hope for me?" I rub my jaw against his finger. My house did feel like a prison when I met Chase, and my response was to try to lose control. Jeff's response is apparently to exercise control over everyone around him.

"Yeah. There's hope." His voice is husky.

Thoughts of Jeff fly out of my head. It's hard to focus on anything but the boy in front of me when he's so close. My gaze falls to his shirt, which is still wet. There are fresh wrinkles in the center, as if he's pulled it off, wrung it out and shoved it back on. Near his collar is a tiny dry patch.

"I missed a part here." I run my finger over the cotton, feeling his collarbone underneath.

His breath catches in his throat. I stroke my way along the bone, dropping into the shallow dip at the base of his throat. I wait for him to stop me, as he always does. But he remains still. My finger continues its exploration, following a downward path. On the surface, Chase is hard—all muscles, tough sinew and bone. But underneath, he has a tender heart. It aches for us. What he wants and what I want are at odds with what we should be wanting.

"You shouldn't do this." The words are raspy, as if he has a hard time forcing them out.

"Yes, I should."

28

I'm tired of being patient. I'm tired of doing things other people think I should be doing. There's nothing wrong with the concept of *us*.

I won't let us be wrong.

I rise on my tiptoes and press my lips against his. He freezes, but then his lips soften. His hand on my chin draws me closer. He makes a sound, one that curls my toes. One that I want to capture on my phone and play on repeat every night until I fall asleep.

I lean into him, drawing from that well of strength that he's built up inside. His arms close around me, and the kiss goes on and on and—

Bark! Bark! Bark!

A wet nose shoves between us. I look down to see Rocco aggressively pushing Chase and me apart. His stubby tail wags furiously.

Chase releases a half groan, half laugh and then bends down and gives the dog a firm scrub behind his ears. "You want a little love, too, Rocco?"

I use the time to collect myself. We probably shouldn't be making out at work. Sandy might frown on that, and I don't want to jeopardize the time Chase and I have here together. These moments are part of the small things that keep me going through the day.

I take a few deep breaths and push myself away from the wall.

Chase actively avoids looking in my direction for the rest of the shift, but I can't keep my eyes off him. And I can't stop touching my lips.

He kissed me back. Christmas came early.

I grin and my smile doesn't leave my face even when I arrive home to two glum-faced parents. I give them both a wave. Dad probably had a bad day at the hardware store and Mom's always complaining about how the agents are terrible with their expense reports. I float up the stairs. I sway in the shower and hum as I change my clothes.

On my phone, I find the mushiest playlist about love on Spotify, lie on my bed and learn there are old bands with names like REO Speedwagon and The Bangles. Who knew?

After an hour of listening to music, I hear my mom yell up the stairs that dinner is ready.

"Any big Halloween plans?" she asks when we're all seated at the table. The orange pumpkin season is upon us.

"Scar might be having a party." Remembering Scarlett puts a small dent in my good mood. I rest my fork on the side of my plate.

Should I bring up Jeff? No, I decide. If Jeff had been a jerk three years ago, my parents wouldn't still be so in love with him now. Dad, in particular, thinks Jeff's the best guy ever. Plus, I don't want to piss them off with the information that Jeff's dating Scar. It's better that they don't know.

I pick up my fork and resume eating.

"That's nice. I guess we'll need to get you a costume."

"*If* we give her permission to go," Dad says tightly. He's been wearing a dark expression since we sat down. He totally must've had a bad day at work.

Mom sighs. "Dave, we discussed this. Beth's been on her best behavior since…" She trails off, but I can fill in the blanks.

Since she went to the police station in defense of our daughter's killer. Since she went to his house after we ransacked her bedroom and did God knows what with that boy.

"Her best behavior," Dad echoes, and I feel a chill, because it sounds more like a question than an agreement.

"And the shelter? How was that?" Mom casts a worried glance in Dad's direction before turning back to me. "You showered when you got home. Did something happen at the shelter?"

"We washed the dogs and I stunk like wet pet hair."

"We?" Dad echoes, narrowing his eyes at me.

The tiniest alarm pings in the back of my head. "The staff," I say, lowering my gaze.

"You and Sandy?"

It's the tone of his voice that makes me look up from my plate. The tone that says, *I know you're hiding something.* I flick my eyes toward Mom first and then to Dad. They know. Or, *he* knows, at least. The alarm is loud this time. *Buckle up, buttercup*, I advise myself. *This isn't going to be pretty.*

"No, me and Chase," I answer. It's the truth, but I'm hoping my parents don't ask who Chase is.

"Who's Chase?" Mom asks.

Too much to hope for.

"He works at the shelter. Nice guy. He's—"

The sound of my father's fist slamming against the table is almost deafening. All the silverware jangles loudly. A freshly baked bun falls off the serving platter and rolls toward my plate. I catch it before it topples off the table.

"It's Charles Donnelly," Dad growls to Mom.

Her eyes widen. "What?"

He scrapes his chair back in an angry rush. "What our *well-behaved* daughter has neglected to tell us is that she's been working with that...that...*criminal* for the past two weeks."

Mom gasps. "Beth, is this true?"

I clench my fork in my fist. "Yes, and there's not much I can do about it, so that's why I didn't tell you guys," I lie. "He's been very respectful to me, though."

My mother's face pales. "He works with you," she says, sounding dazed.

"I have no control over who the owners hire. But you don't have to worry about us working together—"

"We're not worried." It's my dad who answers. "Because he won't be working with you after today."

I drop my fork. It clatters onto my plate. "What do you mean?"

"I called the shelter and told them that if they continued to employ a murderer, I'd make it my business to see that their business was shut down."

My jaw drops. *What?* "No," I say, shooting to my feet. "He needs that job! It's a condition of his probation to have a part-time job."

"That's too bad." Dad's not sorry at all. He hopes that Chase gets sent back to prison.

I take a deep breath, trying to control my rising anger. I can't believe this. How did my dad even find out about—

"Jeff told you, didn't he?" I demand after it dawns on me. And here I was trying to protect the asshole.

"Yes, he did," Dad bites out.

"He's dating Scar, you know," I say snidely. "That's how he found out. Because he and Scar came to the shelter today."

"I know he's dating your friend. Why shouldn't he be? Unlike some people in this house, Jeff has always been upfront with us."

"This is wrong. You're wrong," I tell Dad, but his face is set in stone. So I turn to Mom. "Please, Mom. You know this isn't right. Chase served his time."

Inexplicably, her response is "Why do you call him Chase?"

I furrow my brow. "That's his nickname. He doesn't go by Charlie anymore—"

A booming sound makes me jump. Dad's just slammed his fist on the table a second time. "You do not say his name at our table. You never say it at our table." He flings his arm toward the stairs. "Go to your room, right now, before I do something I regret."

I don't have to be told twice. I don't want to be here with them.

I race upstairs and grab my phone. I dial Jeff's number and the minute he says hello, I unload on him. "Why'd you tell my dad Chas—Charlie works at the shelter? Why do you care so much?"

"Because it's gross how he's just walking around free!" Jeff snaps back. "He needs to be behind bars."

"He was behind them for three years." I seethe.

"He killed your sister, Beth. He killed our Rachel."

I hate that Jeff is throwing this in my face. Like I don't know my sister is dead. Like I don't know that Chase drove the car that struck her. Like I never mourned for her at all.

"Endlessly punishing him doesn't bring her back," I finally say, trying to keep my tone calm when all I want to do is scream at him for being a meddling ass.

"It sounds like you're happy she's dead," he retorts.

"Fuck you, Jeff. Fuck you."

I'm so glad that we're not face-to-face so he can't see the rage tears fall. I hang up and bring up Chase's number, but it rings and rings. I shoot off a text.

I'm so sorry.

I stare at the screen, willing for him to text me or call me. A call comes through a moment later, but it's not Chase. It's Scarlett.

"What?" I snap.

"What's wrong with you?" she yells.

"What's wrong with *me*?"

"You're working with Charlie? He killed your sister!"

"Why does everyone keep saying that? I know this, okay? I know this!" My cheeks are soaked with tears, the anger boiling inside me causing my hand to shake over the phone.

"You don't act like it. Jeff said he thinks you two are seeing each other. That's awful, Beth."

"Why? Why is it awful?" I don't give her a chance to argue. "You know what's awful? Jeff is! He left me at the party in Lincoln. Just took off in his car without so much as looking behind. He stranded me there."

"That's not what I heard," she says, and her smug tone makes me want to reach through the phone and smack her. "I heard he went looking for you for hours but couldn't find you because you were slutting it up at some drug dealer's house."

"First of all, he wasn't a drug dealer. And second of all, I wouldn't have been in any person's house if Jeff hadn't left me on the street." I swipe at my stupid tears. "Plus, he's always telling you what to do. How to do your hair. What clothes you should wear. He makes you sit in a different seat in Calc."

"So you're jealous, is what you're saying. Having the murderer as your boyfriend isn't enough. You want Jeff, too." Her harsh breathing is loud in my ear. "He *told* me you'd probably start talking shit about him because he turned you down. You're creepy, Beth! First you want to bag your dead sister's boyfriend, and then when he doesn't want you, you turn to the guy who killed her? If anyone is sick and wrong and awful, it's not Jeff. It's *you!*"

She hangs up.

I'm left there staring at my phone. Stunned. I cannot believe she said all that horrible stuff to me. Scar and I both have a temper, but we've never, ever crossed the line with each other.

Calling me creepy and sick and awful? That's unforgivable.

I drag my sleeve over my wet eyes and stumble off the bed. Screw this. Screw Scarlett. Screw Jeff. Screw my parents. I don't deserve to constantly be attacked from all directions.

Since I can't go to the mudroom without getting caught, I dig in the back of my closet for a spare pair of sneakers, my mind running a mile a minute.

What have I really done wrong these last three years? I've followed the rules. I've gotten good grades. I've been a good friend to Scar. I've had a part-time job *and* a volunteer position. Yes, I sneaked out to a few parties this summer, but how is that a crime? I'm seventeen years old. I'm allowed to do dumb things every now and then.

And I'm going to do one now.

Chase hasn't texted back. This time, I call him instead of

texting. I half expect it to bump over to voice mail, so I'm startled when his deep voice fills my ear.

"Hey," he says roughly. "Now's not a good time."

"Why? Where are you?"

"Lexington Heights. I'm picking up my paycheck for the work I did last month with Jack."

"Did..." I swallow. "Did Sandy or someone from the shelter call you?"

"Yeah." His tone is clipped.

"Can we talk about it?"

"No. Like I said, not a good time. I haven't seen Jack in a few weeks and he wants me to stay and chill for a bit."

"Good. Stay there. I'm on my way."

He's quick to object. "Beth—"

"I mean it, Chase. We need to talk. I'm on my way." I hang up before he can voice another protest. And when my phone instantly rings again, I press Decline.

Jack... That's the guy who threw the party where I first met Chase.

This is perfect. My parents might go to the mayor's house to look for me and Chase, but neither of us will be there. We'll be at Jack's.

I don't remember his house number, but I remember the name of the street, and that's all I need to give the cab dispatcher as I whisper my request over the phone. Then I delete the call history, because I know that's the first thing my parents will look at.

I leave my phone on the bed. I can't risk taking it with me, thanks to that stupid GPS program my parents put on it. I also decide to throw them off course by scribbling a quick note telling them I'm going to Scarlett's. I leave that on the bedspread, too.

The window will beep when I climb through it, but I don't care. That just means I'll have to be very, very fast.

And I am. In a heartbeat, I have my bedroom window open and I'm shimmying down the lattice lining the side of the house. I know it's strong enough to support my weight because Rachel once used the lattice by her window to sneak out to meet Jeff. I wonder if he bullied her into doing that. That seems to be his thing. Bullying innocent girls.

Asshole.

I'm breathing hard by the time my sneakers land on the grass at the base of the lattice, but I don't let it slow me down. I keep running, daring only once to look over my shoulder at my house. The front door doesn't burst open like I expect. Still, that doesn't mean my parents won't come after me. Just means they probably haven't checked their phone notifications yet.

I don't give a damn if they freak out or send search parties after me. I *have* to talk to Chase. I know him. My dad getting him fired from the shelter will just be another sign for Chase that he should stay far, far away from me.

Well, too bad, because I'm not staying away from *him*.

29

As I requested, the cabdriver picks me up five blocks away from my house. It doesn't take long to get to Lex, and my heart rate quickens as we pull into the driveway of the familiar ramshackle house. Chase is waiting on the front porch for me.

"You shouldn't be here" is the first thing he says when I hurry up to him. His tone is flat, his expression dead serious.

"I needed to see you," I answer, brushing past him toward the front door. I don't want to stand out in the open, just in case.

Chase follows me inside and takes hold of my arm. "Do your parents know where you are?"

I roll my eyes. "What do you think?"

He curses softly. "Go home, babe. You being here is a bad fucking idea."

Despite his harsh words, my body heats up at the fact that he called me *babe.* "I'm not leaving until we talk, Chase. So you might as well stop arguing with me. You won't win."

He lets out another curse.

"Hey now," an amused voice says, "that's no way to talk in

front of a lady." A tall guy steps out of the kitchen and into the hall. Even though we didn't speak or get properly introduced the last time I was here, I recognize him as Jack.

"Yeah, Chase," I mock chide. "Where did you learn your manners?"

"Juvie," he growls. "I learned them in juvie."

Jack and I snicker.

"That wasn't a joke," Chase says in aggravation. He turns to Jack. "This is Beth, the girl I was telling you about."

My heart flips. He was telling his friend about me?

"Right, the one who wouldn't take no for an answer about crashing our bro night," Jack replies with a grin.

I sigh. Doesn't sound like Chase was telling his friend *good* things about me. "I'm sorry for just showing up," I say sheepishly. "It's important, though."

Jack shrugs. "You want a drink?"

"No, thanks."

"All right. If you change your mind, the fridge is stocked."

I smile in thanks. He seems like a really decent guy. I have no idea why these Lex kids get such a bad rep. All the ones I've met are super cool.

"Mind if we go upstairs?" Chase asks. "Apparently we need to talk."

"We do," I say firmly.

Chase glowers at me, but Jack just grins. "Of course. You guys can crash here, too, if you want." He leans closer to slap Chase on the shoulder. "It's been a while since we hung out. I missed you, man."

"Don't think we'll stay over, but thanks for the offer," Chase says, nodding at his buddy.

My heart soars at the exchange between them. It's so awesome to see someone actually want to spend time with Chase. He deserves this. So much.

Chase takes my arm again. "C'mon."

Upstairs, we wind up in the same bedroom where we...

My cheeks scorch.

Chase notices and runs his tongue over his bottom lip. Not in a lewd way, though. It seems more like a nervous gesture.

"I didn't bring you up here to... You know..." He waves a hand toward the bed.

"I know," I say, blushing even harder.

"Good." He crosses his arms. "Now, say what you need to say, and then it's time to go."

I glare at him. "Please don't act like a jerk. I'm risking permanent grounding to be here right now."

"I didn't ask you to risk anything," he grumbles. "That's on you."

"Gee, I'm *so* sorry I wanted to make sure *you* were all right." Sarcasm drips from my tone. "*Forgive me* for caring about you. How *dare* I!"

His lips twitch. "You done?"

"Nope." I inject more snark into my voice and say, "The *nerve* of me!" Then I smile sweetly. "There. Now I'm done."

With a sigh, he leads me over to the bed and we sit on the edge of it. "You don't have to worry about me," he assures me. "I'm fine."

I moan in misery. "No, you're not. You got fired."

"Yes. And I'm fine. I'll find something else."

I moan again.

"Seriously, Beth. It's all good." He nods at the door. "Jack already said I can join him on the crew again for the next few months. Lots of yard cleanups to do and then snow removal season's coming up."

That makes me feel better. Jack had previously hooked Chase up with a job at his landscaping company, but that was only for the summer. "So you'll have a job?"

"I'll have a job."

Relief flutters through me, but it fades into anger pretty fast. "I can't believe my dad called the shelter and had you fired. He's *such* an asshole."

"No, he's just protective of you." Chase's face is grim. "I already took one kid from him."

"Not on purpose. It was an accident."

"Accident or not, I was still at fault. I was driving too fast." His voice cracks slightly. "When she ran into the road, there was no way I could've stopped."

"I wonder why," I say suddenly.

That brings a frown to his lips. "Why what?"

"Why she was running." An ache forms in my chest as I picture Rachel racing into the middle of the dark street, unaware that she was about to die. She and Jeff had been at a party at her friend Aimee's house that night. As far as I know, Rachel wasn't drinking or on drugs.

"Do you think she was upset? Not paying attention?" I ask. An unformed thought floats in the back of my mind, but I can't grasp it.

"It doesn't matter if she was," Chase says gently. "If I wasn't speeding, I could've stopped in time. But I was sixteen and stupid and I hit a girl with a car I stole." He shakes his head, at himself, I think. "Of course your father hates me, Beth. He'll always hate me. He *should*."

Every word hurts my chest, like someone's scraping my heart with a dull razor. I hate how resigned he sounds. Even worse, how he thinks he *deserves* to be hated.

"I don't hate you," I whisper.

"I know you don't." He eases closer and rests his cheek on my shoulder. His soft hair tickles the bottom of my chin. "But you should, too."

"Never," I say fiercely.

Sighing, he lifts his head to look at me. "You're the most stubborn person I've ever met."

"So?"

A grin springs to his lips. "So? That's your answer?"

"What else do you want me to say? No, I'm not? We both know I'm stubborn as fuck."

He chuckles and pulls me toward him, surprising me with a quick kiss on the lips.

My heart jumps to my throat, and I instantly loop my arms around his neck so he can't get away. "That's twice in one day," I tease.

"Twice what?"

"Twice that we've kissed," I clarify. Grinning, I kiss him again and pull back. "Make that three."

He leans in and presses his mouth to mine. When our tongues meet, I whimper.

"Make that four," he rasps against my lips.

After that, we stop keeping count. Neither of us came upstairs for this reason, but we can't fight it. Maybe it's this house, this bedroom, this off-limits neighborhood. Whatever it is, I can't keep my hands off him. And he can't keep his hands off me. At some point, we need to stop.

But not now. Not for a long time.

Unfortunately, I'm the only one thinking that way. Chase draws away, setting me a firm arm's length from his big, warm body. "I think..." He trails off.

I lean in. "You think what?"

He gets up. "I think this has to be the last time."

"The last time for what?" I ask, hoping he can't hear the panic in my voice.

"The last time we see each other."

The panic surfaces in full force. "Absolutely *not*."

"Beth—"

"No," I interrupt. "We're not going to stop seeing each other. We're going to see each other every day for the rest of senior year, and then we're moving to Iowa together. I'm going to be a vet and you'll be a welder and we'll be blissfully happy. End of story."

"Your father will keep coming after me. And if you keep sneaking out to see me, he'll keep punishing you."

"I don't care. He can't ground me any more than he already has."

"He hates me," Chase says flatly. "Everyone in Darling hates me, Beth."

"Then everyone in Darling needs a lesson in forgiveness," I shoot back. "The accident is in the past. You should be able to walk around with your head held high, Chase. You paid for your mistakes. Don't let them judge you."

To my surprise, he laughs. A dark, humorless laugh.

I frown deeply at him. "What's so funny?"

"Nothing. Nothing is funny." He shoves strands of hair off his forehead. "But it's kind of ironic that you're telling me to not let people judge me when that's exactly what *you* do."

My jaw drops. "That's not true."

"Of course it is. You claim you forgive me, but I don't see you telling anyone we're seeing each other. Your friends don't know. Your parents don't know, though now they probably have an idea we might be." He offers a shrug. "At school, you act like we're strangers."

Frustration courses through me. "Because that's the way

you want it!" I argue. "You're constantly giving me signals—
or telling me outright—to stay away from you at school."

"I'm not blaming you for that. Not at all," he says gently.
"But don't talk to me about the past being in the past, and
me needing to walk around with my head held high, when
you're just as afraid as I am of being judged. If you weren't,
you wouldn't be keeping our relationship a secret."

I'm taken aback. Crap. He's right. I *am* afraid of what
people will say.

That's why I've been meeting Chase in secret for the past
few weeks. That's why I don't talk to him in any of the classes
we share. I tell myself that it's because he wants to lie low at
school. And whenever he gives me a shake of the head or a look
that says, *Don't stand up for me,* I grab onto those opportunities
like they're life preservers and I'm drowning at sea. The one
time I stood up for him, after the fire alarm incident, everyone looked at me like I was psychotic, even my closest friends,
and I immediately went back to pretending we're strangers.

Chase gives me the easy way out at school, and I take it.
Every damn time.

"I don't blame you for that," he repeats, because obviously
my shame is oozing from my every pore. "I understand why
you can't be seen with me in public. Why you can't tell people
about us. But…"

My heart clenches as I wait for him to finish. I know I won't
like what he has to say. I know it's going to hurt me really, really bad.

I'm not wrong.

"But…" His blue eyes seek mine in the darkness. "That's
why it'll never work out with us."

30

The rest of the weekend is pure and utter misery.

When I stumble home three hours after escaping through my bedroom window, my parents are there to pounce on me. I don't remember much of what they say or threaten me with. I'm not listening to them because my head is still back at Jack's house. Back with Chase, who told me we're not going to work out.

He didn't break up with me. I specifically asked if that was the case. It wasn't.

He just doesn't see a future for us.

"It's impossible" were the parting words I got before he deposited me into an Uber that he paid for. And those two words run through my mind like a broken record as I sit in the living room and receive the lecture of all lectures from my parents.

They know I wasn't at Scarlett's or with any of my other friends. Fortunately, they also know I wasn't at Chase's. *Un*fortunately, they know this because my dad stormed over there, demanding to know where his daughter was. Apparently Chase's mother was terrified by Dad's outburst. The mayor threatened to have him arrested, and Mom had to drag Dad to the car.

I, of course, am blamed for all of this—total bullshit. Just because I went AWOL doesn't mean Dad had to show up at the mayor's house and yell like a madman.

On Sunday, I'm not allowed to leave the house, not even to go to the shelter. Dad calls in sick for me, which gives me a sliver of hope because at least he didn't outright quit on my behalf again. That means there's a chance I'll be allowed to go back next weekend.

When Monday morning comes, I've never been more excited for school. My parents took my phone again, so if Chase texted me during the rest of the weekend, I have no clue. But I intend on intercepting him at his locker before AP Calc and demanding to know what he plans to do about our relationship.

I don't get the chance. When I near the senior locker bank, Macy races over to me before I can look for Chase.

"Everyone is saying you hooked up with Charlie this weekend!" is her opening statement. Her eyes are cloudy, but I can't tell if she's jealous or disappointed. "Is that true?"

"Of course not," I lie and then cringe when I remember Chase's gentle accusation that I keep our relationship a secret from everyone.

"Then why are people saying it?" Macy demands, hands on her hips.

"Because people are stupid," I mutter under my breath.

"Scar and Yvonne aren't stupid and they're the ones saying it." Her tone grows increasingly haughty. "Scar says your parents called her house this weekend looking for you, because you said you were going there, but really you were secretly meeting Charlie. She's pissed at you."

I'm not surprised Scarlett's mad that I lied to my parents about going to her house, but why do I get the feeling Jeff's the one who planted the Beth-went-to-meet-Charlie idea in her head?

"Well then it *must* be true if Scar and Yvonne are saying it." I'm being snide but I don't care. What gives her the right to cross-examine me? Who I hook up with or don't hook up with is none of her business.

"Macy," a sharp voice hisses.

I turn to see Scarlett glaring at our friend. She doesn't even look my way.

Macy looks from me to Scar. Then she shrugs and wanders to Scarlett's side, literally *and* figuratively. It's obvious which horse she's backing in this race.

"Hey, Scar," I say coolly.

She ignores me, tugs on Macy's arm and the two of them march off, leaving a wave of hostility in their wake.

Hurt, anger and indignation clog my throat. Screw them. If they can dump me as a friend based on a bunch of lies from Jeff and some rumors about me and Chase, then screw them.

Not rumors, a little voice says. *You* are *with Chase.*

Am I? He tried to dump me this weekend. So, no, I don't even know what we are anymore. And I can't ask him, because the first bell rings and I'm forced to book it to AP Calc.

He's already at his desk when I stalk in. Head down, as usual. He doesn't look my way. Neither does Scarlett. Or Jeff. Or Macy. Or any of my other classmates.

I see how it is. I'm public enemy number one, apparently. But I don't give a crap that everybody is ignoring me.

Only one person's opinion matters, and before this day is over, I *will* talk to Chase.

Whether he likes it or not.

Chase does a good job of eluding me for the rest of our morning classes. He shows up late for Physics and stays late to talk to Dvořák after Music History. Coward.

The plan is to track him down at lunch, but Ms. Tannen-hauf throws a wrench in that by stopping me in the hall and saying she needs to see me in her office. She doesn't give me a choice in the matter.

"Your mother called this morning," Ms. T says once we're seated.

My shoulders instantly snap straight. Through clenched teeth, I ask, "Why?"

The guidance counselor clasps her hands on her desk. "She wanted to let the school know that you had a tough weekend."

My jaw falls open. "Yeah, I did. Because of *them*! Did she tell you how they've turned our house into a prison? There are literally alarms on every door and window."

Ms. Tannenhauf studies my expression. I think she sees more than outrage there, because her gaze softens. "She also told me about her suspicions that you're in a relationship with Charlie Donnelly."

I gulp. Dammit. I knew my parents suspected, but having it confirmed makes me uneasy. Also, are teachers even allowed to talk to you about your love life? I feel like that's inappropriate.

And that's my out. "I don't feel comfortable discussing my personal life," I say primly. I arch an eyebrow. "Is there anything else, or may I go eat my lunch now?"

Her expression grows pained. "You may go," she finally says.

I stand up. "Thank you. Nice chat."

"Beth," she calls before I can open the door. "Please come talk to me if you change your mind. You know I'm always here to listen."

I nod and leave her office. I give the library a quick scan in case Chase is holed up there. He isn't. The pointless meeting with Tannenhauf cost me valuable time, and when I hurry back to the lockers, Chase isn't there, either. I know for a fact he doesn't eat in the cafeteria or visit the Starbucks. So where the hell is he?

I spend the entire lunch period scouring the school, but Chase is nowhere to be found. He can't hide from me forever— my last class of the day is Spanish, and he happens to be in it, too. For sure he'll be there. He can't afford to skip any classes and risk another black mark on his record.

Unfortunately, Scarlett's also in that class.

She and Jeff are the first people I see when I approach the classroom. Through the open doorway, I make out an empty room. Chase hasn't arrived yet.

I stop and lean against the wall a few feet from the door. Scar and Jeff throw hostile looks in my direction, then whisper something to each other. A couple more pointed glances ensue. Some more whispering. A couple sneers. More whispering.

Until finally I roll my eyes and address the couple in a loud voice. "If you've got something to say to me, say it already."

"Oh, look, Scar—Lizzie remembers she has friends."

I laugh incredulously. "Right. *I'm* the one who's forgotten what friendship is."

"Yes, you are," Jeff says coldly. "Not to mention you've forgotten what *family* is. You're banging your sister's murderer."

I grit my teeth. "I'm not banging him. I was just working at the same animal shelter as him. Hardly something I could control." Guilt pricks at me as I realize I'm doing it again— distancing myself from Chase by lying about how close we really are.

Jeff's eyes blaze. "Bullshit. *I* was able to get the situation under control in five minutes flat, Lizzie. I called your father and we got that killer fired. You did nothing but flash a wet T-shirt in front of his face like the slut you are."

Scarlett's face pales. I don't miss the way she flinches when Jeff says the word *slut*.

Ignoring the heat scorching my cheeks, I focus on my—former—best friend instead of Jeff. "Is that what you think, too, Scar?" I ask quietly. "That I'm a slut?"

"I…" She bites her lip.

"That's exactly what she thinks," Jeff announces, his tone smug. "Everyone does."

"Shut up," I snap at him. "I'm talking to Scar." I lock gazes with her. "Do you think I'm a slut?"

Jeff plants a hand on the back of her neck, in that possessive grip he's so fond of. "Yes," he says firmly. "She does."

I remain focused on Scar. She's clearly flustered.

But she doesn't go against him.

Disappointment fills my belly. I've known this girl since kindergarten. Over the years, we've laughed together, we've cried together and we've always had each other's backs. Or so I thought. It's obvious Scar would rather stay in Jeff's good graces than have my back. She'd rather listen to him taunt me about what a slut I am than defend me.

Come to think of it, nobody is defending me. Thanks to Jeff, all my classmates believe *I* ditched *him* at that party in Lincoln so I could hang out with a drug dealer. Have Macy or Yvonne or Troy come up to me and asked for my side of the story? Has anyone? Nope.

And meanwhile, here I am, placing so much value in these jerks' opinions. What do I care what they think of me? These people aren't my friends. I thought they were, but they're not. My only true friend is Chase. He's the one who listens to me, supports me, acts like he actually gives a damn about me.

"Look, there's Lizzie's fuck buddy now," Jeff says with a sneer.

My heartbeat speeds up at Chase's appearance. He's wearing all black, and I don't think he shaved all weekend because his face is covered with dirty-blond scruff. He looks incredible. And resigned—he looks utterly resigned as his blue eyes shift from me to Jeff.

The two boys hold each other's gazes. For several seconds, time stands still.

Chase shoves his hands into his pockets and ducks his head.

Jeff visibly gloats at winning the staredown and causing Chase to back down.

Indignation surges through me. No way. No fucking way. Jeff isn't allowed to win *anything* over Chase. Jeff is a controlling asshole who gets off on terrorizing girls and guys who won't fight back.

Chase is a million times better than Jeff Corsen. He's kind and supportive and he's paid for his mistakes. He's been good to me. And he does *not* deserve to be treated the way I've been treating him. It makes me sick to my stomach that he thinks I'm ashamed to be seen with him.

I suck in a long, shaky breath and search for the courage inside me. Finding it, I take a step forward and speak in a clear, even voice.

"Nah, that's not my fuck buddy," I inform Jeff and Scarlett and anyone else in earshot of us. "That's my boyfriend."

There's a scandalized gasp.

A few whispers.

Chase's blue eyes widen at my declaration, but I don't give him any time to sit with that shock. I stride toward him, grab hold of his T-shirt collar and tug his head down.

Then I kiss him in the middle of the hallway, in front of all our classmates, staking my claim.

To hell with what anyone thinks.

Chase is the only one who matters.

31

The kiss is widespread knowledge by the time school ends. Chase and I suffer through the stares and whispers in Spanish class. We endure the muttered, disgusted jabs as we leave the school. We ignore the dirty looks we receive in the parking lot.

My bus isn't here yet, but Chase can't wait with me and he's not happy about it. Since the final bell rang, he's been mumbling about how stupid it was for me to kiss him in view of everyone. How crazy I am for proclaiming that he's my boyfriend.

And yet he hasn't let go of my hand.

"I really wish I could wait to make sure you get on the bus okay," he says grimly. "But Jack's picking me up at the Starbucks in five minutes. We've got two yard cleanups to do today before it gets dark."

"It's okay," I assure him. "I'm, like, the only senior who rides the school bus anyway." Damn my parents for taking away my car again. "Those freshmen and sophs are too scared to get in my face."

That seems to appease him. He nods briskly and says, "I'm

biking home from work in a few hours, and then I'll come by your place tonight." My heart does a happy flip, then plummets when Chase adds, "We've got a lot to talk about."

Yeah, we do. But we're *not* talking about what I think he wants to talk about. We're not breaking up. We're not going to stop seeing each other. Today, I made my stand. I chose Chase Donnelly over everyone else in my life, and it can't be for nothing.

I stand up on my tiptoes and smack a kiss on his cheek. It's so surreal doing that with the autumn sun shining down on us and other students in plain sight. I think it freaks him out a little, too, because the moment my lips touch his cheek, his wary gaze instantly conducts a sweep of the area.

"Iowa," I whisper to him.

"Iowa?"

"Whenever you're feeling panicky about the kids in Darling, just remember that in September we'll be in Iowa and nobody will care if we kiss in public."

He sighs. "I still haven't agreed to go to Iowa with you."

"Sure, you have. You obviously just forgot." I plant another kiss on his cheek. "See you later."

He gives me that guarded half smile of his, hops on his bike and pedals off.

I shift my backpack to one shoulder and wait for the yellow bus to appear. It's just pulling into the lot when Jeff stalks up to me. The tails of his untucked white button-down flap with each impatient stride, and he nearly mows down three freshman girls on his way to me.

"Leave me alone," I say icily.

"No. We need to talk." Jeff grabs my hand hard enough to leave a bruise. When I yelp, he hastily lets go. "Sorry," he mutters.

He's not sorry. He's only saying it for the benefit of the on-lookers whose attention we've captured. Jeff doesn't want our peers thinking he's an abusive ass. He's good at hiding it, too.

But these days, I see right through him. I glower at him. "We have nothing to talk about, because I've got absolutely nothing to say to you."

"Well, I have lots to say to you, yeah?"

Again with that fake British accent. "Well, I don't, *yeah*?" I mock and take several steps toward the line of students wait-ing to get on the bus.

His dark eyes flare with annoyance. He presses his hands to his sides as if he's trying to restrain himself from grabbing me again. Then he exhales in a long, steady rush. "I want to talk about Rachel."

I pretend to be unfazed, but the sound of her name leaving his lips does affect me. It makes me sick that my sister dated this guy for nearly a year.

"Did you hear me?" he demands when I remain silent.

I coolly meet his aggravated eyes. "Yes, I heard you."

His brow furrows. "I said I want to talk about Rachel."

"I don't care," I answer with a big fake smile.

Fluttering my fingers in an equally fake, cheerful wave, I spin away from him and get on the bus.

Dad is waiting for me when I get home. It doesn't come as a surprise, since he'd already informed me last night that, from now on, he'll be leaving the hardware store at three o'clock every day so he's home when I get back from school. His part-time workers must be thrilled for the extra hours. Me? Not so thrilled.

"You can do your homework in the dining room," he tells

me after I kick off my shoes in the mudroom. Rachel's section of the bench, as always, is pristine.

"My laptop's in my room," I mutter.

"No, I already brought it downstairs for you. I'm getting an early start on dinner, so I'd like for you to work in the dining room."

He says it graciously, as if he's actually giving me the option. "Why, so you can watch me from the kitchen to make sure I don't escape?"

"Yes," he says flatly.

I gape at his stiff back as he disappears into the kitchen. Wow. I cannot believe my father. What's *happened* to him?

"This is ridiculous," I yell after him. "I'm going to be gone in less than a year!"

I'm leaving this house and this town and every hateful person in it even if it means not going to college. I can't take another four years of this.

I drag my unhappy ass to the dining room table. The numbers and letters on the page swim in front of me. I can't focus. The television is on in the kitchen. Dad's clinking pans against the stove burners. Morgan barks. I look up to catch a flash of black as he streaks across the yard.

Uh-oh. He must've gotten loose. I throw my pencil onto the notebook and stand up.

Dad appears in the entryway, a dish towel thrown over his shoulder. "Where are you going?"

"Outside." Morgan's tail bumps against Rachel's swing, sending the wooden seat swaying.

Dad follows my gaze. "That fool dog." He snatches the towel off his shoulder and squeezes it between his big hands, likely imagining the fabric is Morgan's neck.

"Wait!" I hold out a restraining hand. "Mrs. Rennick will catch him."

"They shouldn't have gotten that damn dog in the first place. He's not around and she's got no control over that animal." He reaches for the latch.

I throw myself against the door. "Morgan's a sweet dog. He's not doing any harm."

"He's going to knock Rachel's swing down."

"So you can rehang it. What does it matter?" I dig my heels in. I'm not letting Dad out of this house if he's going to hurt Morgan. We've really spiraled out of control over Rachel's death if a dog knocking down her swing is going to cause this much trauma.

I'm no match for my dad, though. He shoves me out of the way with one sweep of his hand and heads for the garage. I'm torn between chasing after him and helping Mrs. Rennick catch Morgan. I choose Morgan and Mrs. R.

"This dog!" Mrs. Rennick cries as I race toward her. The big mutt runs around the tree, sending the swing careening in one direction and then the other.

I wince when the wooden seat strikes the tree trunk. "You go that way and I'll go this way," I tell Mrs. R, pointing to the opposite direction.

"Okay."

We separate and try to corral Morgan between us. He, of course, thinks that we're engaged in a wonderful game and darts just out of reach.

A piercing whistle fills the air. It startles Morgan into a momentary stillness and I leap on top of him. Mrs. Rennick throws me the leash. I quickly affix it to Morgan's collar and hand him over to his frazzled owner.

"I'm so sorry, Dave," our neighbor apologizes as Dad strides forward, a screwdriver sticking out of his front pocket and a ladder hoisted over his shoulder. Morgan strains under Mrs. Rennick's grip. "Morgan got loose again."

He gives her a terse nod at the obvious statement but doesn't stop walking until he reaches Rachel's swing.

"I, ah, better get home. I'm sorry again."

Dad still doesn't respond, instead focusing on setting up the ladder.

"It's fine," I say, trying to cover for my father's uncharacteristic rudeness. As a local small business owner, he's usually super nice to everyone. "Bye-bye, Morgan." I give the doggy a wave. He wags his tail happily, oblivious to the tension in the air.

"Call me if there's a problem," Mrs. Rennick says, although I'm not sure if she's directing that to me or my dad.

I answer again, "Sure thing, Mrs. R."

She gives me a finger wave before hauling Morgan away. Dad climbs down off the ladder only seconds later with the wooden seat in his hands, the rope over his shoulder.

"I should've taken this down years ago. It's a miracle there isn't more damage." He inspects the planks that are worn from the years of exposure to the Midwestern weather.

"It's just a swing, Dad." Rachel's not here. She only swings in our memories.

"It's not just a swing, Lizzie. It's her swing."

I give in. From long experience, I know arguing with Dad about anything is a futile endeavor. Instead, I offer a hand. "I can carry that. Where do you want it? The garage?"

He shakes his head and tucks the seat under his arm, and still manages to fold the ladder closed. "I'll put it in the den."

That's healthy.

I trail behind, frustrated and more than a little hurt that

I'm not good enough to handle the swing. Back in the house, Dad disappears for a second to place the holy swing in his study. My parents are like dragons, hoarding Rachel's things like they're rare treasures.

They need therapy—that's becoming more and more obvious to me. I stopped suggesting it a long time ago, but after everything that's happened lately, I think I need to bring up the subject again. Maybe Ms. Tannenhauf can help me stage an intervention. Or I can see if my old grief counselor can stop by the house for an ambush therapy session.

Either way, my parents need help. They can't keep doing this to us.

My stuff on the dining room table mocks me. There's nowhere for me to go in this house.

"When am I getting my door back?" I ask as Dad reappears on his way to the kitchen.

"When you show yourself to be trustworthy."

"I'm not doing anything bad. I'm not drinking. I'm not doing drugs. I'm not sleeping around. I'm just trying to enjoy my last year of school."

"You were at parties. You were with drug dealers. You have repeatedly disobeyed us." He picks up the knife and resumes his dinner preparations.

"Because your rules are ridiculous!" I have the urge to stomp my feet like I did when I was five.

"I know you think I'm going overboard with you, but I'm trying to protect you," he insists. "I wish you'd understand. The security measures, making sure you don't have contact with filth, the tracking. This is all for your own good. What kind of dad would I be if I didn't protect my little girl?"

"But, Dad, this isn't protecting me. This is smothering me. What happened with Rachel was an accident. It could happen to anyone, no matter where they are. You can't prevent bad things from happening."

"I can do my best," he says grimly. "I wouldn't be able to look myself in the mirror if something happened to you, too. This isn't about Rachel. This is about *you* and how much we want you to be safe. Now, go finish your homework."

With that, he continues chopping. Denial. He's in total denial.

Gritting my teeth, I go back to the dining room and try to concentrate on my homework. For the next few minutes, the only sound from the kitchen is the *tap-tap* of Dad's knife hitting the cutting board, until it's finally broken by the chirp of his phone.

"Hello?" comes Dad's brisk response.

I strain to hear what he's saying but only make out the low murmur of his voice.

A moment later, he walks into the dining room, tucking the phone in his pocket. "Let's go for a drive," he suggests.

A drive? "Seriously? I just tried having a real conversation with you and you dismissed me. Now you want to go for a drive?"

"We can have that conversation in the car, then." He pauses. "We'll talk about the door."

I know he's manipulating me. I know it, but I let it happen anyway.

"Where are we going?" I ask as I buckle into the passenger seat.

"I need to pick up your mother from the office. Her car's in the shop until tomorrow morning."

"This isn't the way to Mom's office," I point out.

"We're making a small detour."

"Where?"

"You'll see."

The cryptic response is a joke, because it doesn't take long to figure it out. When the road gets wider and the houses grow larger, I immediately know who called.

"Jeff and I are not on good terms," I inform my dad.

He nods easily, as if he's heard this before. "He said you two had a falling-out."

"So why are you taking me to his house?"

"Because he has a box of Rachel's things and he asked if you'd be willing to come over and go through it with him."

"He asked *you*, not me. Don't you think I should have a say in the matter?" I ask curtly.

"No, because I agree with Jeff. Sharing your memories of Rachel will help repair the rift."

Jeff is so fucking disgusting. Using my dead sister to gain the sympathy and support of my father? I'm going to punch him when I see him. The box is probably as real as the story he'd told Dad about building an arbor in the backyard.

"Why are you so in love with him? He's a jerk."

"He's a good boy," Dad disagrees. "He loved your sister with all his heart."

"Did he? Because he treats Scarlett like she's a piece of garbage." I know Dad's not going to turn the car around, so I might as well use the opportunity to let Jeff know that he can't go on mistreating my friend like this.

But Dad flat out ignores the accusation. "He told me that you've been unhappy with how he's tried to protect you from that Donnelly boy."

"Oh, I'm sure. Did he also tell you that he pulled the fire alarm at school and tried to pin it on Chase? Or how he's constantly nagging Scarlett about what she wears and how she acts?"

"I'm sure you're exaggerating. He's looked out for you since he got back. He's defended your actions to us," Dad says with a sigh, as if that makes Jeff both an idiot and a saint.

He pulls up to the front of Jeff's huge house.

I'm tempted to run down the lane and over to Mayor Stanton's house instead. It's just a few blocks away—we passed it on our way here, but I'm sure that Jeff would narc on me. He's probably in his living room, peeking behind some curtain. I don't even understand why he wants to talk to me.

"Go on now. I'll be back in an hour."

With a final mutinous look in Dad's direction, I force myself to get out of the car. I trudge to the door and ring the bell.

Jeff's mom answers.

"Lizzie!" She gathers me against her chest in a warm hug.

Awkwardly, I hug her back. I've never said more than two words to Jeff's mom. Hell, I don't even know her first name.

She draws back, cupping my shoulders. "You're looking more and more like your sister."

There's a faint resemblance between Rachel and me. We have the same dark blond hair and brown eyes, but Rachel was taller and thinner than me. We certainly don't look enough alike for Jeff's mom to act like I'm some long-lost daughter arriving home after thirty days at sea.

"Hi, Mrs. Corsen. Apparently, Jeff has a box of stuff to give me?" I say woodenly.

"He's downstairs in the game room." She clasps her hands together happily. "I'm so glad that you two are together. I know some people will think it's odd, but I feel like your shared grief brought you closer. Isn't that right?"

"Together?" My eyebrows scrunch together in confusion. What the hell is Jeff telling his parents?

"Jeffrey was so lost after Rachel died," she says, her tone finally losing some of its cheer. "He just lost control. That's why he had to go to England, you know?"

This is something I didn't know. Something I feel is important, which is why I act like I know what she's talking about. "Yeah, he said he found himself," I lie.

"I hope so. Goodness, I hope so. After the incident with Debbie's son, I was so worried, but he hasn't gotten into any fights since he's been back. And everyone's been so good to him since he returned."

"No. No fights." That's at least true, but I've never heard of this incident with Debbie's son. Debbie's their housekeeper.

"I should have been paying more attention after Rachel's accident, but you know how busy we are." Jeff's dad is some big insurance executive and spends most of his time in Chicago, but his mom has no job as far as I know. Maybe she's busy with charity things or whatever really rich women do with their time.

"Teenagers can be sneaky," I say, wondering what conversation we're having.

She buys it. "The pills were the least of our concern," she admits. "It was the anger that was, well, challenging. Apology gifts only go so far."

"That's true," I agree, but inwardly I'm left wondering. What on earth did Jeff do? What anger issues were so serious that he had to be sent to an entirely different country? When I open my mouth to ask, Jeff's head appears at the top of the stairs.

"Lizzie," he says.

"Beth," I remind him frostily.

"Come on. I have something for you." He grabs my hand and tugs me down the carpeted stairs.

I don't believe him. Or, at least, I don't want to believe him, but my feet follow after his. If he does have something of Rachel's, I don't want to leave it here. I remember how unhappy she was in the days leading up to her death, how she withdrew from all of us.

That indistinct thought I had before has morphed into a huge concern. *Jeff* was the reason for her unhappiness. He was the reason she stopped smiling, stopped talking to us. He doesn't deserve to have any of her things.

"Why didn't you tell me about it before? It's been a whole month."

"I just found it. I forgot I had it."

He leads me down the stairs. His basement is as big as my house. There's a full bar and a room filled with hundreds of bottles of wine. I see a pool table and a wall of windows leading out to Jeff's pool, which is covered for the winter.

We bypass a large sitting area and go into a paneled room with two heavy leather sofas facing each other. At one end is a green felt table. On the walls are pictures of those silly dogs playing cards.

"Have a seat." He crosses over to a cabinet and tugs open the door. "Want a drink?" He holds up a bottle of vodka.

"Where's the box?"

"Do you want to have a drink?" He shakes the bottle lightly.

"No. I want the box."

"Just one drink."

"It's four in the afternoon. I don't want a drink." I check my watch. Only ten minutes have passed. I have fifty to go. I take a seat on the sofa. "I'll have a soda."

"Fine. When did you get to be so uptight?" he grouses but grabs a Sprite for me.

He drops it into my lap and settles in too close. I inch away and check my watch again. Time is moving slower than a turtle.

"Got someplace to go? Your felon boyfriend waiting?" He lifts the bottle of liquor to his lips.

"My dad said he'd be back soon, so you should give me what you have."

"You still don't have your wheels back?" He clucks his tongue. "Be nice and I'll take you wherever you want to go."

"Okay. Take me to my felon boyfriend's house."

Jeff raises the bottle and, for a flash, I think he's going to hit me. But he tips it to his mouth again. I must've imagined it.

"You're a bitch, you know that?" he says, swiping his hand across his mouth.

"Is that supposed to be an insult?"

"What is it with you girls lately? You're a bitch and Scarlett's a slut. You two used to be so good." He slurs the last bit.

I wave a hand in front of my face to get rid of his booze breath. "Maybe it's not us girls who have changed."

"Nah. It's you. It's always you bitches changing. You, your sister, Scarlett. More trouble than you're worth," he mutters. "You all need some education."

I have to spend another—I check my watch again—forty minutes listening to Jeff ramble about how terrible women are? I'd rather pour bleach in my ears. "Thanks for your input, but where's the box?"

"This whole 'females first' shit. That's what's wrong with this world. Y'all turned into man haters."

This asshole. There's obviously no box of Rachel mementos in this basement, or this house. And even if there was, whatever he has of Rachel's is not important. Just like the swing isn't important or the preservation of her space in the mudroom isn't important. Rachel isn't in any of these *things*. She lives in the hearts of the people who loved her.

And Jeff isn't one of those people.

I don't know what game Jeff is playing, but I refuse to participate.

"Whatever. I'm leaving." I'll walk home.

Before I can get to the door, though, Jeff appears in front of me. The vodka sloshes over the side of his hand.

"Goddammit," he curses. "Look at what you made me do."

I shove his arm out of the way. "I didn't make you do anything." My mind is already elsewhere. I need to talk to Scarlett. Even if she gets mad at me, we have to talk about Jeff. He's not treating her right, and all the shit his mom told me upstairs has formed a knot of worry in my belly.

"Rachel always said you were more stubborn than a goat."

I stop, my hand on the door handle.

"She said that you'd be better at volleyball if you weren't so quick to jump to conclusions, too," he continues, and I hear his footsteps moving away from me.

I twist to face him. Rachel did say that about my play—that I was too quick to guess where the ball was going to land. "Why are you bringing this up now?"

"I told you. I just found it." Jeff drops a medium-sized cardboard box onto the coffee table between the two sofas. So he does have a box.

I release the door handle and drift over toward him, but I stop halfway. "Why did you get sent to England?" I ask warily.

"Because I beat up the housekeeper's son," he replies bluntly. "They made me take this bullshit anger management program. Plus rehab for the pills."

I'm surprised at his honesty. "What pills?"

"Just some oxy. No biggie."

"Obviously it was big enough for you to go to rehab." I frown at him. "Why did you beat up that poor kid? What did he ever do to you?"

"He got in my face about Rachel, about how I was partly responsible for her death."

My pulse quickens. "How so?"

"We were fighting, but I think you suspected that." Jeff rummages in the box and pulls out a hairbrush. It's light brown, with blond strands in it. Rachel's hairbrush.

He kept it all these years? I wonder what else he has in the box. I creep closer. "What were you fighting about?"

He slaps the brush against his hand. "I don't really remember. It's been a long time. Plus, remembering is painful."

He tosses the hairbrush aside and pulls out a T-shirt. I can tell by the color that it's a Darling High shirt. Is that Rachel's, too? I move even closer, until I'm only a foot or two from the table.

"I stuffed this all away because I didn't want to think about her, but I think that's wrong. We should think about her. Like, would Rachel want you to hang out with the guy who killed her? I don't think so." His hand whips out so fast I don't see it coming.

He grabs my wrist and twists it painfully. I yelp and then fall to my knees. He's on top of me in the next minute, pushing me onto my back.

"Get off me!" I yell.

"What is it about Donnelly that you like so much? That it's wrong? You sick up here?" Jeff taps me on the forehead. His eyes are wild and blazing, his jaw tighter than a drum.

I struggle underneath him. "Let me go, asshole."

"Girls like you need to start listening to guys like me or you're going to get hurt. I know you don't want to get hurt." He grabs both of my wrists in one hand and stretches my arms above my head.

I turn my face and try to bite his arm, but he moves it out of the way. I've never felt so helpless. Jeff is six inches taller than me and outweighs me by fifty pounds. He's using every ounce to subdue me.

My heart beats wildly against my chest. "Wh-what are you doing?" I stammer. "Let me go."

"Not until you listen to me." He lowers his face to mine, as if to kiss me.

I wrench my head to the side, and this time I'm not stuttering. "Get off of me, you fucker!"

He claps a hand over my mouth. I bite it. He curses but doesn't remove it.

"Listen to me," he insists. "Calm down and listen to me."

I can't breathe. His body is weighing me down, squashing the air from my lungs. A mélange of thoughts race through my head. This is Jeff. My sister's boyfriend. His mom's upstairs. He's dating my best friend.

He's hurting me. He's *hurting* me.

I buck up again.

"This is what that Donnelly kid is going to do to you, *Beth*, if you don't stop hanging around him."

A hand fumbles between us, grappling for the waistband of my pants. I twist enough to make him lose his grip, but he's back again.

"You're the only one who's hurting me, Jeff." I pant. "Stop it." I try to reason with him. "This isn't what Rachel would want."

He laughs. "How do you know? How do you know what she wanted? Did you listen to her? No. It was me who listened to her. I held her hand and dried her tears. I was the one who helped her study, drove her to practice, picked out her clothes, read her texts, listened to her phone calls. And for what? For her to tell me I was being possessive? And awful? Oh no." He tears at my shirt. "I didn't put in all that time with her for her to break up with me! Do you hear me?" He's shouting now. Spit is coming out of his mouth.

I jerk my hands upward, breaking his hold. I scratch at his face and try to wriggle free. When he grabs for my hands again, I roll over, stuffing my arms under my body. He laughs again. It's a terrible sound.

"You want it like this? You want it like a dog?" His hand lands on my butt.

Oh fuck, this is a mistake. I try to roll over again, but he lies flat on top of me.

And then the door opens.

We both freeze and look up to see Mrs. Corsen at the door. She has a tray filled with drinks in her hands. Somehow, it doesn't drop to the floor. But her jaw does.

"Mrs. Corsen!" I cry. "Help me. Your son is hurting me."

"Wh-what?" she stutters in shock.

"That's not true!" Jeff exclaims at the same time.

His moment of panic is all I need to throw him off me and start running. Past Mrs. Corsen. Up the stairs. Out the door. Down the long drive. I stumble on something. My shoe falls off.

It's dark out and I can barely see the street because of my tears. I keep running.

This is how Rachel felt. I know it. That night, she was trying to escape Jeff. She might've been crying. I swipe a hand across my face and stagger forward, the tears still obstructing my vision.

I hear the screech of brakes.

Honk!

I look up to see a pair of headlights headed straight for me.

32

Before I can react, a big object slams into my side, pushing me out of the road. I land hard on the sidewalk, the wind completely knocked out of me.

"Ouch!" I cry.

"Are you all right?" an urgent voice asks.

At the same time another one roars, *"Get away from her."*

I catch a brief glimpse of Chase's face before it's replaced by my mom's.

"My baby. Oh, my baby."

Mom throws herself onto the sidewalk and gathers me in her arms. She's crying as she clutches me against her chest. Just beyond her I see my dad looming, one hand on his hip and the other holding a phone to his ear. I try to peer around Mom for Chase. I swear I saw him.

"9-1-1. Yes, this is Dave Jones. I'm reporting an assault by Charlie—"

"No!" I push Mom aside and lunge at my dad, grabbing the phone from his hands. "There's no need for any emergency services." I gasp into the phone. "No one is injured." I disconnect the call and then throw the phone as far away as I can.

"Goddammit, Elizabeth. What are you doing? Give me your phone, Marnie."

Mom looks at him uncertainly.

"No. No. No." I shake my head. "You've got it all wrong. I wasn't running from Chase. I was running from Jeff."

I point toward Jeff's house, only to see him at the end of the driveway, blinking at us like a deer caught in the headlights.

"You fucker," Chase growls, appearing from behind my father's stiff frame.

The threat lights a fire under Jeff's heels. He turns and starts booking it toward his house. I run after him, but Chase beats me by a mile, tackling Jeff to the ground. Chase straddles Rachel's ex, grabbing Jeff's T-shirt and twisting it around his throat.

"What'd you do?" Chase thunders.

"She was asking for it," Jeff pants out. "She's been teasing me since I came back to school, telling me how much she wanted me. She was always jealous of Rachel. She always—"

Out of nowhere, my mother flies forward and slaps Jeff across the face. "Don't talk about my girls like that!" she spits. Breathing hard, she turns toward me and asks, "What happened, baby? What did he do to you?"

"Jeff attacked me. He was going to rape me." I lift a corner of my shirt so they can see it was torn.

Behind me, my dad moans in dismay.

"He conned Dad into driving me over to the house by saying he had a box of Rachel's things. But really, he just wanted to get me alone," I say shakily. "He was mad that I've been ignoring him. He said that Rachel was like that, always thinking she knew what was best instead of listening to him. Jeff was going to tell me…"

"I'm going to kill him." Glaring murderously at Jeff, who's still lying beneath him, Chase pulls back his arm.

I throw myself on Chase's back and grab his arm. The last thing I need is for his probation to get revoked. "Don't. He's not worth it."

"*I'm* going to kill him." Dad thrusts both of us out of the way. "You little motherfucker. You hurt my girls." He hauls Jeff upright and dangles him like a worm over the ground.

"Mr. Jones." Jeff gasps, clawing at Dad's grip. "I can't breathe."

"And my little girl is dead." Dad punches him, and that's all it takes for Jeff to pass out. With an anguished noise from the back of his throat, my father shakes the boy's limp body and then drops him to the ground in disgust.

He walks away, as if he can't bear to look at any of us, and stares into the dusky sky. The sun has set, but there's still enough light out for me to make out my father's grief-stricken profile.

"I think they were fighting that night," I tell Chase. "The night that you stole your coach's car. Rachel ran out on the road because Jeff was chasing after her. I think that's what happened. He said that I was just like her and he was going to teach me the lesson that Rachel never learned. She ran away from him, like I did. It was an accident." I implore him with my eyes. "An accident," I repeat.

"Yeah, I know."

"If you know, then why do you keep saying it's your fault?" I cry.

"Because I am at fault, Beth." He rubs his hands up my arms to cup my shoulders. "It doesn't matter if Rachel was upset or if she was crying or if she was running away. I was the one behind the wheel. I took her life." He gently sets me aside and approaches my mom. "I'm sorry. You'll never know how sorry I am."

Mom takes his hand between hers. "Yes. I know that, Charlie. I know you're sorry."

"Dad?" I prompt.

He refuses to turn around. My stomach sinks, because I know in the pit of it that he'll never forgive Chase.

"It was an accident," Mom says. Her voice trembles. "Wasn't it, Dave?"

Dad sighs, clearly loathing speaking the words. "Yes, it was an accident."

"We almost hit you, Beth." She's weak with emotion.

I place an arm around her and she immediately leans into me. I'm surprised at how frail she feels.

"We were arguing about how we were treating you. Your dad wasn't looking at the road." She pushes away from me and grabs Chase's hand again. "Thank you for saving our girl."

He nods weakly. "It's a damn good thing I was coming home from work at that exact moment. I saw Beth run out and jumped off my bike to get her." He gestures to the bicycle lying five feet away.

"Thank you," Mom repeats. She raises her voice. "We're very grateful, aren't we, Dave?"

There's a pause and then "Thank you." He turns on his heel and walks back toward his car. It's as far as he can bend today.

"I'll give you a moment," Mom says.

"A moment?" I start to argue.

"Thank you," Chase tells her.

"But—"

Chase drags me aside. "Baby steps, Beth."

"They should forgive you," I whisper. "You never should've spent a day in jail."

He shakes his head. "I'm glad I went to prison. I'm glad I was punished. I mean, yeah, I hated it while I was there. I felt sick and sometimes I felt like I'd lose my mind, but being punished helped me live with myself. I stole a car. I killed your sister, Beth. I couldn't live with myself if I hadn't been punished. There's got to be balance in this world. I don't know if three years is enough to make up for what I did."

I see the earnestness in his eyes and hear the sincerity in his voice. Underlying all of that, though, is the guilt that weighs him down. Chase has his own demons to grapple with. I won't ever truly understand his perspective. But I can try and sympathize.

I think that's what he's asking for here—for understanding. This battle within himself isn't about me. It's about him. My fight is with my parents. I have to repair the torn relationship and Chase needs to deal with his guilt.

And we can't really be together until both of those things happen.

"Okay," I say softly. "Then do this for me."

"What?"

"First, move out of the basement. You hate it down there and it's stupid of you to keep punishing yourself like that."

He gives a slow nod. "I can do that."

"Good. Second, transfer schools." He starts to object, but I hold up a hand. "Hear me out. You talk about balance and how you need to be punished for your actions, but my question is, when does the punishment stop? Because the court gave you your sentence and you served it. What good does it do anyone for you to go to Darling other than to cause yourself more pain? You suffering isn't going to bring Rachel back. My parents pretending that she's just on some extended school trip won't bring her back."

I hear a soft, wounded noise from behind us, and I know my mom must've overheard the last remark. No, the accusation.

I lower my voice and keep talking. "Me acting like I didn't care that she died isn't going to make her less dead. The best we can do is to live what life we have left in the best way possible." I gulp. "For me, that starts by recognizing I'm not the only one in pain. For you, it means not punishing yourself anymore. You need a fresh start. A new school, where you're not suffering every day."

He rakes a hand through his hair. "Where I don't get to see you every day."

"We still have the tree," I tell him, trying to smile but failing. "The swing isn't there anymore, though."

No, it isn't there. Because Rachel is gone. But she lives in my heart. In my parents'.

And even in Chase's.

He takes a deep breath and when he meets my gaze, his eyes are full of pain. "I think it's best if we don't use the tree. It's too hard for me." His voice sounds hoarse. "You should spend your time rebuilding your relationship with your folks. And I...I need to heal myself. The next time I see you, I want to be with you guilt-free. I don't want my guilt or Rachel to be between us."

"That's what I want, too."

"I guess that leaves us with—" his voice drops to a whisper "—Iowa."

I'm startled for a moment, and then I give him a sad smile. "Iowa," I whisper back.

Our gazes lock as we each let it all sink in. I know this is right, but it feels terrible. Like he's rending my heart in two.

I kiss him. In front of my parents. In front of Jeff. In front of anyone who might be passing. I'm kissing him because this is going to be the last time for a long time.

"I'll wait for you," I murmur. "I'll be there when you're ready. When we're both ready."

"I know." He visibly swallows, and then he gives me that rare, gorgeous half smile that I love so much. "You waiting for me is the one small thing that will keep me going."

33

Iowa State is a six-hour drive across the most monotonous stretch of land known to mankind. Mom and Dad wanted to go with me. I wanted to make the trip myself. My parents see a therapist twice a week now, but although our relationship is better, the events of last autumn left a hole that can't be forgotten no matter how well healed it is.

Rachel's death is like that. It's a hole in my heart that's healed over, but odd things will always remind me of her and sometimes those memories make me sad and sometimes they make me happy.

I arrive at the dorm midafternoon. There are parents everywhere. A momentary regret pings through me that I'm by myself, but this is the way I wanted it. I wanted to start new and fresh, as much as I possibly could.

In Darling, I would always be the girl whose sister died, and my actions and reactions would always be measured against that watershed moment. It's why I needed to get away from Darling. Just like Chase.

We both needed a fresh start.

He transferred schools the week after he saved me from getting hit by my parents' car.

I heard he went to Lincoln, and I was happy for him. The Lincoln kids gave him a welcome-back party; the Darling kids gave him a cruel nickname. That gorgeous girl, Maria, seemed nice. So did his other friends.

For the rest of our senior year, Chase didn't call or text. He didn't work at the shelter. I assume he worked with Jack. We got a lot of snow that winter, so the crew would've been kept busy.

Another girl would've thought Chase had forgotten her. Another guy might've strayed. But we were each other's one small thing and that will never change.

One night, in early December, I drove by his house. It didn't look like anyone was home, but then Mrs. Stanton came outside to roll the garbage bins off the curb and into the garage. She noticed my car and gave it a strange look. I hunched over and tried to make myself invisible. I don't know if she saw me.

Over the holidays, my parents and I went to Colorado to ski and see my dad's sister.

For March break, I joined Scarlett's family in Daytona Beach for a week of sun and fun. We're good now, Scarlett and I. She dumped Jeff the day after he almost forced himself on me; she was the first person I called when I got home that night, and to my surprise, she actually picked up the phone. She's known me long enough to sense when I'm truly upset about something—and I was hysterical that night. She drove right over without a second's hesitation.

Scarlett said that hearing about Jeff's actions served as the wake-up call she needed, made her realize that how he had been treating her was wrong. The next morning, she was there holding my hand at the police station as my parents and I filled out a restraining order after all—against Jeff.

Last I heard, he's in another anger management program. Dad wanted me to press charges against him, but I didn't want to go through a messy trial, especially since it would've been a case of he-said, she-said. Because despite having caught her son red-handed, Mrs. Corsen suddenly "forgot" everything she'd seen that night. The rich protect their evil young, I guess. But the cops in Darling have their eyes on Jeff now, and, with a restraining order against him, I hope he learns to control his anger. I also hope I never, ever see his face again.

I'm happy to see my friends, though. Ever since Scar got rid of Jeff, she's back to her old self, and she doesn't let any guy boss her around anymore. She admitted that she let the fact that Jeff's older and so "sophisticated"—her word, not mine—blind her to his many, many faults. It's a mistake she's vowed to never make again.

Macy is still her flaky self, unable to make a decision about which school to attend. Yvonne got into Harvard. She's over the moon. We all brag about it, as if we collectively made it to the Ivy League school.

My friends don't ask me about Chase, and I don't tell them about him.

There've been days when I inwardly raged at him for not contacting me.

You coward. You love me and you ran away. I hate you.

But I don't hate him. I love him, and I miss him, but we both made the decision to part ways. He needed to learn how to forgive himself, and I needed to prove to my parents that I'm not a selfish, reckless child who needs their protection. I wanted them to feel comfortable about letting me go off to college.

And now here I am, at Iowa State. I've got a car and a phone and what I assume will be a door to my dorm room. I'm one step closer to being a vet. A small step, but I focus on the small and manageable these days, not the big and out of reach, remember? I focus on what I can control, and what I have to live for.

Because there's always something to live for. Something to be thankful for. Something to look forward to.

That's the biggest lesson I learned from Chase.

I lift the hatch and reach inside the trunk for my first load.

"Need a hand?"

The smile that stretches across my face is almost too big to be contained. I haven't heard his voice in months.

It's the most beautiful sound in the world.

"You're here," I say with immense satisfaction. I never had any doubt that he would be here.

"Where else would I be?" Smiling back, Chase steps closer and tucks a loose strand of hair behind my ear. He's not wearing all black, but faded blue jeans and a sky blue T-shirt a few shades lighter than his mesmerizing eyes.

My heart nearly explodes in my chest. And then, right on cue, the tears start to fall.

"Aw, please don't cry," he says roughly.

"I can't help it," I say between sniffles. "We've already discussed this—I've got a crying problem."

He laughs, and I take it back—*that's* the most beautiful sound in the world. Chase is laughing. Chase is here. He's actually *here*.

I hated not seeing him. I hated not talking to him. I hated waiting so long for this moment, for the promise of "Iowa" to finally come true. But being an adult is painful, I've learned. I guess I just have to live with that.

I'm alive. Rachel isn't. I have to keep going no matter what, because she never got the chance to do so. I have to live for *her*. I have to be grateful for what I have. One small thing every day, just like Chase taught me.

So yesterday, the small thing I clung to was the beautiful sunset that Scar and I watched while eating ice cream on the hood of her car. Our last hurrah before she comes to visit me next month.

The day before that, it was Mom taking down Rachel's name above the chalkboard. The week before that, Dad hung Rachel's swing back up.

And today?

It's *him*.

★ ★ ★ ★ ★